WINTER
KILL

A JOHN HENRY
COLE STORY

WINTER KILL

A JOHN HENRY COLE STORY

BILL BROOKS

First Edition: 2016
ISBN 978-1-5046-8536-8

1 2 3 4 5 6 7 8 9 10

Blackstone Publishing
31 Mistletoe Rd.
Ashland, OR 97520

www.downpour.com

CHAPTER ONE

All the horses froze that winter. All the cattle. They froze to death where they stood, caught in the teeth of a seven-day storm that rattled windows and doors and killed every living thing that stood in its path. The snow and wind closed all the roads leading into and out of Cheyenne. You could have shot a pistol in any direction and not hit a living soul. Temperatures plunged to sixty below and the cold was so bone-deep, even whiskey couldn't fight it. Men went crazy and women wept with fear because it was like a white death had descended on that place. Children stared wide-eyed as if they were frozen, too.

Nothing moved among the drifts of snow, and the wind howled like mourning women. Horses and cattle weren't the only creatures that died that winter. They found Wayback Cotton frozen to death in a snowbank; the only thing exposed was his head, the eyes a milky glaze of white. And when they dug him out, they found the neck of a shattered whiskey bottle in one hand, the snow stained brown around him. Someone said his craving for liquor had finally killed him. He was the first one the winter killed.

Shorty Blaine's wife Cleopatra grew sick and took to her bed, and Shorty wrapped her in blankets and a mangy buffalo robe and placed warmed bricks at her feet, trying to save her. She cried in her delirium that the angel of death rode a pale horse and was coming for her. Against good sense, Shorty went out in the midst of the storm to fetch the town's only doctor. When he slammed the door behind him, an icicle rattled loose from an overhang and pierced Shorty's neck and bled him out; his blood froze and formed an irregular pool of crimson ice beneath him.

Bart Bledsoe, performing his duties as city marshal, braved the killer storm to go and quell a fight between two prostitutes who were fighting over a miner snowed-in on his way to the gold fields in the Black Hills. The whores had gone into a rage from opium and greed to get the miner's poke, and that, along with the storm that had forced them to stay together, had turned them crazy. One of the whores had a straight razor and slashed the other, cutting the miner in the act. Bart Bledsoe made the mistake of getting between them just as the miner pulled a belly-gun to kill the whore. Bart was felled with a bullet through his eye and a razor cut to his throat. His dying finger squeezed off a shot and killed the other whore.

John Henry Cole was three miles away on his small ranch, waiting out the storm that was quickly killing his cattle and horses, and starting to feel a little crazy himself. Everything he owned was dying before his eyes and there wasn't anything that he could do about it. There wasn't anything he could do about his friends, either. He might as well have been a thousand miles away.

When the storm finally blew itself out and the Chinook came, he surveyed his losses and knew there was nothing left for him in Cheyenne. He had spent every dime he had buying the ranch and a herd of longhorns whose bodies lay facing south in dark clumps amid the dissipating drifts. His dreams of a settled life were as dead as everything else. The winter had killed them all in one way or another. He knew it was time to move on.

He put the ranch up for sale and watched as the gray wolves and coyotes came and made short work of the carcasses of his cattle and horses. He watched the ice dripping from the eaves and drank bitter black coffee and weighed his options. He was down to thin pockets and no future, a situation he had become well accustomed to for most of his life. He knew one thing, though. Cheyenne and John Henry Cole were quits. Any reason he had to stay was gone. When finally the weather grew warm enough, he took one last walk up the hill to the cemetery with Cleopatra because she'd asked him if he would. The warm winds tugged at their clothes and the sun lay at low angles across the winter landscape and made the slopes of ice look blue in places. As they climbed the grade to the little boothill, they could look back and see snow on the roofs of the town and black wisps of smoke curling from stovepipes. It was a peaceful scene, if you didn't know better. Death was surely as present among the living as it was on that little cemetery ridge.

"I'd as soon it had been me that died than him," Cleo said, her voice quavering like a wire in the wind. She coughed into a small silk hankie and it tinged red. "All these years, I waited for a good man to come along ...." Her voice lost its strength and she coughed again and knuckled the dampness from her eyes. Her pale features stood in stark contrast to the black mourning dress she wore.

Cole understood what it felt like to be willing to trade places with the dead. He counted the graves of his friends and it was like ticking off time, each one representing a memory, a good time, a shared glass of liquor, a laugh, a sense of indescribable loss.

"I know he loved me," Cleo said, standing before the rock cairn of Shorty Blaine's final resting place. The ground was still frozen and the dead had to be buried under rocks until the thaw, when graves could be dug. Shorty Blaine, Wayback Cotton, Bart Bledsoe. Three good men had come to a bad end.

"I know he loved you, too," Cole said to Cleo.

"He left me the café," she said. "But I don't know that I'll stay. I was thinking of selling it and moving east ... Boston, maybe." Cleo had been a prostitute that Shorty had met and married only a few short months before. Maybe she thought she needed to run it past Cole, her plans to leave Cheyenne, since Shorty and Cole had been friends for the better part of twenty years.

"You don't need my permission," Cole said. "Shorty would want you to be happy. Slinging hash for cowboys and living up here in this high lonesome country isn't much of a future for a woman."

She put her hand through the crook of his arm. "Thank you for saying that, John Henry," she said. "Walk me back down the hill to town and I'll fix you a good breakfast before you go off to wherever it is you're planning on going."

* * * * *

John Henry Cole was staring at his reflection in the mirror of the Ar-buckle's coffee in his cup while Cleo was in the kitchen fixing up what she called a "hellacious" breakfast, when the door to the café rattled open before closing hard against the hard wind. A man wearing a greatcoat and a bowler stood there, looking about.

"We're not open for business yet, mister," Cleo said, popping her head out from the kitchen. "There's been a death in the family."

"I didn't come here to eat," he said. Then, looking directly at Cole with dark, feral eyes under a massive brow, he said: "You John Henry Cole?"

"Who's asking?"

Cole noticed he had a slight limp as he approached the table.

"Teddy Green," he said. He looked at Cleo just long enough to make an appraisal, but it wasn't the usual sort of look a man gives a woman; there was nothing to indicate he had that sort of hunger in him.

"I don't know you," Cole said, taking his makings from his waistcoat to roll a shuck.

The man's gaze switched back to Cole. "You've heard of me, though," he said.

Cole had. Teddy Green had a legendary reputation as a cowboy, lawman, buffalo hunter, and Indian fighter. "Yes, I've heard of you, Mister Green."

"You mind?" he said, indicating the empty chair across from Cole. Cole nodded, and Green took the seat, setting his bowler atop the table. Cole noted the rings he wore—silver and gold, one on each of his pinky fingers. He unbuttoned the greatcoat and Cole saw the butt of a pistol in a shoulder rig under his left arm. Walnut grips and a brass strap hung in the well-oiled leather.

"I saw a lot of dead cattle and horses on the way up," he said. "Saw the same thing once before in the winter of '68. You could walk clear across Montana on the backs of dead beeves and never once set foot on the ground."

"I know you didn't come here to talk about the weather," Cole said.

He twisted his mouth like maybe he had a tooth that was aching. He had a face like granite that had withstood the weather for some time.

"I'm looking for a woman," he said.

"A lot of men are."

"I'm looking for a *particular* woman," he said. His eyes lacked amusement, but, then, it wasn't an amusing time.

"What does that have to do with me?" Cole asked.

Cleo came out of the kitchen, carrying a plate of eggs, salted slabs of ham, hot biscuits, and a jar of sorghum, and set it down without taking her eyes off Teddy Green.

"Did we meet somewhere before?" she said.

He looked at her again, those dark eyes registering everything about her, every curve and wisp of hair and the way she stood there with her fists balled on her broad hips.

"I think I would have remembered," he said.

"Kansas, maybe," she said. "Perhaps Dodge City."

"No. Least not whenever I was there."

"I have a good memory for faces," Cleo said. "And you sure look like someone I met once."

"You got me confused, sister. Sorry to say."

That seemed to satisfy her curiosity. Cole was splitting open the warm biscuits and drowning them in sorghum. Seven days waiting out the storm and doing his own cooking had left him famished for a regular meal, something that wasn't burned black or whang-leather tough.

"She looks sickly, that woman," Teddy Green said after Cleo had retreated to the kitchen.

"It's been a hard winter," Cole said. "Her man died, and now she's got lung fever."

Teddy Green smoothed the sides of his hair with the palms of his hands, then lightly rested them atop the table next to his bowler. They were hands that had seen hard work, but none lately. The lining of the hat was white silk.

"I never liked it this far north," he said. "Hard country to carve out a living."

"Then why did you come?"

He watched Cole cut into the biscuits with his fork, watched the sorghum run to the edges of the plate and soak into the eggs.

"Like I said, I'm looking for a woman."

Cole put down the fork.

"You want to tell me what this has to do with me, Mister Green? I'd like to have at this meal before it grows cold."

"I'd like to hire you to help me find her," he said.

"You believe it takes two men?"

"Two men with grit and a reason to find her. I know she came here, know about the two of you. Figured you could lead me to her." He had a rather sure way of speaking, as though he'd done it a lot—used his voice to command attention and to strike bargains.

"This woman," Cole said, "what's her name?"

He waited for Green to tell him the name and, when he did, something the size of a fist caught in his chest.

"Ella Mims," he said. "That's the woman I'm looking for. At least that's the name she was using from what information I've been able to gather."

"You want to tell me why you're looking for her?"

"You knew her, didn't you, Mister Cole?"

"If you already know that, why ask?"

He cocked his head slightly, twisted his mouth again. He was clean-shaven but the shadow of a beard darkened his chin and cheeks. A small scar cut through his left eyebrow and another the shape of a quarter moon welted his right cheek.

"She's not who you think she is, Mister Cole. So, if you think you're protecting her from me, you've got it wrong."

"Why don't you tell me what I don't know, Mister Green?"

"She's wanted for murder. That's why I'm looking for her."

He pulled back the flap of his greatcoat to reveal a Texas Ranger badge pinned to his waistcoat. Cole could also see that the pistol hanging from the shoulder rig was a double-action .44, a Colt Frontier model.

"You're a little out of your territory," Cole said, and went back to concentrating on his breakfast.

"I go where I need to go," Green said.

"Well, good luck in your search." Cole made an effort to keep his voice level, to act unaffected by the news Green had brought, but his mind was turning over the information fast.

"You haven't heard me out," Green said.

"I've heard enough."

"If you fell in love with her," Green said, "you wouldn't be the first. Ella's an easy woman to love."

"How would you know *that?*"

"I know because she's my wife," he said.

Suddenly the eggs and everything else seemed as cold and uninviting as the waning winter to Cole. A light rain began to peck at the window.

"Her married name is Ella Jane Green," he said. "It has sort of a nice ring to it, doesn't it?"

Cole wasn't buying it. If you share intimacies with a woman the way he had with Ella Mims, you don't just throw it all away because of a stranger's accusations.

"Look, I've run out of trail. I'm willing to pay for your help to find her. Five hundred for the information, or your gun to back me up, depending on what you know."

"Five hundred or five thousand, it won't buy anything from me," Cole said.

"I'm not the only one looking for her, Mister Cole. If I find her first, she'll get safe transport back to Denver and a fair trial. If the others looking for her find her first, they'll make sure she doesn't make it back to Denver."

Suddenly he had Cole's full attention.

"Who are these others and why do they want her?" Cole asked.

"She was involved in the killing of the son of an important man."

"Who's the man?"

"A federal judge by the name of Thaddeus Beam."

"What does Ella have to do with it?"

"She was reportedly in the escort of another man at the time, a real wild wind. They both knew the dead man and had been seen in his company the night of the killing."

"For being married to her," Cole said, "it doesn't sound like you kept a tight rein on her."

Green shifted his weight in the chair, touched the brim of his upturned bowler, and seemed to study it for a moment. "We were married a long time ago, Mister Cole. It didn't work out. She went her way. I went mine. Trouble is, we never actually got around to a divorce." His gaze fell into the hat like he was looking inside it for something, a lost marriage perhaps.

"So this judge hired you to find her?" Cole said.

"No. He hired others to do that. I got word of it and decided I'd better round her up before his hired men did."

"Why trouble yourself?"

"Because she's still my wife and I know the assassin the judge hired to find her."

Cole waited for him to give a name.

"You ever hear of Colorado Charley Utter?"

All Cole knew of Colorado Charley Utter was that he had paid for Wild Bill Hickok's funeral and a grave marker to have the notorious gunfighter buried in Deadwood, that they'd been pals for a short time, and that right after the funeral, Utter had disappeared. That wasn't much to know about the man.

"What about him?" Cole asked.

"He's deadly, and intolerant of wayward women. Rumor has it"—Green leaned a little over the table—"that he doesn't like any kind of women."

"You seem to know a lot about him."

"I ran into him and Wild Bill in Kansas one time. Bill was the law there before they fired him for shooting his deputy. Charley was there and there was some talk about his unnatural desires."

"You get around."

"I was a lot of things and have been to a lot of places before I turned to rangering. I know most of the worst of humanity that roam this frontier. I've put my share of men in the ground or in prison. I'm good at what I do, Mister Cole, make no mistake about it."

He stood then, took up his bowler, replaced it atop his head, and tapped it lightly.

"I'll be staying the night at the Inter-Ocean and leaving first thing in the morning. I could stand your help in finding Ella," he said. "And you look like a man who could use a stake. And in case you know where she is and are thinking about getting a jump to warn her, just remember, Mister Cole, there're others that are after her … and they're all professional gun artists. If they weren't, they wouldn't be riding with Colorado Charley. You'll not want to go up against them alone. If you care at all about her safety and welfare, you'll throw in with me. The two of us might stand a chance, at least a better chance than if we go it alone."

"I wish I could help," Cole said.

Green turned as he reached the door. "Another thing you ought to know," he said. "That man I told you Ella was involved with, the one I believe had a hand in the killing of the judge's boy … his name is Gypsy Davy and he broke jail before they could hang him. My suspicion is that he's also looking for Ella, probably to make sure she keeps her mouth shut about what happened the night of the murder."

He left and Cole sat there, staring after him through the window, watching as he crossed the street with that slight hitch to his gait and headed for the hotel. Cleo came out of the kitchen and said: "You look like a ghost has jumped into your hide. What did that man want?"

"His wife," Cole said.

"Good Lord, don't men know that when a woman disappears on them, she's not looking to be found?"

Cole stared out the window onto a half-frozen world that was as forbidding as a bitter heart, and he knew he'd have to find Ella and learn the truth no matter where that truth led him. He would be leaving Cheyenne, but not in the way he'd planned.

If Cole knew anything at all about her, Ella Mims wasn't the kind of woman to commit murder no matter what the circumstances. But if he didn't find her before the others did, there would be no way to prove that. He knew Teddy Green was right about their chances of going it alone as opposed to throwing in together, but he'd learned a long time ago that you didn't buy a pig in a poke. He had to make sure Teddy Green's story wasn't a pig.

Every time Cole got to thinking the dance had ended, the old grim fiddler started it up again.

CHAPTER TWO

Cole walked to the telegraph office and sent a wire to a man he knew in Denver—a one-armed old cowpuncher from his droving days who'd ended up striking it rich by marrying a wealthy widow twice his size. Now, instead of sleeping in his soogan on a muddy trail somewhere along that thousand-mile stretch between San Antonio and the Kansas boom towns, he was sleeping in a canopy bed on satin sheets. His name was Harve Ledbettor. He'd lost his arm while serving as a city constable in Rock Creek, Wyoming, nearly chopped off by a madwoman with a hoe after her man shot him through the jaw. Harve told Cole later it had been a bad day all the way around and had convinced him that he wasn't cut out to be a peace officer. He'd gone to Denver to a hospital to recover and it was there that he had met the rich widow who was volunteering as a nurse. Her name was Zerelda Beechcomb and she took to Harve like a preacher to whiskey. Harve called it a case of mad love.

Cole knew all this because the last time he had been in Denver with Bill Cody, they had run into Harve Ledbettor in an outlandishly opulent restaurant Cody had insisted they eat in—they had an oyster bar and Cody liked to be seen by the blue bloods. Cody's surprise was such that when he saw Harve, leaning against the bar wearing a fancy black suit and a cravat with a ruby stickpin, he dropped an oyster into his lap. Cody called Harve over and asked him what bank he'd robbed. Harve brayed like a mule and bought a round of drinks and told them the story of his good fortune.

"I fell into it, boys, like a mud cat into a two-holer. I was lost, and now I'm found."

He looked blissful. Cody looked envious. Cole figured, if a man lost something as dear as his arm, he had a right to whatever good fortune came his way after that. The three of them got as hammered as a keg of roofing nails. Every time Harve tossed back a tumbler of gin rickeys, he would flap his empty sleeve and crow for the waitress to bring them another round.

Cole thought about that night now, as he waited for the telegrapher to send the telegram, the stuttering clack of the key of small comfort to him. He was grasping at straws, trying to find out what he could about Ella's life in Denver. He needed to learn what he could about the killing and Harve Ledbettor was his only source of hope. His mind still wasn't accepting the things Teddy Green had told him about Ella. Part of him wanted to believe Green was a man with a mission but not necessarily the one he claimed. If it was true that he'd been married to Ella, maybe she was running from him, and maybe she had a reason. Cole needed to get to the truth and find out what he could. And if anyone knew anything about the sins of the high and mighty in Denver, he figured it to be Harve Ledbettor. He was married into it. Cole was counting on Harve's being able to tell him something he didn't already know about the murder and the players involved.

"Make sure and tell the operator at the other end to send someone to deliver that message *pronto*," Cole said.

The telegrapher peered at him from under his green eye shade, then tapped out some more code, and sat back and waited. "May take a while to get a reply back," he said.

"I'll check in with you later," Cole told him, and headed up the street to the railroad station. He needed to buy a ticket on the next flyer to Ogallala. From there, he'd rent a horse and ride out to the ranch that Ella Mims's aunt owned. That was the last place he'd seen Ella, the place he'd left her while he went off to find Ike Kelly's killer. He'd wanted to go back long before now, but the winter had come and killed everything. When he'd left her last, whatever future they had talked about was hanging by a thin string. Ella had told him when he left that she wouldn't wait forever for him to make up his mind. Now Cole was sorry as hell he'd taken so long.

He was halfway to the station when he ran into Karl Cavandish, the town's undertaker. He'd buried some of Cole's enemies and most of his friends, and as soon as the ground thawed, he was going to bury a few more. His features were more gaunt than usual and his stovepipe hat was battered and muddy and angled to one side. His gait was unsteady and he smelled like a saloon.

"Awful early to hit the juice, ain't it, Karl?"

Cavandish's eyes tried to focus on Cole but were having a devil of a time doing it. "John Henry?"

He started to topple, and Cole caught him before he landed in the mud. "Easy, Karl."

Through the broadcloth coat, Cole could feel bones. Cavandish seemed like a man without flesh, his frame as starved as a lobo after a hard winter. He hadn't shaved or had a haircut in some time and had the odor of the unwashed mixed with the stink of liquor. That stench caused Cole to shift downwind of him. He knew Cavandish as a man who normally took fastidious care of his person, and certainly not a man given to displays of public drunkenness.

Cavandish gripped Cole's shoulder with one claw of a hand and steadied himself. "I'll buy you a whiskey if you'll drink it with me," he said.

"It's nine o'clock in the morning, Karl."

"Oh," he said. "Well, hell then, we'd better get started before they close up the saloons."

"It's none of my business," Cole said. "But if you fall down in the street and don't get up, a wagon might run over you, or you could suffocate in all this mud."

Cavandish swayed slightly, looked about, then settled his gaze on Cole again. "Hardly would make a difference if I did, John Henry." His eyes welled with tears and his hands began to shake.

"José?" Cole said.

Cavandish nodded. The kid he'd been taking care of, the one Long Bill Longly had shot through the spine and crippled, had apparently also been claimed by the harsh winter.

"When?" Cole asked.

"This morning," Cavandish said, his voice quavering. "I went in his room and found him staring at the ceiling."

"You did what you could for the boy, Karl. Maybe it's for the best. His suffering is over. We've still got ours."

"I know," Cavandish said. "I know to hell it is, and he is in a better place than this crap hole. But it don't stop me from wanting to get drunk and go dig up Long Bill and shoot him in the god-damn' face for what he did to José!"

"Well, hell. If it will make you feel better," Cole said, "let's go get some shovels and do just that."

Cavandish looked at him for a moment, saw that Cole wasn't just making fun, then smiled at Cole like a proud father. "You'd do it, too, wouldn't you?" he said. "Go dig him up with me so I could shoot him in the face?"

"Hell, yes. I've got nothing better to do right now anyway except buy a train ticket."

"I'm glad they hanged that son-of-a-bitch," Cavandish said. "But I'd still like to shoot him in the face." He seemed to be talking more to himself now than to Cole. He muttered something Cole couldn't make out, then looked at Cole again like it was the first time he knew Cole was standing there. "Ticket?" he said. "You leaving?"

"For good this time, Karl. The winter took all my livestock and killed off all my friends but you. I've got no reason to stay. I guess I wasn't cut out to be a rancher. What I know about raising cows you could stick in your hat. A man ought to stick to what he does best. Besides, there's some business I have got to take care of."

"Hell," Cavandish said, looking all around him, "we all got reasons to leave this god-forsaken place!"

"You going to be OK?" Cole asked. "If I turn loose of you, you won't fall down in the street and get run over by a wagon or smother in the mud, will you?"

Cavandish straightened himself mightily and Cole felt his bones go stiff. "I may be miserable and drunk," he said. "But I am too dignified to fall down and let some damn' ignorant teamster run over me or drown with my face in the mud."

"Good," Cole said. "I don't need to lose any more friends."

"None of us do," he said. "By the way, where you taking the train to?"

"Nebraska," Cole said.

Cavandish blinked, staggered a step, caught himself, and said: "Pitiful choice."

Cole waited until Cavandish had made it across the street and into the Blue Star before going to the station to buy his ticket. The next train to Ogallala wasn't for another two days. When he came out of the station, Cole saw Teddy Green standing across the street, smoking a cigar. He nodded and Cole kept walking.

CHAPTER THREE

Cole's horse was hitched to the rail in front of Shorty's Café, but his gear was stowed in a back room of Sun Lee's laundry just across the street. He'd thought last year, when he'd bought the ranch, that he'd never have to sleep in a room the size of a jail cell again, that he'd have plenty of space to sprawl his lanky frame and let fly his elbows, and lots of windows to look out of. And for a time on the ranch he did. Now Cole was right back where he'd started the first day he'd set foot in Cheyenne. Texas was beginning to look good to him again, and for him that was a bad sign.

The old Celestial was spooning some soup into his puckered mouth, drops of it glistening on his chin whiskers, when Cole walked in and closed the door behind him.

"Mistah John Henly, you back already," he said. "You want me to fix you some soup. It's got some chicken in it?"

"No thanks," Cole said. The soup was a thin yellow water and he sure didn't see any chicken floating around in it. "That must have been a pretty small chicken, Sun."

He grinned until his eyes disappeared behind the waxy folds of his skin. "Most the chicken gone now, just some of the feet all that's left. But still pletty good."

Chicken feet soup had never been a favorite of Cole's. Sun Lee couldn't have weighed more than ninety pounds with lead in his pockets. It wasn't surprising; all the man ever consumed was soup and tea. "I'll be leaving the day after tomorrow," Cole said. "You can rent out my room after I'm gone."

Sun Lee looked up from his bowl. It was a glass bowl with little blue fat-bellied figures painted on it, the same as the ones on his teacup.

"You leave for good, Mistah John Henly? You not coming back?"

"First train out," Cole replied. "I'd like to settle up with you for the room."

Sun slurped down more of the soup and watched Cole with the curious gaze of a cat. "Three dollah," he said. "Should be enough."

Cole took the money from his waistcoat pocket and set it on the table next to Sun's teacup.

Sun eyed it for a moment, then went back to eating his soup.

"Sorry to see you go, Mistah John Henly. You a funny man, always make Sun laugh. Ha, ha."

Cole had never understood why Sun Lee thought him a funny man, but then there was a whole lot he'd never understand about him. You would look into his eyes and you knew that they'd seen some strange and mysterious events, things you'd like to ask him about. But perhaps like Cole's, or like any man's, Sun's private world was better left undisturbed. "You'll have to give me the recipe for that chicken feet soup," Cole said.

Sun's laughter sounded like rice paper being ripped apart.

Cole packed what few possessions he owned, but his mind was still turning over the events of the story Teddy Green had told him. It didn't seem possible that Ella could or would be involved in murder. And it seemed even less likely that she'd be running with the likes of Gypsy Davy, a notorious individual, according to Teddy Green. The question for Cole was—who was Gypsy Davy and why was Ella in his company?

Cole made a shuck and smoked it slowly and stared out the one lone window that looked onto an alley. The snow lay in dirty clumps, but above the roof lines he could see a triangle of flawless blue sky, the world in contrast between its beauty and its ugliness.

Cole wondered how he could have been so wrong about Ella, then he realized that, the truth be told, he'd known the woman for a total of only six days—plenty of time for a man to let himself be fooled, especially if the object of his foolishness was a russet-haired beauty with soft hands and a warm smile. But he also remembered looking into her eyes and knew that what they'd shared couldn't have been a total lie. Somewhere between the idea and the reality stood the truth, and now Cole aimed to find out what it was. Regardless of what secrets or sins there were, he felt he would be damned before he allowed any harm to come to her.

There was a knock at the door, and, when he opened it, a kid stood there with a telegram in his hand. He was a waif with dirty cheeks and rolled-down socks who Cole recognized from around town running odd jobs and errands. He'd heard his folks died of diphtheria and he was an orphan, twelve, maybe thirteen years old. The West was full of orphan kids, and they were forced to grow up fast or perish. This one had the eyes of an old man, tired and distrustful.

"Telegram, mister. Old Man Kersaw told me to bring it to you."

He stood there after handing Cole the telegram and Cole gave him half a buck. He looked at it, then put it in his shirt pocket and thanked Cole.

"Hey, kid. What's your name?"

"Eli, mister. Why you asking?"

Cole's own son would have been about this boy's age had he not died of the milk sickness as an infant. "No reason, kid," Cole said. "Thanks for bringing me the telegram."

Cole waited until he left, then read the wire.

God damn and Jesus. I heard you was dead, killed and buried in that hell hole Texas! Stop. I guess you ain't. Stop. I got information you requested but will deliver it in the living flesh. Stop. Catching the afternoon flyer. Will be in Cheyenne tonight. Stop. Don't leave till I arrive. Stop. Loaded for bear and ready for adventure. Stop. Yours, H. Ledbettor, Esquire.

Cole read the telegram again, disbelieving the message. He wondered— what the hell was that crazy fool up to? He hadn't requested that he come to Cheyenne, nor did he want him here. His plan was to travel fast and light. Unless he was wrong, Teddy Green would be on the same morning flyer to Ogallala, dogging Cole's steps. That was fine, because Cole planned on renting the fastest horse in Nebraska and shaking him off his tail once he was mounted. He went directly to the telegraph office and sent a wire to Denver.

"Just two words?" Kersaw asked when he looked at what Cole had written.

"Send them," Cole said.

Kersaw nodded and tapped out the words—Don't come.—then charged Cole a nickel.

"You could have gotten a full line for the same price," he added, but Cole was already halfway out the door. The last thing Cole needed was a Texas Ranger and a one-armed cowpuncher riding his heels while he looked for Ella Mims.

CHAPTER FOUR

Strange things happen when men are left with too much idle time on their hands. The Chinooks were easing the cold and warming the air enough that icicles dripped steadily from the overhangs, turning the main drag into a slop of mud. But even warm winds weren't enough to relieve some of the madness the killing winter had wrought.

Cole had walked across the street to Shorty's Café to get a cup of coffee and tell Cleopatra that he was leaving on the next flyer and that, if she was smart, she would sell the café and leave, too. The place was full and she was busy. Cole had to stand around until a pair of bachelors vacated a table near the window.

Cleo had hired one of the local prostitutes to help her in the café after Shorty Blaine's death. The whoring business had nearly died along with everything else that winter. It was an arrangement that suited both women.

The younger woman's name was Katy O'Brien. She had copper hair, green eyes, and a shanty Irish brogue. The way Cole had heard it was that she'd come from Brooklyn, New York, and worked her way West with a theatrical troupe. In Cole's view how she had ended up in Cheyenne was just a matter of misfortune, like almost everybody else who'd ended up there, himself included. Cole found her pleasant to look at, and after he took a seat, she came to his table. She wore a prim but simple calico dress and a white apron; her hair was bunched atop her head and held with Spanish combs.

"'Marnin', sar," she said, and offered Cole a half-hearted smile.

He ordered coffee and she poured him a cup from the pot she carried and asked if there would be anything else. For a full moment their eyes met, then Cole nodded that the coffee would be all, and she left. He forced himself not to let his gaze follow the swing of her hips. The winter had been long and lonely and Katy O'Brien was the only other woman in the place besides Cleo. But his mind was on another woman and he needed to keep it there. As he thought that, he looked out the window and saw more of what the winter madness had wrought.

Two men were rapidly approaching each other from opposite directions—one from the east end of town, the other from the west. They had their pistols drawn and aimed. One of the men was Sam Harrison, the other Jim Levy, and both had reputations as shootists. Cole knew them slightly but couldn't attest to their abilities with side arms, for he'd never seen either of them shoot so much as a prairie dog. He couldn't hear what they were shouting as they closed the distance between each other, but from about forty paces apart they began firing at each other.

The sudden eruption of gunshots made the diners drop their forks and dive for shelter under the tables. Cole counted seven shots before he saw Harrison fall. He tumbled to the mud and lay there for a moment, then struggled to rise. Then Cole watched as Levy hurried to the wounded man, stopped a foot from him, aimed his pistol, and fired a final round into Harrison's skull. Levy did this as casually as if it had been a turkey shoot. He then knocked the spent rounds from his revolver, re-loaded, and sauntered off toward the Blue Star, leaving Harrison sprawled in the muddy street. Cole didn't know what their differences had been and it really wasn't any of his concern, but it angered him that one man would kill another in such an indefensible position as Levy had just done.

Several patrons rushed outside once the shooting subsided and pretty quickly a crowd had gathered around the body of the slain man.

"Well, isn't somebody going to do something?" a woman said. She was holding the hand of a child who stared wide-eyed at the dead man. "Doesn't any of you have a sense of decency?"

"Don't know what you'd have us do, Anne. We ain't got no law since Bledsoe was murdered," a man in a brocade vest said. "'Sides, the way I saw it, it was a fair fight. Sam just wasn't as good a shot as ole Jim was."

"Pick this man up and take him to Karl Cavandish's," Cole said, joining them. "The woman's right … decent people don't leave dead men lying on the street."

It took a moment before several of the bystanders grabbed up the corpse and carted him off to Cavandish's Funeral Parlor.

Cole surmised the woman was mistaken about his intentions, for she approached him and said: "I'm glad that somebody is willing to do something! Will you go and arrest the killer of that poor man?"

"They were both armed," Cole said. "No judge or jury would convict him."

She glared at Cole for a moment, then turned sharply and pulled the child after her.

Cole walked over to the Blue Star, entered, and approached the bar where Jim Levy stood drinking with several men who were talking about the gunfight and buying him drinks. He didn't seem to mind all the attention. Cole took a place along the oak. It wasn't any of his business. That's what he told himself. "Hell of a piece of gun work out there," he said.

Jim Levy turned toward Cole. "What say?"

"The way you walked up and shot that man in the head once he was down … hell of a piece of gun work."

Levy stiffened. "I never shot two men in one day, mister. Don't push your luck."

"No, Levy, you haven't shot two men in one day and you won't today, either, unless you're a hell of a lot luckier with me than you were with Harrison."

His eyes narrowed. "I know you," he said. "You was one of Ike Kelly's men. John Henry Cole, that's it."

"Yeah, that's who I was."

"You looking to mix it up?" he demanded.

Some of the men surrounding him looked eager to see Levy kill his second man that day. It had been a long, boring winter.

"No. Just saying it doesn't take a lot to walk up and shoot a wounded man."

"Well, maybe I ought to shoot you," he said.

"Yeah, maybe you ought to," Cole said. "But I won't miss like Harrison did, so you better not, either."

Levy's features slackened and Cole knew the starch had gone out of him.

Somebody standing to Levy's right whispered to him that Cole was the one who'd killed Leo Foxx, the previous city marshal, and had sent Bill Longly to the gallows. That took some more of the starch out of Levy.

"It was a fair fight, Cole," Levy's crony said. "We all saw it."

"Yeah, it was a fair fight," Levy said. "The son-of-a-bitch stole a shirt of mine and I called him out on it."

"You killed a man over a shirt?"

He nodded. "It was wool," he said.

"Jesus Christ," Cole said, and walked away.

Cole spent the rest of the day buying a new Mackinaw and a pair of boots for his trip to Nebraska and generally trying to kill time that was crawling by more slowly than a mud turtle. He knew, if he let himself, he could get drunk as sin just to forget why things were the way they were. At one time in his wild days, he'd known the bottle a lot better than he had known his own name. Two years of fighting for a losing cause in the War Between the States, then losing a wife and a son to milk sickness had left him adrift in a world where only Tennessee sipping whiskey and the hollow affections of whores could come anywhere close to easing the pain and keeping the nightmares at bay.

John Henry Cole was forty-one years old and he'd already outlived most of his contemporaries. He felt like a man alone in the world and the hand of desire for old escapes kept knocking at his door—all he had to do was answer. And he almost did answer it that night when Katy O'Brien showed up at his room in the back of Sun Lee's laundry.

"I saw the look you gave me this marnin'," she said. "I know when a man is interested."

Cole felt ashamed of himself because she was right. He had looked at her like a man who was interested.

He'd been lying on the bed in the darkness when he'd heard the knock. Out of habit, he had slid the self-cocker from its holster and told whoever it was to enter. The dim light from the hall behind her was enough to make him ease the hammer down on the pistol and lay it aside. That's when she told him that she noticed the way he'd looked at her.

"I won't lie to you," Cole said. "But I'm not looking for any company tonight."

"I am," she said, closing the door behind her. Cole sat up on the side of the bed and lit the oil lamp and watched the flame climb up the glass chimney and spread a soft yellow glow in that corner of the room.

"I've brought a bottle of whiskey," she said. "For us."

She set a three-quarters full bottle of Red Thunder—a bust-head liquor made of alcohol, plug tobacco, and snake heads—next to the lamp, then Cole watched her remove her black wool capote and scarf and toss them on the foot of the bed. She still wore the calico dress he'd seen her in at the café. It rustled when she moved.

"Will you pour me a glass?" she said.

Cole excused himself and went out to the laundry and found a pair of teacups in a cupboard where he knew Sun kept his plates and bowls. He had no intention of involving himself with Katy O'Brien, but he knew the look of loneliness when he saw it and understood the need for company on a desolate night, so he didn't turn her out like he felt he probably should have.

"I sometimes think of killing myself," she said, sitting on the edge of the bed next to Cole. The glass cup in her hand cost more than a whole barrel of the cheap whiskey held inside it. "Life, you know, it gets hard sometimes."

Cole watched her drink from the cup, putting it to her lips and taking a deep swallow before holding it out for him to refill it.

"I came all this way for a man only to discover that the man I came all this way for didn't want me after a few months of having me. Strange creatures, men are. They hound you and hound you until they get what they want, then, when you give it to them, they don't want it any more. Like little boys, really."

Her Irish brogue was tinged with deep bitterness.

"After that, I quit trying to figure it out," she said. "I had to eat, to live, you know? And there's only one thing a man will pay a girl for 'way out here ... anywhere, for that matter. So when Garrity left me, I figured why should I give myself to the next man who wants me, only to wind up in the same boat? Why should I do that now?" She turned her face directly toward Cole.

"I can't think of any reason," Cole said, and poured himself half a cup of her whiskey.

"You are damn' right," she said. "So I began charging for it, and I defy anyone to tell me it's wrong to want to survive."

Cole didn't know what Katy O'Brien wanted, so he just listened.

"Thing is, a garl can kid herself for only so long. And after a time, after she's got herself enough of a reputation, you know, ain't no man going to want to take her for his wife ... not when he can get what he wants for a dollar or two and not be troubled with the rest of it."

Cole tossed back his drink and reached for the makings.

"Would you mind rolling me a cigarette, too?" she said.

He rolled each of them one and they smoked in silence, the slow burn of the paper replacing whatever words they might have shared for that time. She drank her whiskey and asked for more, and Cole filled her cup again and she drank that. Then she leaned over to set her cup down next to the bottle, and, as she did, she kissed him. Her mouth was soft and wet and her inexperience at such an intimacy proved itself in the awkwardness of the kiss. Cole didn't kiss her back, and he didn't pull away. He was torn between his own loneliness and hers, knowing for her, at least, it didn't matter who or what he was, just as long as he was willing to drink with her and listen to her and share the empty hours with her.

The kiss lingered but a moment, then she pulled away and looked at him.

"You saying you don't want me?" she asked. "Am I not woman enough for you, or is it because I'm a prostitute?"

"You're young enough to be my daughter," Cole said.

"I thought men liked that. Men are always telling me how much they like it that I'm young."

"Maybe some men, Katy, but not all of us are like that."

"You don't have any desire for me?" she said, her hand resting on Cole's knee.

"Yes, I have some desire for you, and for that I'm ashamed. I'll drink with you, and I'll sit here and talk with you and listen to you, but I won't sleep with you."

She looked duly disappointed.

"I've come to that," she said. "Where a decent man won't have me even for free."

"How much is passage to New York?" Cole said.

"What?"

"I'll be happy to buy you passage back to New York, if that will help."

"Do you think a garl like me will fare any better in New York than out here on the frontier?" she wondered. "Ha, the only thing different would be that back in New York I'd have a pimp to see I worked and gave him every dime."

"Then what's the answer for you, child?" Cole asked.

She lowered her gaze and let her hand slide from Cole's knee. "Answer," she said. "There is none. I am what I am, what the fates have made me. I'm a young whore who will soon be an old one and we all know what happens to them, eh?"

"It doesn't have to be like that."

"Oh, surely it does, sar. How else can it be?"

Cole took $20 from his saddle pocket and placed it in her hand.

"You can do with this what you want, Katy. You can spend it on liquor or opium, or buy yourself passage back to New York. It's not much, but it could be a start."

She stared at the money for a long time.

"I don't want it," she said, and tried to give it back to him.

Cole curled her fingers into a fist. "Keep it," he said.

"I'd like to do something for you," she said.

"Maybe someday you can."

She kissed him again, then stood and put on her capote and scarf, and took what was left of her whiskey and said: "I thought it would surely be a cold day in hell before a man ever gave me money without me giving him something in return."

"Judging by the sound of that wind outside," Cole said, "it surely is."

"Cheyenne and hell," she said. "It's all like the same place, ain't it?"

"One and the same."

"Yes, exactly." She laughed and waved her bottle and slipped away.

Cole lay on the bed for a long time and stared at the darkness and listened to the wind chattering against the glass, and it sounded like the teeth of hunger gnawing at his soul.

CHAPTER FIVE

A hard knocking and a loud feminine voice shattered the dream Cole was having. He opened his eyes to the dull, margaric light of morning that angled its way through the window of his room. It took him a few moments to get his bearings. The dream had been about a woman and a moonlit river that ran red.

"John Henry! John Henry!" The voice was Cleopatra's.

Cole pulled on a pair of drawers and opened the door.

"You've got to come!" she said. "It's Karl Cavandish!"

"What's happened?" Cole asked as he put on his shirt and boots.

"You won't believe," she said. "Come quick!"

When he emerged from Sun Lee's, he could see a crowd gathered at the far end of the street and directly in front of the Blue Star saloon.

In his rush he had grabbed up the self-cocker but had left without his hat. A man on the streets of Cheyenne without his hat wasn't considered fully dressed. Cleo hurried ahead of him toward the crowd, holding her skirts and high-stepping through the mud. For a crowd, it was a quiet bunch. Cole pushed his way through and that's when he saw Cavandish and Long Bill Longly—well, the corpse of Long Bill Longly, stiff as a board and trussed to a hitching rail with baling wire. Cavandish had himself a mean-looking shotgun that he was aiming at the dead man.

"You killed that boy, you evil son-of-a-bitch!" Cavandish cursed. There was a dried rose in the lapel of Long Bill's black suit that looked fresher than its owner, and all in all it was a real strange scene.

"Karl," Cole said.

The undertaker looked around and Cole could see he was, if anything, drunker this morning than he had been the day before.

"I dug the bastard up, John Henry, just like I said I was going to. Now I'm going to give him some of his own medicine, going to cash in his chips for what he did to José."

"Looks to me like Long Bill's chips have already been cashed in, Karl. You really think this will make you feel better ... blasting him with that scatter-gun?"

"God damn, it took me half the night to dig him up, but I did it! I want the whole town to see what happens to trash that kills innocent boys!"

Cavandish's clothes were splattered with mud, even the seat of his pants. Tears ran down his cheeks and his hair stuck out wildly. He was a sorry and pathetic sight. Cole looked around at the crowd but no one said a word. From the far end of town, the engineer on the morning flyer from Denver cut loose the whistle as he approached the station and the sharp blast caused several people to jump.

"Karl, this would be unseemly if you were to shoot a dead man," Cole said. "Folks around here would find a thing like that hard to forget."

"I don't want them to forget!" Cavandish shouted. He had a hard time maintaining his balance and staggered about like he was stepping in post holes, trying hard not to topple over.

Cole was worried that he'd fall and accidentally shoot himself. "Why don't we go have a drink and talk about this," he suggested.

Cavandish blinked, looked around, looked at Long Bill, whose eyes were closed and oblivious to the undertaker's rancor, then back at Cole. "Soon as I fry his hash!" Cavandish said, trying to steady the twin barrels on the stony figure of Long Bill. Death had not been kind to Bill. Some of the skin was sloughing off his hands and cheeks. His color had turned an ash-gray and his hair was stringy.

"Maybe you should use this," Cole said, offering him the self-cocker. "Makes less of a mess." Cavandish started to protest the offer of the pistol until Cole reminded him that there were women and children in the crowd. "You don't want to leave those little ones with nightmares all the rest of their days, do you, Karl? That's no way for people to remember you. Besides, some of those pellets might miss their mark, hit someone innocent."

Cavandish looked sheepish and a bit contrite. "You're right," he said, and started to trade his shotgun for the pistol.

Just then a voice like the sound of gravel in a bucket stirred from the crowd. "Jesus Christ! I've seen about everything now!"

A voice like that you don't forget in a lifetime. Parting the crowd of gawkers like Moses parting the Red Sea came Harve Ledbettor, Esquire, formerly of Texas and lately of Denver high society, fully decked out in a beaver hat, buckskin jacket, and striped trousers tucked down inside a pair of fancy hand-tooled boots. He had a hog-leg with a twelve-inch barrel strapped to his hip in a silver-encrusted holster. The gun was a Ned Buntline Special. He even wore a checkered cape like the one Wild Bill Hickok used to wear. He looked for all the world like he'd just stepped off the front cover of one of Dewitt's Ten Cent Romances, an actor about to give his greatest performance. Wild Bill and Bill Cody would have laughed out loud.

"Karl Cavandish, when the hell did you start supplying your own business?" Harve cawed. "Why, that man looks deader'n Stonewall Jackson, God rest his soul."

It took Cavandish several seconds to recognize Harve, but as soon as he did, tears formed in his eyes. "Harve, is it really you?" Then, seeing the empty sleeve, he said: "Where's your arm?"

"Left it up in Rock Creek to a woman with a hoe, nothing but a bone by now, I suspect, all the meat chewed off by the coyotes and wolves. I aim to go back there someday and see if I can find it, take it, and have it bronzed now that I can afford to. Now let me ask you something, why the hell are you getting ready to plug a dead man?"

Cavandish looked at the shotgun in his hands as though seeing it for the first time. Harve looked at Cole and said: "John Henry, how you been?"

"You didn't get my wire not to come?" Cole said.

"What wire?" Ledbettor said with a mischievous grin.

Cole knew it was pointless to say anything more about the man's arrival.

"I was just going to shoot Long Bill," Cavandish said.

"Why?" Ledbettor asked as he took a closer gander at Long Bill, then wrinkled his nose and added: "This feller's putrid."

By now, the crowd was beginning to grow restless, unsure of whether there was going to be a show or not. Some had disappointed looks on their faces, realizing that they might not get a good story to tell their grandchildren about how a drunken undertaker dug up a dead man and shot him right there on the streets of Cheyenne. They would say it was the result of the terrible winter, how it turned men crazy, even men like Karl Cavandish, who was a paragon of propriety. There would be lots of stories to tell about that winter, but none would be quite so interesting as that of seeing a dead man shotgunned. So they were growing a little restless, waiting for Cavandish to fill Long Bill full of buckshot.

"Of course he's putrid," Cavandish said. "He's been dead since last autumn."

Ledbettor shook his head as he continued to inspect the corpse. "I heard you had a bad winter up here," he said. "Just never knew how bad until now. Did he pop up out of the ground himself, or did someone dig him up?"

"What difference does it make?" Cavandish said.

"None that I can see," Ledbettor said, then looked at the pistol in Cole's hand. "He must have been a bad piece of work for you to have dug him out of the ground so you could both shoot him."

"This is foolish," Cole said. "Karl, give me that shotgun before you shoot your feet off."

Without so much as a word, Cavandish handed Cole the shotgun. Then Cole asked some of the men to get a wagon and take Long Bill back up to boothill. Turning to Ledbettor, he said: "If you came here to help, you can start by helping me get Karl sober."

"Hell, I knew the minute you sent that wire," Ledbettor said, "you were ass-deep in trouble of some sort or other." He took an arm and Cole took an arm and together they marched Cavandish to his house where they tried to pump him full of hot black coffee.

Cavandish sputtered and cursed and carried on, then passed out on the bed from exhaustion.

Ledbettor looked at him a long minute, then said: "Do you think he's passed over?" He put his ear to Cavandish's chest and listened, then added: "Nope, he ain't dead."

"Why'd you come, Harve?" Cole said. "I sent you a wire telling you not to."

Ledbettor produced a silver flask, unscrewed the cap, and took a pull, then handed it to Cole who declined. "I've not had my breakfast yet."

"This is breakfast, son. A cowboy's breakfast, or have you forgot?"

"It's been forever since we were drovers, Harve."

"It ain't been that long, son. We ain't that far removed from what we was. Look at me. I'm a rich man, but I still spit in the street. And look at you, you ain't changed a lick. Still tall in the saddle, restless as tumbleweed. Why ain't you married and settled down with a bunch of ankle biters?"

"You look like you're doing OK for yourself, Harve … that fancy jacket and the new boots," Cole said. "And that hat had to cost you thirty dollars. And if you came here to talk old times, you've wasted a trip."

Ledbettor took another pull, looked at the flask, which had HHL, Esq. engraved on it, then said: "That's twenty-dollars-a-bottle firewater, son. Sweet as honey, smooth as a woman's teat, but it'll sneak up on you and kick you like a mule." Then he smacked his lips and flapped his good arm and the empty sleeve that held his stump, crowing like a rooster. "Look here at this piece of iron old Ned Buntline gave me. Son-of-a-bitch will shoot the eye out of a gnat at a hundred paces. I came loaded for bear, son. Came to help you do some killing."

"Who said anything about killing?" Cole demanded.

Ledbettor looked at Cavandish, passed out on the bed, then at Cole, his whiskey flask in one hand, his Buntline Special poking down along the leg of his trousers and said: "If I know anything at all about you, I know we're going to do some killing."

CHAPTER SIX

A strong wind blew out of the north and Ledbettor said: "Jesus Christ, this is cold country." He pulled at his flask. "Twenty-dollar whiskey," he said with a shudder. "God damn, never thought I'd be drinking twenty-dollar whiskey."

"You want to tell me what you learned that made you hop a northbound freight and come all this way?" Cole said.

They had left Cavandish stretched out on his bed, snoring peacefully, and had walked over to Shorty's Café. Katy O'Brien was hustling flapjacks and slabs of bacon to some of the same faces Cole had seen in the crowd a few minutes earlier who had been waiting to see a dead man get shotgunned.

"That's a fine-looking woman," Ledbettor said, watching Katy O'Brien hustle tables. "Lot's of hip and thigh to her."

"You mind?" Cole said.

"Soirées, John Henry?"

"What the hell is that supposed to mean?"

"It's what the rich people do in their free time ... attend soirées. Zerelda, God rest her soul, loved nothing better than to throw a soirée and she threw lots of them."

"Harve, if you caught the flyer up here just to tell me about Denver social life, I'm not interested."

Cleopatra came from behind the counter where she'd been cooking and ventured over to them. Harve ran his gaze over her like she was a piece of grazing land he had in mind for a thousand head of hungry longhorns. She eyed him askance and shook her head. "You boys want coffee?"

"Just enough to spill some of this sipping whiskey into, sis," Ledbettor said.

Cole glanced across the room and saw Katy O'Brien waiting on a fat man and several of his cronies, one of which was Jim Levy, who had his back to them. He saw Levy reach out and take her by the wrist and pull her toward him, then say something to her before loosing his grip.

"Why dilute good whiskey?" Cleo asked, referring to Harve Ledbettor's admiration of his liquor.

He snorted and lifted the flask in a salute and said: "Sis, you're just the ticket."

"You'd not be the first one to come along and try and charm the bloomers off me, mister."

He found that humorous. Cole found it distracting. "Bring us coffee, Cleo, and don't turn your back on this one-armed reprobate."

"Cut off my other arm," Ledbettor said, "and I'd still have eyes."

"Tell me what you found out about the murder," Cole said. "Before you wear my ears out."

Harve snuffled and leaned forward. "Those soirées I was trying to tell you about," he said, "are where the rich and powerful let their hair down, and sometimes their drawers. A man can learn a lot of dirt by just listening."

"You know, Harve, listening to you get the facts out on the table is like riding to Austin backward on a bony mule. Spit out what you're getting at."

"You've gotten irritable in your old age," he said.

Cole leaned back and rolled himself a shuck while waiting for his coffee and Harve to tell him what he knew about the murder.

"Judge Beam and Chief of Police Tommy Murphy was among the regulars who attended Zerelda's soirées, so I knew them about as well as I cared to. And it was Murphy who led the investigation into the judge's boy's murder. The boy's name was Tyron and he was just the opposite of the judge in every respect when it came to his morals and reputation. They say he liked to beat up whores, for one thing. Maybe that had something to do with them finding his body in the red-light district."

Cole felt a dull throbbing just behind his eyes.

"And there was something else, too," Harve said. "His ears was missing."

"Missing?"

"Somebody cut them off and took them." Ledbettor had a vacant look in his bloodshot eyes like he was trying to see a dead man without any ears. "You ever hear of a wild hair called Gypsy Davy?" he said.

Cole told him about Teddy Green and how he had dropped the same name on him.

"Seven shades of humanity," Harve said, spilling some of his whiskey into his coffee cup, then adding three spoonfuls of sugar.

"What's this man have to do with the killing?" Cole persisted.

"Gypsy Davy is a 'breed, but worse than that, he's an educated 'breed … went to Harvard, which is somewhere back East. The boy has himself a law degree and they say he was also some sort of a doctor, too. Dark-haired and dark-eyed, handsome devil and women fall all over themselves at the very sight of him."

"This doesn't sound like the same man Teddy Green told me about," Cole said.

"He tell you Gypsy Davy is a stone killer?"

Cole nodded.

"Well, he is that, too."

"How do you come by this information, Harve?"

"Gypsy Davy was … until the murder … the most popular feller in Denver. Hell, Zerelda and all the other rich matrons in the city couldn't wait to invite him to a soirée, that's how I come to know him."

"So the thinking is that he killed the judge's boy, this Tyron?"

Harve shrugged his shoulders. "Well, he was arrested for the killing, then broke jail. Word has it he said this woman was to blame, that he was innocent."

"Tell me about her," Cole said, feeling a coldness trickle through his blood.

"She was a looker," Ledbettor said, smacking his lips after sipping his coffee. "What was her name?"

He squinted the name into memory. "Ella, I believe it was," Harve said. "That's all the name I got on her. She was seen in his company at one of Zerelda's soirées and between the pair of them, you didn't need no gaslight to see by. They lit up the room."

Ledbettor described her and Cole was having a hard time denying that it was Ella Mims, the same woman he'd fallen in love with.

"What about this business with the ears?" Cole asked.

Harve shifted his weight in his chair. "They say Gypsy Davy keeps himself a necklace of ears from the men he's killed. I think that's what put Chief Murphy onto him as a suspect … the kid's missing ears and that necklace."

"Tell me you're pulling my leg on this one, Harve."

Ledbettor shook his head. "Wore 'em once to one of Zerelda's soirées. Looked like black prunes. Only he claimed he'd bought them from some natives in Borneo when he was traveling the world."

"How the hell does such a man get invited to rich folks' parties?" Cole asked.

"The rich are easily bored, John Henry. Anything out of the ordinary, they're interested in it. And a fellow like Gypsy Davy with his handsome looks, fancy talk, and educated ways fits right in. That string of ears helped make him a curiosity. Sorta like a big rattler, dangerous and fascinating as hell all at once, if you know what I mean."

"Tell me something. Why isn't a man like that swinging from the end of a rope instead of drinking champagne and rubbing elbows with the wealthy?"

Harve looked at him, then said: "That's a good god-damn' question and I don't know, except to say that wealth brings its own perversity to the table."

There was a commotion and a shattering of glass and Cole looked around in time to see Katy O'Brien stumbling backward and Jim Levy rising out of his chair, his face flushed red. He didn't have time to push her again before Cole hammered him over the head with the barrel of his pistol and dragged him outside.

He sputtered and struggled like a man hell-bent on getting himself killed will do, but Cole had a good grip on him. When Cole turned him loose,

Levy landed in the mud. He managed to struggle to his knees and feel around for the knot on the back of his skull before recognizing who it was that had done the damage to him.

"Cole! You son-of-a-bitch!" His fingers came away, smeared with blood, and this incensed him even more. He managed to rise halfway before Cole hit him again, cracking the barrel atop his collar bone and that put an end to his cursing. He howled like a scalded dog.

"Next time you want to get rough with somebody, Levy, come see me," Cole said, and turned to go back inside the café. Several diners had followed them out and stood there with napkins stuffed in the collars of their shirts. If they weren't going to get to see a dead man get killed, maybe they could at least see one or two live ones end up dead.

Somebody yelled something and before Cole could turn back around, two pistol shots cracked the air almost at the same time. The plate glass window behind Cole shattered into a rain of broken glass. He looked that way and then down, where he saw Jim Levy lying face down in the mud, smoke curling from the barrel of a pistol in his left hand. Ten feet away stood Teddy Green with a policeman's model Colt still aimed at the back of Jim Levy's spine.

Cole watched as Teddy Green slipped the revolver back into the shoulder rig under his greatcoat, then tipped his plug hat in Cole's direction.

"You should have killed that man when you had him down," Teddy Green said. "Lucky thing I came along or it'd be you in the soup, and I'd be out a man to help me find those people I'm looking for."

Those people, Cole thought.

Harve Ledbettor was right. There was going to be killing and it had already begun.

43

CHAPTER SEVEN

That night John Henry Cole drank a whiskey alone in the Blue Star and thought about the train ride to Ogallala the next morning. He had a lot of questions to ask Ella Mims, or was it Ella Green? Whoever she really was, she'd done a damned good job of capturing his heart. And he wondered if it wasn't a case now that he'd just been too lonely for too long and had let himself be blinded by a pretty lady with a soft voice and a warm bed. He hated himself for even thinking that way about her. The whiskey tasted good but it wasn't doing its job of making him forget.

Earlier, Harve Ledbettor had gotten drunk by noon, and Cole had let him pass out on the bed in his room behind Sun Lee's laundry. It was just as well. Cole didn't crave company, his or anyone else's. He thought about the men who were after Ella, thought about what Teddy Green had said about Colorado Charley Utter and the assassins the judge had sent to find Ella and make sure his own brand of justice was carried out. Cole thought about Gypsy Davy and wondered how it was Ella had come to be involved with a man who would wear a necklace of dead men's ears.

Cole had kicked around for a lot of years and never heard or came across anything to match the things he was hearing now. He thought of Texas and the old friend he'd shot down there near the border over a woman, thought about his late wife and son. He was a man with no home and no place to go and the last good thing he'd found in life was a woman named Ella Mims who people were now telling him was involved in an ugly murder with some really bad company. He didn't want to believe it and he wasn't going to believe it until he heard it from Ella. That was if he could find her before Judge Beam's assassins did. Teddy Green sat at a table in the far corner by himself, and Cole knew he was dogging Cole's every move, but unless he walked up and shot him, there wasn't much he could do about it. He grabbed the neck of the Jack Daniel's and walked over to Teddy Green's table.

Green didn't say anything. Cole poured out two whiskeys and set one before him. "It's not much for saving my hide out there on the street today."

Green nodded and tossed the liquor back before wiping off his mustache. "You were the law down in Del Río at one time," he said.

"How'd you know?"

"I heard about the killing. You did the state a favor by putting that *hombre* in a deep hole."

He was talking about Francisco Guzman, the old *amigo* and border bandit Cole had killed over a faithless woman. "We ever meet before?" Cole asked.

"No, but word gets around. I was with Company A of the Texas Rangers back then, running down the last few wild Comanches that still had enough fire in them to raise hell."

"And now?"

"I'm still a Ranger, but I'm not chasing down Comanches any longer. Rounded up the last of them in Palo Duro Cañon. They went home to roost and we caught them there."

"Just chasing women these days."

"One woman," Green said. He eyed the bottle in Cole's hand, and Cole poured him another drink, the liquor like amber oil under the yellow light, and watched as he washed his throat with it.

"If you don't mind my prying into your business," Cole said, "what happened between you and Ella that she would leave you?"

He offered a tight smile. "I was off chasing wild Comanches, remember."

Cole nodded, tossed back a glass of Mr. Daniel's sipping whiskey, and rolled himself a shuck.

"We were young," he said. "Put a young woman out alone on the Texas frontier, you can't expect much good to happen." His eyes crinkled in the corners, the skin permanently burned by wind and sun. He stared off into the past, seeing old memories flame to life again. A spot just below his right eye ticked. "We were married less than a year," he went on, his voice now a rough whisper. "I'd been gone on a long campaign, and when I came home, she told me she was leaving. I helped her pack, bought her passage to Denver. She'd always wanted to live in Denver. I reckon that's where she must have first met this Gypsy Davy." He found a cigar in the pocket of his greatcoat and bit off the end and held it between his fingers a while before lighting it. "She wrote me a couple of letters. But then they stopped coming, and I never heard from her again or anything about her until I was up in Dallas and read about the killing in the *Dallas Herald*, saw her name." He shifted the cigar to his mouth. "I learned she ran a hat shop here in Cheyenne, but it burned down. I wondered maybe, if the fire had something to do with the killing in Denver."

Cole nodded and told him the story about how he'd come to Cheyenne to work for his old friend, Ike Kelly, who had operated a detective agency; how Ike had been murdered, his office set on fire with him in it, and how the fire had burned down Ella Mims's hat shop in the process. "That's how we met," Cole said. "Ella and me, the first time. I questioned her about the fire, what she saw that night. We went from there. It didn't have anything to do with Denver."

"I'm relieved to know that," Green said.

"What connected you to me?" Cole wondered.

"I didn't know her long," Green replied. "So I didn't know that much about her, about her past. But I learned recently she had an aunt in Ogallala and I sent a wire inquiring about Ella, stated that there had been some serious trouble, and that I was looking for her. The aunt wired back and said Ella had been there but had left. She also mentioned that Ella had a visitor while there and gave me your name. It's the only lead I have. I came here to find you, hoping you could tell me where she was." Green must have seen Cole's look of surprise, for he said: "You don't know where she is, do you?"

"I figured she was still in Nebraska," Cole said.

Green shook his head. "Not according to the aunt. The trail runs out right here in Cheyenne with you. The aunt figured maybe she'd come back here, looking for you."

Cole ran the possibilities through his mind and came up with nothing. "I guess I can cash in my ticket to Ogallala," he conceded. "If she's not there, I don't know where she is. It's a big country, Mister Green."

"Unless the aunt is lying," Green said.

"She didn't strike me as a dishonest woman," Cole told him.

Green shrugged his shoulders, stood up, and buttoned his coat. "What would you do to protect someone you loved?" he said. "Ogallala is all we've got, Mister Cole. You want to take the chance the aunt's telling us everything she knows? And if she does know something more than she's telling, better we find her before Colorado Charley Utter and his boys, or Gypsy Davy."

It wasn't what Cole had had in mind, throwing in with Teddy Green.

"Train leaves eight-fifteen," he said. "I could use the help."

"Tell me something," Cole said.

"What's that?"

"Do you still love her?"

Green twisted his mouth and removed the cigar stub, examined the ash, and finally said: "You don't love a woman like Ella, then just stop because she left you. You ever been hard in love, you know that much, Mister Cole."

Cole thought that he knew exactly what Teddy Green meant.

CHAPTER EIGHT

A cold rain driven by a hard wind had the three of them huddled around the potbelly stove at the train depot the next morning. Cole had tried to talk Harve Ledbettor out of coming with them, but he'd simply waved that Ned Buntline Special of his in the air and declared he was up for excitement.

"You don't have an investment in this," Cole had argued as he had packed his saddlebags.

"Seems to me you are trying to look a gift horse in the mouth," Ledbettor had said. "I only got this one arm left, but I can shoot like a son-of-a-bitch."

"You can get shot, too."

"Looky here," Ledbettor had said, pushing the beaver hat down squarely on his head. "I've lived all the life one man can stand. I've been down to hardtack and river water coffee and I've et fish eggs on crackers. Had me ugly women, tall women, fat women, skinny women. I've ridden behind the ass of cows and slept in the saddle and I've slept in beds with satin sheets, too. Drank horse piss from a boot and champagne from a slipper. I guess I ain't missed a thing if I was to get shot before breakfast. I'm willing and you need guns, if you run up against Colorado Charley Utter and his bunch, or that ear-wearing Gypsy Davy. 'Sides, I'm a freeborn man and can go where I damn' well please. So finish up packing, John Henry, and let's stop jawing."

"OK," Cole had said, "but you ought to know I've not had much luck with friends lately … most of them are up there on boothill taking a long *siesta*."

He had winked and said: "But not me."

Teddy Green was already at the depot waiting for Cole when they came in. He looked at Harve, looked at the flap of his coat sleeve, then at Cole. Cole introduced Harve, and Harve said: "Teddy Green. Hell, I've heard of you."

"I'm from Texas as of late," Teddy Green said. "But I was a lot of places before Texas."

"Seems to me I recall you killed the Harris brothers in a barn in Missouri," Harve said. "All three of them on the same day."

Teddy Green warmed his palms over the potbelly stove. "Killed the ones that was there, yes, sir."

"Never did hear why you killed 'em," Harve said, trying not to act overly inquisitive but primed for some juicy conversation. "But I'd read plenty about their exploits as bank robbers. Those boys claimed they robbed more banks than Frank and Jesse James."

"They robbed a few."

"I see," Harve said, and warmed his own hands over the stove.

Teddy Green pulled a big silver pocket watch from his waistcoat, snapped open the face, read the time until he was satisfied, then closed it and slipped it back in his pocket.

"You were with the Pinkertons as I recall," Harve said, not content to let a potentially good story go by the boards, now that his curiosity was up. "On the scout for Jesse and Frank when you come up on them Harris boys. Leastways, that's the way I read it in the *Police Gazette*."

"Yes, sir, I was with the Pinkertons at the time."

"You just catch them boys in that barn, or was you waiting for them?"

Teddy Green leaned forward a bit, arched his back, and said: "The beds at the hotel are pretty soft. I prefer a hard bed, keeps my back from aching."

Harve took the hint that Teddy Green wasn't much interested in talking about the Harris brothers of Missouri and tugged his flask from inside his coat and held it forth.

"Anybody care to have a nip of old Tose?"

They heard the train's whistle and gathered up their gear in preparation of boarding. The cold rain pecked at their necks as they stood on the platform, and Harve finally turned to Cole and said: "Don't the weather ever grow pleasant in these parts? I ain't seen the sun but once, and that was in my dreams."

It was a six-hour ride from Cheyenne to Ogallala, and when they finally unlimbered themselves, the rain had stopped but the sky was flushed gray and a strong wind was blowing up from the Platte. A few waddies with nothing better to do than hang about watching the comings and goings of strangers gave the three of them a careful once-over.

"We'll need to rent saddle horses for the trip out to the aunt's place," Cole said.

One of the waddies leaned and spat from a plug in his cheek and called out to Harve: "Hey there, old-timer, you lose your arm in the war?"

They were just slothful youths, rag-tag boys without enough to keep their minds occupied. Harve was content to let the comment pass, conceding that they were ignorant and disrespectful street trash.

They went up to the livery stables but found the old man there had only one horse to rent at the time.

"Have more in the morning," he said. "All the others I got is let out at the present." Then he started to tell them the names of those that had rented his other horses and why they'd rented them, but the trio turned and headed back up the street to find a place to eat dinner.

"That feller must be dang' lonely to tell us his business," Harve said. "But from what I've seen of Nebraska so far, I can understand why. This looks like one of the loneliest places I've ever been."

The last time Cole had been to this territory, it wasn't Colorado Charley Utter or Gypsy Davy that had troubled his mind, it was a man by the name of Tom Feathers, the son of a rich man who wanted Ella's attention, and more than just that. Cole had figured that once he was out of the scene, Tom Feathers would move in and stake his claim. He might be a good man to look up, if they couldn't find Ella, a piece of information he decided to keep under his hat.

They found the rooms at the Big Muddy Hotel. There was a bar downstairs and a dining room that served oysters and freshwater mussels and Harve insisted on treating them all to some oysters and steaks the size of elephant butts.

They ate until they could barely push themselves away from the table, then went to the bar where Harve further insisted that he treat them to a few after-dinner drinks, which turned out to be gin rickeys. Cole didn't care much for anything but good Tennessee sipping whiskey and so, after the first gin rickey, he ordered some mash and stayed with that.

Teddy Green said that he wasn't a drinking man by nature and turned in his drink for some black coffee. Cole saw his gaze take in everything and everyone. It was the gaze of a born lawman. In a far corner sat a group of men, playing poker with a circle of other men standing around them so that you could barely see who the card players were.

"Must be a high-stakes game going on," Teddy Green said. Then Cole caught a glimpse of one of the card players and knew why there was such a crowd.

Bill Cody was wearing a beaded buckskin jacket and under the yellow light above the table his finely trimmed mustache and Vandyke gave him the appearance of an actor, which he had been—him and Texas Jack and Wild Bill before Wild Bill had jumped a train back to Kansas. Once there, Hickok promptly got married and headed for the gold fields in the Black Hills, where he was murdered and had left a widow that hardly knew him.

Cody had told Cole on his last trip to Nebraska how damned scared Wild Bill had been in front of Eastern audiences. His fear of making a fool of himself, Cody had said, was what got him killed. If Hickok had been more like Cody and Texas Jack, he'd probably still be alive and living well from his fame. As it was, the only ones living well from Wild Bill's fame were the dime novelists who wrote about him. Men like Ned Buntline, who was also sitting at the table to Cody's left.

"You met Bill Cody?" Cole said to Teddy Green.

"That him?" he said, pointing with his chin toward the table.

"That's him."

Harve said: "God damn, he ain't aged a lick."

51

"He's a lot smaller than I imagined him," Teddy Green said.

"Bigger than life," Cole said.

"I heard he met the queen of England, Victoria," Teddy Green said.

"He gave her a pair of silver spurs," Cole replied.

"Heard he killed a Cheyenne war chief name of Yellow Hand." Teddy Green's interest bordered on disdain, as though Cody's fame didn't scratch much dirt with him.

"What would the queen of England want with a pair of silver spurs?" Harve asked, two steps behind the conversation because of the number of gin rickeys he'd put away.

Bill Cody was holding court more than he was playing a simple game of stud poker. He enjoyed the attention and was in his element when surrounded by admirers. Cole imagined that the long winter had made him as restless as everyone else to leave the confines of his big house up near North Platte and come to town and do a little celebrating and give folks a chance to have a look at him. From what Cole knew from the last time he'd visited him at his ranch, Cody felt like the prophet who was honored everywhere but in his own home. He loved his wife and daughters, but they saw him only as a husband and father and provider, not quite the way he saw himself or the way he preferred to be seen.

"We could have used him down in Texas fighting Comanches," Teddy Green said, turning his back and leaning his elbows atop the bar. Cole wasn't sure how Teddy Green meant this comment. With Teddy Green, it wasn't easy to tell what he was thinking.

"Comanches are a fearsome bunch," Harve said, hoisting his gin rickey. "Here's to them poor sons-of-bitches!"

Teddy Green nodded and said: "Don't toast them too hardily, Mister Ledbettor, they killed plenty of Texas Rangers and a lot of other folks as well, before accepting their medicine."

"Yes, sir," Harve said. "They were a *fearsome* bunch."

Harve left them standing at the bar and went over and plowed through the knot of spectators around Cody's table and began slapping him on the back and calling him Cuz. It took Cody by surprise, then he recognized the old drover, and whooped and cleared a place for him at the table, ordering a fresh round of drinks.

"You want to join your friends," Teddy Green said, "go ahead. I'm thinking of taking a walk, getting some fresh air."

"No," Cole said, "I think I'll grab some shut-eye. I'd like to get an early start in the morning."

Teddy Green nodded, shifted his weight within his greatcoat, and walked out the front door. Cole headed for his room, knowing that Harve and Bill Cody would be up most of the night, drinking and telling grandiose stories, each of them slightly envious of the other's position—Harve wanting to be widely known, and Cody wanting to be wealthy.

As for John Henry Cole, he just wanted to find one woman. It didn't seem like a lot to want in a world full of wanting.

He was asleep when Harve pounded on his door and shouted: "Teddy Green's just killed a preacher!"

Rain hit the window and Cole thought: *Good god damn, what else can go wrong?*

CHAPTER NINE

Cole followed Harve to the bad part of town—the red-light district of cribs and bagnios. Every town had a bad side and Ogallala was no exception. Whores and pimps and dope fiends lurked in the shadows, men who would crack your skull with a lead sap while their women would pluck you like a chicken.

"What the hell was Teddy Green doing in this end of town?" Cole asked Harve, who only shrugged and said: "Same as any man I expect, looking for some comfort."

The odd thing for Cole was that Teddy Green hadn't struck him as the sort of man who would find his comfort in a red-light district.

A sizable crowd had gathered outside a false-fronted building; torches flared and sputtered under a soft rain. There on the porch, looking as dead as a Nebraska winter, was sure enough a man dressed like a preacher, half his jaw shot away, blood staining his white collar. He was staring at the rain, but he wasn't feeling any of it.

Teddy Green was there and so were three deputies with shotguns aimed at him.

"Man, 'Creek ain't gonna like it you shot a preacher in his town," one of the deputies said to Teddy Green just as Cole and Harve walked up. "'Specially *this* preacher."

Teddy Green's shoulder rig hung empty. Cole saw his pistol in the belt of one of the deputies. Green shot him a glance when they parted the crowd and stopped just shy of the porch where the dead preacher lay.

"He's a preacher, then I'm Abe Lincoln," Teddy Green said to the deputy.

"You don't understand, mister," the deputy said. "That feller ain't only a preacher, he's the city marshal's son-in-law."

"What happened here, Green?" Cole said.

"That man," Teddy Green said, pointing at the dead man, "is no preacher, or if he is, he wasn't when I knew him. He's wanted in San Antonio for murder and robbery."

"What in hell are you talking about?" the deputy said. He seemed to be the only one of the three that could, or would, talk. They were, all three, jug-eared and slack-jawed with their hats tugged down low. "That there is the Reverend Elihue Morral, Bittercreek Newcomb's daughter's husband."

Harve Ledbettor started to ask a question when a stir swept through the crowd and a man well over three hundred pounds pushed his way to the forefront. He stopped just short of the body, looked at it, and spat.

"This the son-of-a-bitch that did it?" he said to the talking deputy while nodding at Teddy Green.

"Yes, sir. That's him. Me and Hedge and Roy were just next door when we heard the shooting. Saw this man standing over Elihue with a smoking pistol in his hand, Elihue's jaw blowed off. That's some of it over there in the mud puddle."

The big man turned and saw the chunk of bloody flesh and bone floating greasily in the rainwater, then turned back to Teddy Green. "That there's my baby's husband, mister. And he's a god-damn' preacher to boot! You double-sinned tonight."

"He's a wanted man in Texas for murder and rape," Teddy Green said flatly.

"Well, you know something, you dandified son-of-a-bitch? This here ain't Texas and you ain't the law. I am. And what we do with murdering sons-of-bitches is hang 'em from the hanging tree." He pointed off toward a large cottonwood a hundred paces distant that stood like a lone sentinel, like a tree that was waiting to hang its next man. "Get a rope!"

Cole knew Bittercreek Newcomb from down in Oklahoma Territory where Cole had spent a year working out of Judge Parker's court in Fort Smith. How a man like him had ever gone from illegal whiskey peddling and petty thievery in the Territories to city marshal of Ogallala was a mean trick—a big, tall bastard with a dark face and curly black hair who looked like he wouldn't know what it was like to crack a smile. Maybe all that whiskey peddling and crime he pulled off in the Territories had made him a sour and bitter man, like his name.

"No rope," Cole said, and that spun Newcomb halfway around on his heels. Cole already had the self-cocker drawn and aimed at the center button on Bittercreek's shirt. "This man's a Texas Ranger," he said, nodding toward Teddy Green. "And if he says that dead preacher was wanted down in San Antone for crimes, then I believe him. You best, too."

Harve Ledbettor had slipped up on the porch behind the talking deputy and had placed the long barrel of his Buntline Special just behind the deputy's ear and thumbed the hammer back.

"I believe him, too, boys. Don't make this into a bloody mess," Harve said.

"What the hell business is this of yours?" Bittercreek bellowed like a bull, but all the bellowing in the world wasn't worth a wooden nickel against an ounce of lead.

"Green's with me," Cole said. "And there will be no hanging."

"He god-damned killed my sweet baby's husband and I won't stand for it!"

"You'll stand for it or join him," Cole said.

Newcomb gave Cole a hard eye and said: "Do I know you from somewheres?"

"I arrested you and Emmett Dalton once in the Nations for selling snake-head liquor to the Indians."

Newcomb shook his head; he didn't remember because it had probably been more than once some federal marshal had hauled his bacon into court. His recourse was to blink like he had a cinder in his eye. He turned back toward Teddy Green.

"What proof you got that Elihue is wanted in Texas?"

"These," Teddy Green said, pointing to his eyes. "I never forget the face of a wanted man. Got a memory as long as the hind leg of a dog. When he was in Texas, that fellow went by the name of Dirty Bob Braddock."

Bittercreek Newcomb was breathing hard now without having done anything; his chest heaved and fell beneath the greasy duster he wore; his sombrero was battered and mud-stained; his face was as red as a beet. "Looks like what we got here is a Mexican stand-off," he declared.

"No, sir," Cole said. "What we have here is a bunch of dead men if you don't release this man and back away."

"Well, you'll be just as dead as the rest of us," Bittercreek sputtered.

"Maybe so, but so will you and that deputy with the Buntline Special behind his ear … that's a fact."

There was a long moment when the only sound was the patter of the soft rain on the tin roofs of the whorehouses and into the puddles where it collected, then Bittercreek Newcomb let out his breath and said: "All right, god dammit. Hedge, Roy, you help Pat here get my son-in-law up to the funeral parlor … take his jawbone, too."

The deputies didn't move immediately and Bittercreek had to tell them again before they lowered their shotguns. Cole nodded to the one who had Teddy Green's pistol in his waistband and the deputy handed it back to Green, his eyes full of regret but full of relief, too; he would get to go home and see his wife and children that night.

"I'm gonna wire the police down in San Antone," Bittercreek said. "And if I find out they ain't never heard of no Dirty Bob Braddock, then I'm coming to arrest you for the murder."

"You won't arrest me," Teddy Green said.

"Why not?"

"This job can't pay enough to get yourself killed over a murderer and rapist, even if he was married to your daughter."

"Who says *I'd* be the one getting killed if I was to come looking for you?" the fat lawman said.

"Don't come looking for me, mister." Teddy Green said it as calmly as if he were ordering a dog to sit and not move, then turned and walked away into the descending rain.

"Let it go," Cole said to Newcomb. "That feller may have been a good husband to your little girl, but he sure as hell isn't worth getting killed for."

Bittercreek Newcomb leaned to the side and spat and didn't bother to wipe his chin. "I can round up a hundred men if I have to," he said.

"A hundred won't be enough," Cole said. "Leastways not where you're concerned. Let it go."

"I still don't remember you from down in the Nations," he said, as though that was still troubling his mind. "What are you doing up here?"

"Just passing through, Marshal. Just passing through."

*   *   *   *   *

They had gotten halfway back to the good side of town before Harve said: "Hot damn, but we come close to shooting the ribbons out of those yahoos, didn't we, John Henry?"

"We came close to dying, Harve, that's the way I saw it."

"Hell, dying, living, it's all the same thing in the end, ain't none of us getting out of this world alive."

"I'd just as soon die in my sleep than out here on these muddy streets, if you don't mind."

"Hell, I'm ready for a drink. How about you, John Henry?"

"We'd better just sit tight and stay off the streets. Bittercreek Newcomb might still want revenge for Teddy Green killing his son-in-law."

Harve grumbled his assent and didn't say anything until they'd reached their hotel.

"You know what I saw back there?" Harve asked.

"No, what?"

"The prettiest Chinese whore I ever laid eyes on, and I've been to San Francisco."

"You better lie low, Harve."

"'Cause of Bittercreek?"

"No, I think maybe Cleopatra has her eye on you."

Harve looked struck dumb for a moment, then he grinned like a beaver. "You think?"

"Well, I think she was at least warming to you by the time we left Cheyenne."

"Well, then, I'd best be careful and get me safe on back to that sweet woman when this is all over."

"You can go now, if you want," Cole suggested.

"No, sir … we ain't finished the job yet, and I intend to be there at the end. 'Sides, I ain't killed nobody yet."

"You have a one-track mind, Harve."

"Well, sir, my daddy raised me right. He said … 'Don't try to ride a horse and a woman at the same time.'"

"I don't know what that means."

Harve smiled and said: "Neither do I, but it means something."

They reached the hotel and Cole started to head for his room when he caught a glimpse of a man in a bowler hat and a greatcoat, sitting in the shadows of the bar. He told Harve he'd see him first light, and went over to where Teddy Green was sipping coffee.

"Did you have to kill that man?" Cole inquired, taking a seat across from him.

"I never kill anyone I don't have to."

"If you try and arrest everyone you see that's wanted for a crime in Texas, we might be a long time finding Ella."

His gaze held steady over the rim of his cup. "It's not likely I'll run into that many," he said.

"That's not the point."

"It couldn't be helped," he said.

"What were you doing at that end of town?"

He lowered the cup and embraced it with both hands. "I thought maybe I might find her there."

"Ella?"

He twisted his mouth and looked at his reflection in the cup. "It's a long story," he said.

"I'm listening."

"Maybe another time. It's late. I'll see you in the morning, John Henry."

He didn't move and Cole knew their conversation was over, at least for the moment. He didn't want even to guess about the reference to finding Ella in the bad part of town. Right then Cole needed a whiskey, some time alone—they all did. But the questions kept running through his mind like wild horses across the high sage flats: *Where was Ella? What was her involvement with Gypsy Davy and the murder? What did Teddy Green know about her that would make him seek her out in the red-light district?* The only way Cole would find the answers was to find Ella, but the real question was, did he want to know the answers? He still loved her and maybe the truth wasn't what he really wanted. When the bar dog asked him what he was having, he told him to bring him a bottle, then took it to his room.

CHAPTER TEN

The next morning they rode out of Ogallala on three rented horses, heading west to the aunt's house under a stormy sky. Harve complained that he hadn't seen the sun shine since he'd left Denver and wondered openly if Nebraska was good for anything other than boredom until they spooked some sandhill cranes near the river. When the big birds lifted into the air, Harve said: "Good God Almighty, them's big chickens." Of course he knew what they were; he was just trying to lift the somber mood that had overtaken them. Nobody laughed but Harve.

The aunt's house was about ten miles outside of Ogallala and every mile seemed like twenty. Then it commenced to rain hard and something made Cole think that even the gods were going to be against him this time around.

The place was just as Cole had remembered it: a two-story white clapboard with black shutters and a porch on three sides with the summer kitchen out back. The memory brought with it the scent of stored apples and the long kiss Ella and he had shared there in that small room with the spring sun coming through the windows.

They reined in and Cole said that, since he knew the woman, he'd knock on the door. Harve shifted under the stiff wind coming out of the northeast and drew up the collar of his coat while Teddy Green sat on his horse, stoically taking in his surroundings. He seemed immune to the conditions, the rain beading on the crown of his bowler.

Cole's knock brought no reply, but he'd seen the hack near the rear of the house under a lean-to and the piebald mare in the corral, so it seemed likely that the aunt would be home. He knocked again and this time his eye caught a glimpse of women's shoes through the tatted curtains of the parlor window. The shoes had feet in them and his heart skipped a beat.

He tried the door but it was bolted. He went around back and saw the broken window to the summer kitchen and the door ajar. He found the aunt there on the floor of the parlor, strangled, her eyes staring at the wainscoting, a harness strap knotted around her neck. There was something else he noticed, too. He unbolted the front door and motioned Harve and Teddy Green to come inside. He wanted them to see the dead woman.

"Jesus Christ," Harve said when he looked down at her.

"Gypsy Davy," Teddy Green muttered as he squatted next to the aunt.

"He's cut off her ears," Harve said.

"If she knew where Ella was," Teddy Green said, "you can bet she told him."

"Now what?" Harve said. "The trail looks like it ends here."

Cole did not claim to be an expert on dying, but it looked to him as though the aunt had died a hard death. Teddy Green was undoubtedly right; if she had known anything about Ella's whereabouts, the aunt would have told it.

"I've got one card left to play," Cole said. "It's not much, but it's something."

Harve pulled his flask and took a pull, then offered it around. Teddy Green and Cole both declined.

"We'll need to let someone in town know," Cole said.

"Play your card," Teddy Green said.

They rode to the Feathers spread. It was a thin chance that Ella would have gone to Tom Feathers's for refuge, but then how well did Cole really know her in the first place? The rain had stopped, but the wind had increased and dark clouds scudded so low it seemed they were riding right through them.

The main house lay in a valley between swelling mounds of brown winter grass. When they topped a ridge, they could see it there, quiet and seemingly undisturbed except for a wisp of black smoke curling out of the chimney before it got swept away by the stiff wind. It was a raw day in every respect and none of them had gotten the picture of the dead woman out of their minds.

"Seems awful quiet for a cattle operation," Teddy Green said.

They'd ridden through a large herd of the new shorthorn cattle a mile from the main house. Harve had hawked and spat his disdain when seeing them.

"A cow without long horns ain't much in my book," he had said.

It was true. There was no activity surrounding the house as you might expect. They saw a blood trail from the front porch leading to the barn just as they rode up.

Teddy Green jerked the pistol from his shoulder rig and said: "We've ridden into some bad business here, John Henry."

They found three men hanging from a rafter. The cold gray light silting through the roof shone mutedly on their twisted faces. They were dressed like drovers and their tongues lolled out of their mouths, black and thick. Like the aunt, their ears had been sliced off.

"Son-of-a-bitch," Harve muttered.

"You know any of these men, John Henry?" Teddy Green said.

Cole didn't. They were no doubt hired hands who had gotten caught unawares.

Teddy Green's gaze took in the scene, then his eyes trailed toward the back of the barn where a door swung in the wind. "The blood trail continues out that way," he said.

The trail led to a well twenty yards beyond the barn. They heard a strange sound from the depths of the well, but it didn't take a scholar to figure out it was the labored breathing of a person. Something the size of a fist knotted in Cole's stomach. The only person he cared about might be lying in the bottom of the well, dying.

"We'll get a lantern and tie it to a rope and lower it down," Teddy Green proposed.

That's what they did. They didn't have to lower the lantern far, for there about ten feet down was Jake Feathers, Tom's rich father. His face was bloody, and, when the light neared his eyes, they grew stark and wide with fright. He uttered something unintelligible and screamed.

"Feathers, if we lower you a rope, can you get it tied around you so we can haul you out of there?" Cole shouted. He moaned and Cole asked him again.

Then he said in a weak voice: "I'll ... try."

It took a good half hour before Feathers got the rope knotted around himself well enough that they could haul him up, and once they almost lost him. When they did get him out of the well, he looked like he'd been dragged by horses. Harve found a tarp and they laid him on it and carried him to the house. He was in bad shape, bad enough shape that Cole knew he'd die no matter what they did—a dying man gets a certain look in his eyes, and Jake Feathers had that look. They did the best they could for him, wrapped him in blankets, and fed him whiskey, most of which spilled from his lips.

"Tom," he kept saying over and over. "Tom ... Tom."

Cole asked Feathers where Tom was and his eyes grew startled and shifted from Cole to Teddy Green to Harve and back to Cole. "Is Ella with Tom?" Cole asked.

He blinked several times, and Cole asked again.

He nodded his head. "Gone," he said. "All gone."

"Where?"

Harve spilled some more whiskey in him, then took a pull himself.

"Where are they?" Cole said again. "Where are Tom and Ella?"

Feathers looked toward the door, then up to the beamed ceiling.

"Gonzales ...."

Cole wasn't sure if he heard him right, but Feathers repeated it. The name didn't make any sense, but nothing did.

"Who did this to you, old-timer?" Teddy Green said.

"Hi- ... him ..." he muttered. "Man ... knife ...."

"Gypsy Davy?" Cole said.

Jake Feathers looked at Cole, looked at Harve, at Harve's empty sleeve, then rolled his eyes, took a breath, and died.

"Who's this Tom?" Teddy Green said.

"His boy," Cole said.

"You know him well?"

"Well enough."

"Can he fight, John Henry? Can he stand up to a man like Gypsy Davy?"

"I have my doubts."

"Then we'd better get going."

"Where?" Harve said.

"Any ideas, John Henry?" Teddy Green said.

Before Cole had a chance to think about it, the ground thrummed with hoofs. They went to the front door and there, topping a ridge, were maybe a dozen riders.

Teddy Green stared at the bunch and said: "That would be Colorado Charley Utter and his assassins."

"How can you tell?"

"Their hats," Green said. "See the way they wear them pinned back?"

CHAPTER ELEVEN

Colorado Charley Utter was a short, thick-set man who wore a cream-colored sombrero with the front brim pinned back to the crown. He also wore a heavy buckskin jacket that had beadwork, fringes, and doeskin gauntlets. He wore a brace of pearl-handled revolvers and Cole could see the brass-fitted stock of a long-range Winchester rifle like the one he owned tucked into the boot of his saddle. He was a grim-looking man who looked loaded for bear. The men with him were typical waddies: broad-brimmed hats pinned back like his, chaps and spurs, and equally well armed. Cole counted ten of them.

"We're looking for a man named Feathers," Utter said. "One of you him?"

"He's in there," Cole said, "but he's not up to conversation just now."

Utter leaned forward, resting his hands on the pommel of his saddle. "Why ain't he?"

"He's as dead as Moses," Harve said. "Some feller tossed him down a well after he dragged him."

Utter looked beyond the three of them as though he were trying to see through the log walls of the main house, trying to see if Jake Feathers was really inside, dead as they'd said he was. Then he said something to the man next to him, a tall, lanky cowboy wearing batwing chaps and three pounds of pistol on his hip. He told the man to go see how dead Feathers really was. The man sniffed the air and swiped at his sandy mustache before climbing down from his horse and going inside. He came right back out again.

"Son-of-a-bitch's dead, Charley, these fellers weren't lying. And his ears is cut off."

Utter took off his gloves and slapped them together, then said: "Well, ain't that a piece of bad news." Then he looked at John Henry Cole and said: "We're looking for a lady. Don't suppose you've seen a woman about?"

"Saw no woman," Cole said before Harve or Teddy Green could say anything. "Why are you looking for her?"

Utter looked at Cole with his dark, buggy eyes, the lids half closed, as though he were already tired of the conversation. "That'd be none of your business, mister."

"You're the man who buried Hickok," Cole stated.

He blinked. "You heard of me, huh?"

"I know who you are."

"Then, if you know anything, you know I'm a serious man. If you know about this woman I'm looking for … her name'd be Ella Devereaux … then you'd best tell me about it. I find out otherwise, me and my men here might just come looking for you boys."

"You don't want to come looking for me," Teddy Green said in his flat voice that was as cold as iron.

"Oh, you don't believe so, eh?" Utter replied.

"You don't want to come looking for me, mister," Teddy Green repeated. "You want to track down women to hang them, you go ahead. Maybe that's your speed, but you don't ever want to come looking for me."

Some of the riders visibly shifted their weight, but not Colorado Charley Utter—he was a man with too much bulk to shift easily. He tapped his gloves in one hand and measured Teddy Green, measured his speech and the level empty gaze.

"You know why I'm after her, then," Utter said at last. "I find out you boys know the whereabouts of this woman I'm after, I won't forget that."

"We don't know anything about this woman," Cole said, making sure to cut off Teddy Green's challenge to the man. Getting into a shoot-out wasn't going to serve anyone's purpose, especially not theirs, considering they were outgunned three to one.

Utter tugged on his gloves, took up his reins, and turned his horse back in the direction they'd come and rode out. The other riders followed, slapping the ends of their reins over the flanks of their mounts, throwing up clods of dirt as they peeled up the ridge.

"Maybe I should have killed that man here and now," Teddy Green said. "Might have saved us all some future troubles."

"Maybe so," Cole said. "But a wise man has to pick and choose his place and time and this was neither the place nor the time."

Green shifted his gaze from the distant riders. "We'll meet those men again, John Henry. And when we do, we'll have to kill or be killed."

"I've already counted on it, Mister Green, but maybe next time we'll have the odds a little more in our favor."

"What now?" Harve said. "We going to ride or are we just going to stand out here and watch it rain and talk about shooting guns?"

"I'm with you, Mister Ledbettor," Teddy Green said. "We're just burning daylight, standing around here."

"Well, we might find us a way to narrow down just exactly where Ella and Tom Feathers are headed," Cole said.

They both looked at him and Green said: "How?"

*　*　*　*　*

They rode back into Ogallala and stopped in front of the city marshal's office. Bittercreek Newcomb was sitting inside, his feet in a pan of hot water. He looked up when they walked in, wide-eyed and ruddy-faced. He was already working up a sweat at just the sight of them.

"What the hell you yahoos doing back here?" he shouted.

"Keep your feet in that pan," Harve said. "Or I'll pull this hog-leg and shoot you in both of them wrinkled dogs."

Newcomb grimaced at the threat.

Cole told him about finding Ella Mims's aunt and Jake Feathers and his men.

Newcomb got a sour look on his face. "Cut off their ears?"

Harve started to go into detail about Gypsy Davy and his penchant for human ears, but Cole stopped him before he could get windy. "The man who killed them," Cole said, "is someone we need to find before he finds Ella Mims and Tom Feathers. The old man's dying word when we asked him the direction they were headed was 'Gonzales'. You want to tell us what that means?"

Bittercreek looked at the three of them like they were rotting buffalo hides some fool had dropped off in his office as a practical joke. "Well, even if I did, you think I'd give two shits about you boys finding them, or anybody else, for that matter?" His gaze was fixed stonily on Teddy Green. "You know how hard my daughter cried when I told her you killed her husband? You know what my baby's tears felt like running over my hands as I tried to wipe them from her eyes? You got any idea how much she loved that man?"

"This ain't about that," Cole said. "Maybe next time she will have better judgment in men and won't marry a killing rapist."

Newcomb's gaze shifted to Cole with as much vehemence as it had held for Green. "I aim to kill you boys, just thought you ought to know."

"Go ahead and shoot him in the feet, Harve," Cole said.

"Hell, yes!" Harve said, and pulled his Buntline Special. "When I finish with you, you'll have to crawl for your supper and sit to take a piss."

"Hold on now!" Newcomb cried.

"Tell me what you know about this Gonzales," Cole said.

Bittercreek grumbled for a moment, then saw that Harve would have no trouble crippling him by shooting him in the feet. Convinced, he told them that he'd seen Feathers and Ella passing through town three days before on the south road with luggage tied to the back of Tom Feathers's hack. "Jake owned a cattle spread in Gonzales, Texas," Bittercreek said. "That's all I know about it."

"That road they took, where's it lead?" Harve asked, still aiming his long iron at the feet of Bittercreek Newcomb.

"Take you all the way to the god-damn' Gulf of Mexico, I reckon, if you stayed on it long enough."

"Kansas, then across the Oklahoma panhandle, and on into Texas," Teddy Green said. "We better get after them."

"They ain't alone," Newcomb said. "Feathers has got a nigger hand of his with them … one who can shoot in the dark."

Harve blinked. "Nigger that shoots in the dark?"

"That 'un can," Bittercreek said. "The old man hired him special, had him brought up here from the Nations 'cause of his reputation. Fact is, I'm the one who told Jake about that nigger … how he can see in the dark good enough to shoot a man at a hundred yards. You give him daylight, he'll kill you from a mile out with his buffler gun."

"That doesn't mean spit to me," Teddy Green said, already turning to leave.

"Maybe that nigger will shoot you in the dark and save me the trouble," Newcomb said. That was when Teddy Green came around in one forceful motion and struck the lawman hard across the cheek bone, knocking him out of the chair and his feet out of the water pan. "You want to shoot me, get to it, you fat tub of guts, or keep your mouth shut."

That was all there was to it. Bittercreek Newcomb didn't say another word as they turned and walked out of his office.

"We have to look at it this way," Cole said as they walked their rented horses back to the livery. "If Feathers has got an extra man with him who can shoot, it can't hurt if Gypsy Davy or Charley Utter catches up with them before we do."

Harve chimed in by saying: "I knew a trick shot in Fresno who shot glass balls off his wife's head while wearing a blindfold."

"That's damned risky business on her part," Teddy Green said.

Harve laughed and said: "No, he wasn't wearing the blindfold … she was."

It broke the mood somewhat, Harve and his stories. They needed to buy horses and asked the owner of the livery if he had any for sale. He clapped his hands and said: "I do."

They bought three of his best, which were of average horseflesh, but they'd have to do.

"You think these mounts will hold up under a hard ride?" Teddy Green said as they saddled up. The horses had cost them $20 each, the saddles $40.

"Only one way to find out," Cole said.

They rode until dark and made a dry camp by a branch of the Platte. A meal of beans and river water coffee, a quick shuck, and a pull from Harve's whiskey flask to ward off the chill, and they found themselves in their bedrolls, staring up at a half moon behind shifting silvery clouds. As he lay there watching the big emptiness overhead, Cole kept thinking about the surname Utter had given Ella—Devereaux. The more he learned about her, the more he understood how little he knew.

CHAPTER TWELVE

They rode three days south into Kansas. One thing about Kansas is that there's not much to take up your attention, just endless seas of prairie grass and hardly any trees. If you wanted to hang a man in Kansas, you'd be hard pressed.

"This is a godless place," Teddy Green said after lonely hours and days of riding and seeing little more than an occasional soddy. "What would possess a man to bring his family way out here?"

"Free land," Cole said.

"It's not hard to see why it's free," Green said. "Who'd want it?"

Harve rode along, whistling happily until he ran out of bug juice. "Need to stop and buy some supplies," he said, holding forth the empty flask, trying to shake out the last drops.

They rode on. Eventually they came to a burg called Sweet Jesus—it was painted on a board a hundred yards from the nearest set of raw lumber buildings. Cole counted four in all.

"It ain't hard to see how it got its name," Harve said as they rode past the sign. "The first feller probably stopped here and said … 'Sweet Jesus, I can't go no farther! And, Sweet Jesus, there just ain't no reason to.'"

Among the buildings there was a whiskey den, a mercantile, a restaurant, and a blacksmith—everything a prairie town needed to survive, it would seem. Harve wanted to go straight to the whiskey den, but Cole suggested they might do well to have a meal at the restaurant, that all the hardtack and beans they'd eaten on the trail were getting plenty tiresome.

"Well, I'll meet you boys at the hog house," Harve said. "I've got to warsh my throat."

Teddy Green and Cole rode over to the restaurant while Harve tied up in front of a place called Big Mary's. They went inside and grabbed chairs at a table near the window. Cole had a need to sit by windows where the light was good and he could observe the street—it was an old habit from his days as a lawman, and also from his days while on the dodge.

They sat there a long time without anyone taking notice, even though they were the only patrons. Then finally a man came out of a back room, wiping his hands on a greasy apron. He had a head full of thick hair and was as big around as he was tall and, when he saw them, he came right over.

"'Scusa," he said. "I'm in the back and don't hear you gentlemen come in."

He had the same accent as Bill Cody's wife—Italian.

"Two plates of grub," Teddy Green said. "Make it steak, if you got it, and no beans!"

"*Sì, sì, signore.* I fix them right up for you."

"Wonder how it is a man comes all the way across the wide ocean to end up out here on this godless frontier?" Teddy Green said. "Think of all the places a man could end up. This place doesn't even seem like it would be on the list."

"Maybe he was trying to get to California or Oregon and just couldn't go no farther, like Harve said."

Teddy Green reached in his pocket, took out his watch, and wound it. He checked the time, then put it away again.

"You catch the name Colorado Charley used when he spoke of Ella?" he said.

"Yeah, Devereaux," Cole said. "Was that her maiden name before she married you?"

"No, it was Simpson, leastways that's what she told me at the time."

73

"Then she's using an alias," Cole said.

"Sounds like."

"You as concerned about her as I am?"

Green looked at Cole for a long hard moment. "You forgetting who it was came to you for help in the first place?" he said.

"No, I haven't forgotten."

They ate their steaks in silence. They gnawed the meat off the bones as if they were pilgrims just landed, which in a sense they were, only instead of an ocean behind them, they were in a sea of grass.

Cole was rolling a shuck when he saw something he didn't believe. It was a naked man riding a flea-bitten mule down the center of the town. Naked, that was, except for his hat, a pistol belt and a revolver, and his boots.

Teddy Green saw him, too.

"I thought I'd seen everything," he said. "I was wrong."

Cole called the waiter over and asked him who the man was.

His eyes got big and he said: "Oh, that's *Signore* Allison."

"Clay Allison?"

"*Sì*, that's *Signore* Allison. Sometimes he comes to town like that."

Cole looked at Teddy Green. "The last I heard Clay Allison was in New Mexico, married, with a wife and several children."

"Last I heard he was in jail in El Paso," Teddy Green said. "Somebody ought to go tell him to put some clothes on before he's spotted by a decent woman."

"Be my guest," Cole said.

Green looked at Cole in that hard flat stare of his. "Maybe I just will."

"Let it go, Teddy. Why risk getting killed because the man's a fool?"

"Doesn't this place have any law?" Teddy Green asked the waiter.

He nodded sadly. "*Sì*. We got *Signore* Redbird, but he's asleep a lot or drunk and asleep. Sometimes he's a fishing in the river, too."

"Where's his office?" Cole asked.

"Over there." He pointed toward Big Mary's, the saloon Harve had gone into to drink his lunch.

They found Ned Redbird stretched out on the pool table, asleep. Harve was chatting with a woman in a red dress in a far corner near the piano and paid little attention to either Clay Allison, who stood along the bar with his bare buttocks sticking out like loaves of unbaked bread, or Cole and Teddy Green when they came in.

Teddy Green shook Ned Redbird awake. He sat up, scratching his eyes, and said: "Who are you and why are you disturbing my sleep?"

Teddy Green pointed toward the naked gunfighter. "Is it your custom to allow lewdness in public?"

Ned Redbird looked at Clay Allison, then back at Teddy Green. "Why, hell, that's Clay Allison. What'm I supposed to do? That man's killed more people than the pox. You think I'm going to tell him he has to dress up to come into my town?"

"You're the law, aren't you?" Teddy Green said.

"Am the law, but that don't mean I got to die being it. Besides, what's the harm? He ain't shooting or stabbing nobody. Wake me up if he starts shooting or stabbing somebody." Ned Redbird stretched back out on the pool table.

"Why? Does that mean you'll go arrest him if he starts killing folks?" Teddy Green said.

Ned Redbird opened one eye and peered disdainfully at the Ranger. "No, it just means that, if he starts stabbing and shooting people, I want to get on down the road before he stabs or shoots me."

Teddy Green uttered an oath, then looked at Cole and said: "That is just plain indecent."

"Let it go," Cole warned him again. "You see anybody complaining except you?"

The woman Harve was talking to laughed suddenly and Cole saw Clay Allison look in their direction.

"Naomi, you damn' cheating bitch!" Allison bellowed.

"That's it," Teddy Green said, and crossed the room to where Allison stood against the bar.

"Mister, you are a damnation to look at. Why don't you go put some clothes on like a decent man?"

Clay Allison drew his head back sharply as though he'd ducked a punch. He blinked, probably unaccustomed to having anyone say anything to him about his appearance or manner. Cole eased his way into position to shoot Allison if he went for his pistol. If he did go for his gun, some of them might die.

Seeing for the first time Clay Allison's state of affairs, Harve cawed from the table: "What's that you say, you bare-assed son-of-a-bitch?"

Allison's gaze shifted from Teddy Green to Harve. Cole's movement in taking up a position on him also caught his attention. Suddenly he looked like a bad dog surrounded by three other bad dogs. *Which one to fight?* That may have been what was going through his mind.

"Let it go, Clay," Cole said. "You pull your iron, one of us is going to kill you."

His gaze came to rest fully on Cole, at least what he could see of him, standing where he was, where the light was bad and off to his left.

Harve had moved away from the table where the woman seemed to shrink herself as small as she could. There wasn't a back door and no place to run except past Clay Allison, so she stayed where she was.

"That," he bellowed, "is my god-damn' woman sitting with that one-armed son-of-a-bitch, and I don't allow no man to sit with my woman, especially one-armed sons-of-bitches!"

"He didn't know," Cole said. "He does now."

Harve was itching to pull his hog-leg and let fly, but Cole knew Allison would probably kill him before either Teddy Green or he could shoot the man down.

"Ease off, Harve," Cole said.

Teddy Green and the gunfighter were no more than three feet apart. Cole kept waiting for one of them to make a move, hoping the whole time that Clay Allison would see he was in a delicate situation.

"Three against one, Clay," Cole said. "Even a blind man can see those are poor odds. Why die like this, naked in a saloon? Think how your wife and kids would feel, hearing the news."

He gave it one more moment, then tugged his hat down hard enough to bend his ears, and stomped out. Green and Cole walked to the door and watched as he mounted the flea-bitten mule, cursing to himself as he did so, then rode back out of town in the same direction as he'd come.

"He's likely to get good and chafed," Harve said, joining them, his arm around the waist of the woman. "That man don't have no sense."

"I can't wait to get back to Texas," Teddy Green said, shaking his head. "Men in Texas don't ride around in their altogether and they don't insult women. Kansas is a raw and untamed place, godless as any I've yet seen."

"Maybe it's all this nothingness they got out here," Harve said. "Maybe so much nothingness makes folks crazed."

The woman, Naomi, said: "That's twice in three days that I've seen a crazy man. First there was that man wearing a string of ears around his neck, then today my lover comes riding in naked as a jaybird. I believe he must be on dope or something."

It got their attention, the part about the man with the ear necklace.

CHAPTER THIRTEEN

Naomi said a tall, handsome stranger had come through a few days earlier and had stopped at Big Mary's and drunk a bottle of whiskey and offered her $20 to give him a bath and scrub his back and wash his hair.

"Twenty dollars to give him a bath?" Teddy Green asked incredulously.

"Yes," Naomi said. "At first I thought he was fooling. Most cowboys want to buy my services, but the last thing they want is a bath. Fact is, most of them would rather shoot off their big toes than take a bath. Whiskey and fun, that's what they come here for, not baths. But this man wanted a bath and so I gave him one. For twenty dollars, wouldn't you?"

"I surely would not," Harve said. "I wouldn't give a man a bath for a thousand dollars."

"Well, that's you, honey, that ain't me. Out here, money is as scarce as trees. Somebody offers you twenty dollars for anything, you take it. He offered and I took it. Hell, he could have had the whole package for five … bath and all."

Ned Redbird stirred from his position on the pool table and sat up again. "A man can't get no decent sleep any more," he groused. "Might as well go cut me a willow pole and go fishing."

"Where you going to find a willow pole when there's not a tree to be seen in any direction for a hundred miles?" Teddy Green asked, his mood still sour over the encounter with Clay Allison. "I didn't even see a creek for any fish to be in."

"Well, there is a pond about a mile from here that's got fish in it and I got a willow pole I brought with me from Ohio. I just don't know where I left it. But if I can find it, I'm going fishing."

"Go right ahead, mister," Teddy Green said. "Maybe you are better at catching fish than you are at catching criminals and keeping the laws of decency. This woman says there was a man through here a couple of days ago … tall man wearing a necklace of ears. You see this fellow, see which way he went when he left?"

Ned Redbird scratched himself all over and muttered he was feeling gamy.

"Well, did you?" Teddy Green repeated.

"Yeah, I saw somebody riding a big white horse. I didn't see if he was wearing ears around his neck or not. I never seen a horse that big afore. Must have been eighteen hands tall if he was an inch. All white, except he had a black tail and mane. And that feller's saddle was covered in silver. Had more silver stuck to it than what they had down at the bank before it got robbed and burned to the ground."

"In what direction did he go, that's all I care about," Teddy Green said. "I don't care how tall his horse was or how much silver he had on his saddle or even how much money there was in that bank."

"Well, I had fifteen dollars in that bank when it got robbed and burned down," Ned Redbird said bitterly. "It was my life's savings. Those dirty, ornery Canadian River boys came through and robbed it and burned it and I'm once more broker than a hard-shell Baptist."

"Canadian River boys?" Teddy Green said. "I've never heard of them."

"Well, you're lucky you ain't. They're the meanest bunch of yahoos I've ever seen in my life. They shot everybody in the bank, then robbed it, then burned it down."

"Where were you when all this was going on?" Teddy Green said. "You're supposed to be the law."

Ned Redbird scratched at a spot inside his shirt, then withdrew his fingers and checked them. "I was fishing. And it's a good thing I was, or I might have lost more than just my life's savings. Those Canadian River boys murder any lawmen they see just for the fun of it. Them boys is all 'breeds … Mexicans and half-Injuns and coloreds … and they hate lawmen, white lawmen especially."

"You're a disgrace to that badge," Teddy Green said.

"Here, you want it?" Ned Redbird unpinned it from his cowhide vest and held it forth.

"All I want from you is to tell me which way that man on the tall horse went when he left here."

Ned Redbird pointed with his nose. "That way, south," he said. "And good riddance to him and good riddance to the Canadian River boys as well. I hope not to see hide nor hair of any of them. Fact is, if I can save me another fifteen dollars, I'm going back to Ohio. There is nothing out here on this frontier but grass, people who live in mud houses, and wild gangs of thieves and murderers."

"Maybe it's best you do," Harve said. "How did you get to be a lawman in this burg in the first place, scared of your own shadow as you are?"

Ned Redbird looked duly contrite for a moment. Then Naomi said: "He took it off of Two-Finger Gus."

"Who's Two-Finger Gus, hon?" Harve asked.

"He was my common-law husband and owner of this whole durn' town and everything in it till he passed on. He was also the mayor, postmaster … though we don't have a post office yet … justice of the peace, and town marshal. 'Course, a town like this doesn't need much law … there's only eight folks lives here … was eleven but three got shot and killed during the bank robbery. That's how Gus met his end, fighting those Canadian River boys. They shot him full of holes and left him out on the street dead as any dog." At this, Naomi spilled a tear from her eye and Harve was quick to wipe it dry with a fancy red neckerchief.

"Now, now, hon, take it easy. I'm sure those Canadian River boys will try and rob the wrong bank and end up swinging from ropes before too long. Not to worry."

"Well, how long do you intend on standing around comforting this woman?" Teddy Green said. "I'd like to get moving. What else can you tell us about this feller that had the ear necklace?"

She sniffled and laid her gaze on the Ranger like she was a cow looking at new grass. "He had good skin," she said. "I seen that when I was giving him his bath."

"I don't care about the good skin he had," Green snapped. "I want to know, did he tell you anything, where he was going, was he chasing somebody, anything like that?"

Naomi blinked several times, then said: "I remember asking him what was a fine, handsome man like himself doing 'way out here at the edge of nowhere, and he said he was after a woman, a lady friend of his, and he thought for sure she'd come through here not long ago. Yes, I believe those were pretty near his exact words."

"Let me ask you something," Cole said. "Didn't you think it was a little strange, giving a bath to a man wearing a necklace made of human ears?"

She looked at Cole then like he'd just asked her if she knew how to fly to the moon. "Well, he wasn't wearing them at the time. He only wore them when he came into town and when he left again."

"Fine, fine," Teddy Green said. "Enough of this jawbreaking. Let's get moving."

Cole looked at Harve. "You staying here with Naomi?" he asked.

"No, sir, I'm not one to quit a job before it's finished." He turned to her and said: "You'll just have to wait on me, hon, and hope I get this way again, and if I do, I'll pay you to give *me* a bath and I won't be wearing no string of ears around my neck, either. How'll that be?"

"I can't make no promises," she said. "The wind could come through and blow me away, or who knows? Those Canadian River boys could come back and steal me and take me off to their hide-out and make me their slave and who knows what all. You want me, you better take me with you now."

"Well, what about your boyfriend, the naked feller?" Harve said. "Won't he be broken-hearted if I was to take you away with me?"

"Him!" She snorted. "He's nothing but a dope fiend and a married man to boot. What future would I have with someone like that? I'd be better off marrying a cow."

* * * * *

Teddy Green and John Henry Cole were already riding the south road when Harve caught up to them. He had a wide grin on his face.

"Boys, that's some woman, ain't she? Last woman I knew like that who had pretty white hair and a sweet smile like Miss Naomi's was Squirrel Tooth Alice, who is now married to a Calvinist and lives a stark and pious existence. You'd never know it to look at her that she'd bedded about every rannihan that ever rode up the Chisholm Trail."

"I'm not interested in your experiences with womanhood, Mister Ledbettor," Teddy Green said. "It's not a decent thing for a man to discuss his doings in public, even if it is with whores."

"Suits me to a tee. I just thought it might help pass the miles, I was to tell you about my experiences with Squirrel Tooth Alice, but if you'd rather just ride along and be bored to death, that's fine by me."

"I'd rather be bored plum out of my hat than to listen to a man discuss his private doings with a woman," Teddy Green concluded.

They rode for another few hours like that, hearing nothing more than the creak of saddle leather and the plod of their animals' hoofs and the swish of prairie grass when the wind washed over it.

"You thinking about Gypsy Davy?" Cole said to Teddy Green, who looked deep in thought, his brow furrowed, his gaze fixed straight ahead, where there was little more than grass and horizon and you could see fifty miles in any direction.

"I know where Gypsy Davy is," Green said. "Ahead of us somewhere."

"Then what?" Cole asked.

"What I don't know is where Colorado Charley Utter and his bunch are." Green turned his attention to Cole for a brief moment. "You know they're out there somewhere. Thing is, where?"

"It's something to think about," Cole agreed.

"You know what I'm concerned about?" Harve said. Before either Green or Cole could answer, he added: "Why that Gypsy Davy didn't cut the ears off Naomi after she gave him his bath?"

"Maybe he's got no more room on his string," Green said irritably. "Maybe his string is too full and he just couldn't fit another pair of ears on it."

"Hadn't thought of that," Harve said. "But you could be right."

Two crows flew out of nowhere and crossed overhead, casting their winged shadows over the grass.

"That's a bad sign," Harve said, looking up, "seeing two crows together like that."

"Who says?" Green inquired. "I've seen lots and lots of crows and I've never known it to be a bad sign. Fact is, there is even an entire tribe of Indians named Crows. Fierce warriors known for their strong medicine. A handsome people, too."

"I don't know about none of that," Harve said. "All I know is every time I've seen two crows flying close together without cawing and on a cloudless day such as this, trouble has soon followed."

"I'll keep that in mind," Green said, and spurred his horse on ahead, as though he didn't want to hear any more about crows and bad signs and Harve's encounters with women.

In the meantime Cole's own ears were getting a little sore from so much talk. All the palaver about crows and whores and bad men didn't take his mind off the fact that ahead of them somewhere was a woman he thought he was in love with, one who was running from something terrible, and with a man Cole much disliked. It was a bitter pill for him to swallow, knowing that she had sought out Tom Feathers for help. But then, Cole was beginning to realize there was a lot about her that he didn't understand. He didn't want to believe that he'd let himself be fooled or that everything he thought he knew about Ella Mims was a lie.

They rode until the dusk chased them into a dry camp beside a stream and settled in for the night. Off in the distance you could hear the rumble of thunder. The plains were like that. One minute the weather was peaceful and the next it was at war with you. There were no trees, no sort of shelter if a storm did strike them. Maybe Ledbettor had been correct in saying that the two crows were a portent of bad things to come. Cole had seen men drowned in rivers, trapped by sudden wildfires swept by high winds, and hammered until bleeding by hailstones the size of apples. But the worst thing he had ever seen was an outrider struck by lightning. It had killed him and his pony in a heartbeat and fused his spurs together.

The rumble of thunder came closer, as if it were marching right in their direction. Cole watched streaks of lightning snake through the sky off to the west and thought of the outrider who had been dozing in his saddle one minute and struck dead the next instant. The lightning had also set his hair and shirt afire. Then he felt the ground rumble and knew they were in for it.

CHAPTER FOURTEEN

"There's a cyclone coming, boys! Run for cover!" Harve was already out of his soogan, shouting at them above the wind, its roar like a fast moving train.

"Damnation!" Teddy Green swore. "This is the most godless and inhospitable country I've yet to be in!" At that instant the wind snatched his bowler and carried it off into the darkness and driving rain.

"There's no place to run!" Cole shouted. "No place to hide, except we immerse ourselves in that creek!"

"That's good enough for me!" Harve cawed, and dived in, belly first.

The water was cold, but they hugged it while the lightning, wind, and rain rushed over them, the wind growing so loud they could barely hear each other.

"The horses!" Teddy Green shouted.

"Nothing we can do!" Cole yelled in return.

"My ears feel like they're exploding!" Harve cried. Bolts of lightning struck the ground all around them, then the rain turned to hail the size of prairie chicken eggs and pounded down while the creek water churned and frothed over them.

"Good Lord! Look at that, would ya!" Harve cried during a strong series of lightning flashes that lit up the prairie in a strange ghostly light. Through squinted eyes Cole saw a gray funnel cloud not a hundred yards distant, their horses running ahead of it, but it was plain to see in that moment that they weren't going to outrun the funnel of wind. Then the darkness closed in again and the roar made it impossible to hear one another as they clung to the muddy sides of the creek under the assault of hailstones and a pounding rain and waited.

In minutes it was over, except for the rain. They climbed out of the creek, soaked to the skin, and stood there, trying to see into the dark.

"You reckon it took the horses?" Harve said.

They listened for a time without hearing anything more than the claps of thunder as the storm receded into the darkness.

"Nothing we can do until morning," Teddy Green said. "It's wet and we can't even find a tree to build a fire. Damnable place, this Kansas is."

"I wonder if that cyclone went through Sweet Jesus and blew all the buildings away?" Harve said. "I wonder if it blew Naomi away? She said a big wind might come through and blow her away, or that the Canadian River boys might come and steal her. Maybe she's one of those people who can tell the future."

"That wind took my hat," Teddy Green said. "That was a pretty good hat. I bought it just before I left Amarillo. I used to wear a Stetson, but I sort of liked the way that bowler looked on me when I put it on. Now it's gone, taken by that cyclone along with our horses and every blasted thing we had."

They stood, alone and defenseless, drenched like kittens someone had tossed in the creek.

Teddy Green's wrath was plain in his croaky voice. "Come daylight, I'm going to go look and see if I can find my hat and whatever else that wind swept away. I don't like going about bareheaded."

"Could be we'll find Naomi, too," Harve said. "Along with your hat and our horses. She might have gotten blown clear to China, and maybe so did your hat."

"Mister Ledbettor," Green said, "I think it's time you passed around that whiskey flask you keep in your pocket. I'm terribly wet and cold and it's going to be a long night without a fire to dry our clothes. I'm by nature a temperate man on most occasions, but I reckon the good Lord will forgive me for drinking some of that devil water."

Harve gladly pulled his whiskey flask from his pocket and passed it around and they were for once mighty grateful for the whiskey. It was small comfort, but comfort nonetheless.

After a long, restless night, day broke with a line of silver clouds off to the east and they took survey of their situation.

"Good Lord," Teddy Green said. "That wind blew away our entire camp. Why, we don't even have a saddle between us, nor a gun or rifle. Even our footwear has been blow away!"

It was true. The cyclone had plucked them clean as chickens at a Mormon picnic. Even the grass was cut like a gigantic scythe had bored along, inches above the ground, and they could follow the cyclone's path like a crooked green road.

They began walking, following the path laid out before them. They had little choice if they were to find some of their gear or their horses. They were in sad shape, worse than beggars, wearing nothing but the wet clothes they had had on when the cyclone hit. They were bareheaded and barefooted and without weapons or horses. They would have been easy prey for road agents or renegades. Fortunately it was an empty land, devoid of much life. In three hours of walking, they didn't see as much as a single antelope or coyote.

"I told you those crows we saw yesterday were bad luck," Harve said finally as they shared the last of his whiskey. "I know now why they were flying so low and fast ... they were trying to outfly that storm."

"I'd at least like to find my hat," Teddy Green said. "My head's beginning to broil under this hot sun."

With the passing of the storm, the sky had turned to a pure blue without a single cloud and the sun had turned fierce. Another mile on they found the horses. They were dead, piled one atop the other in a small arroyo, their bodies twisted, their legs stiff and sticking straight out.

"Well, least we found them," Harve said. "If we had a knife among us, we could cut us some horseflesh and eat it like the Apaches do when their horses is kilt or they've run them to the ground."

"Well, we've no knife, nor wood to build a fire to cook with," Teddy Green said. "Unless you want to try and eat those animals right off the hoof."

"I ain't walked that far or gone that long without a meal that I'd eat a dead horse raw," said Harve.

They moved on. Another mile and they found a single boot, but it wasn't one of theirs.

"Who do you reckon this boot belongs to?" Harve said, trying it on, only to learn that it was too small and wouldn't fit.

"Maybe, if we're lucky, it belongs to Gypsy Davy," Teddy Green said. "Maybe the storm caught and killed him like it did our horses."

"Have you taken inventory of our luck lately?" Cole asked.

"Yeah, you're right," Green said. "We wouldn't be that lucky, would we?"

"Well, whoever it was had mighty small feet," Harve said. "I've always prided myself on the size of my feet, but this feller's got me beat." He tossed the boot aside.

"We're in a tight here," Green said. "We could walk a thousand more miles and not see a living soul. I guess the government didn't give away enough of this free land, or else we would have come across one human being by now."

"We could always walk back to Sweet Jesus," Harve said. "It can't be more than fifty or sixty miles."

"If that cyclone hit through there," Cole said, "it would be a wasted walk. Best we keep moving south, forget about finding any more of our camp."

"Poor Naomi," Harve said. "She was a sweet woman, even if she was a whore."

"Well, we can only guess whether the cyclone blew that town off the map or not," Green said. "Your lady friend aside, it would be no great loss to the world if that big wind blew Sweet Jesus clean to Texas, which is where I wish I was right now. In fact, if that cyclone blew away all of Kansas, it wouldn't be any great loss in my book."

"Too bad we ain't cows," Harve said. "We could eat some of this grass."

"And if we had wings, we could fly," Teddy Green said sourly. "Like those crows."

"I wish I was a crow," Harve said. "I'd fly and find us a place to get some grub and buy some horses."

"I guess we can complain all the way to the Gulf of Mexico," Cole said, "but that won't make the trip any shorter."

They fell into silence after that and continued to walk due south, considering that, if they walked long enough and far enough, they'd end up in Texas. Late that afternoon, as the sun was beginning to angle low and cast their shadows into long dark shapes over the beaten grass, they espied a soddy, black smoke curling up from its lone stovepipe. There were two sorry-looking horses staked nearby—a bay and a swayback stud.

"We've been saved," Harve said. "I never thought I'd be saved by folks who lived in a dirt house."

"We're not saved yet," Teddy Green declared. "Those folks might not be friendly, and, if they are, they might not be friendly to three half-dressed and shoeless men. Look at us. We look like bums."

"But we ain't bums," Harve said. "I'm a rich man, thanks to my late wife."

"You don't look rich," Teddy Green said. "You look like a bum of the worst sort."

"Well, I ain't no bum."

They approached the soddy to within fifty yards and Cole helloed the house. After walking all day, there was no sense taking chances of getting shot by a nervous sodbuster.

"What you boys want?" came a man's voice from behind the long barrel of a musket poking through an open window.

"We were caught in a bad storm last night!" Cole called. "It swept away our horses and gear, left us afoot as you can see!"

"How do I know you ain't those Canadian River boys that's been raiding all over Kansas?"

"Mister, take a good look at us," Teddy Green said. "We don't even have a single horse among us or a pistol, neither. How you figure we'd be raiders?"

"You look like trash to me," the man said.

"We ain't trash, either," Harve said. "I'm a rich man from Denver."

"Shit," the man cursed. "You a rich man, then I'm Ulysses S. Grant and I got old Abe Lincoln in here and we're discussing the Congress."

"Look," Cole said, "we just need some grub, maybe buy a horse or two if you have some you'd like to sell."

"Nearest town's forty miles one way, sixty the other. You came from the north, you went through Sweet Jesus ... that's the one's sixty miles. The other's south of here ... Hump Dance ... outside of Dodge City. It's the Sodom and Gomorrah of Kansas. Full of cut-throats and painted whores and whiskey dens. I'm betting you can buy all the grub and horses you want once you get there, or steal them. Better move along before you miss the party."

"The only thing that cyclone didn't blow away was my pants with my lucky gold piece in them. I'll give you that twenty-dollar gold piece for a pistol and some bullets and one of those sorry-looking horses," Harve said. "We could at least protect ourselves from road agents and the like if we had us a pistol."

The man snorted. "Road agents? What would road agents want with you bums?"

"Now look here ..." Teddy Green started to say.

Cole cut him off before he could rankle the man further: "Mister, we'd be grateful to you for something to eat. This man's a Texas Ranger and we're after a pretty bad actor. And maybe, if you'll help us, we'll catch him before he comes along and kills you and whoever else lives here with you." Cole was hoping to play to his sympathies, and if not his sympathies, then his fears. There was a slight pause while the man thought.

"He'll cut your ears off, if you ain't careful," Harve said. "He likes to cut the ears off folks and wear them on a string around his neck."

"Anybody comes around here trying to cut off my ears, I'll give him a gutful of lead," the man said. "Now git along afore my finger gets itchy and I start shooting you boys to ribbons."

Cole saw the scowl on Teddy Green's face. "Come on, let's keep moving."

They walked until dark, then stretched out on the open prairie with nothing but stars for a blanket and the ground for a pillow, but at least they weren't having to sleep in a creek or in wet clothes.

"We walked a damn' long way today," Harve said.

"Farthest I've ever walked at one time," Green said. "And I don't aim to walk this far tomorrow. I might just go back and confiscate that man's horses."

"Then you'd leave him in the same condition we're in," Cole said.

"I know. It's all that kept me from doing it in the first place."

"How far did that man say it was to Hump Dance?" Harve asked.

"Forty miles," Cole said. "Less what we walked since then."

"Forty miles." Teddy Green said it like a curse.

CHAPTER FIFTEEN

Noon two days later they saw something.

"What is it?" Harve wondered.

Someone was moving across the prairie on foot, pushing something.

"Without my hat to shade my eyes," Teddy Green said, "I can't hardly make out who or what it is."

Cole helloed and the figure stopped and seemed to look in their direction, then after a moment or two sat down.

"Let's go," Cole said.

When they reached her, the woman looked like she'd walked as far as she was going to go. She was old and thin and wore a dirty gingham dress and a Mother Hubbard bonnet from which peered a pair of the most forlorn eyes Cole had ever seen. She had a plain and simple face that was long and narrow, and reflected, no doubt, every weary, mournful year she'd spent on the prairies. The thing she'd been pushing was a wheelbarrow with a dead man in it.

The man was as thin as she, dressed in faded denim coveralls and a cotton shirt that was frayed at the collar and cuffs. His brogans were dusty and his skin was grayish. His bony limbs hung over the edges of the wheelbarrow.

"Madam," said Teddy Green, "why in God's name are you pushing a dead man around in a wheelbarrow out here in the middle of nowhere?"

Her eyes flicked white in the shade of her bonnet as she took in the Ranger. She seemed almost too weary to answer, but then said: "Taking him to town."

"What on earth for?"

"Taking him to his harlot," she said.

"Harlot?" Harve asked.

"He loved her, not me. Let her bury him. I won't."

The three of them looked at each other.

Teddy Green was shaking his head. "Strange country, John Henry. Must affect people's minds."

"How far is this town, ma'am?" Cole asked.

She turned her head and stared into the distance, toward a horizon that offered little but grass and sky. The wind ruffled her bonnet.

"Another mile, maybe two. It's hard to say when you're pushing a heavy load like Judiah here. He may appear slight, but he's all deadweight. You ever try and push deadweight more than a mile or two?"

"No, ma'am, not in recent memory," Cole said.

"Well, 'tain't no easy chore, I can assure you that. God damn and son-of-a-bitch, I don't believe we should have ever left Indiana and come to this country. This is a god-damn' useless place that just eats up a body's soul. And now that harlot has eaten up Judiah and she can god damn' well have what's left of him."

It was rare to hear a woman use such language, but she did a right smart job of it.

"What he die of," Harve said, "your mister?"

"Syphilis is what the doctor said he had," she said. "I reckon it was that. It wasted away his brains. The last few days he talked all sorts of crazy talk, tried to jump off the roof to kill himself, only the roof wasn't high enough to even break a leg and all he done was jam his knees and complain about that. Tried to drown himself in the well, but only managed to get stuck and I had to winch him out. Night before last found him standing on a pail trying to screw the milch cow, calling it Jezebel and slapping its flanks. I had to strike him with a shovel to get him to stop. Milch cows is hard to come by this far out … almost as hard to come by as husbands."

There were four bloody dots on his shirt front.

"Looks like buckshot holes," she said. "But they ain't. I didn't shoot him. What finally happened was he rammed himself into a pitchfork and that finished him. Judiah never had that much sense to begin with. The screwing disease poisoned what little mind he had. Pitiful way for a man to come to his end, but that's what sin will do to you … bring you to a pitiful end."

"You don't look like you're going to be able to wheel him to town," Teddy Green said. "Better just leave him right here and go back home, ma'am."

She sat there, staring at the horizon.

"This is the bitterest place I've ever been," she said, then began to weep.

"Where is your place, ma'am?" Cole asked.

She pointed over her shoulder and they saw the soft rut that the barrow's wheel had cut, leading off toward the east.

"Let us help you take your husband back there and bury him proper," Cole suggested.

"I wanted her to have him," she said. "His Jezebel."

"Well, the dead deserve our respect," Harve said. "Even if they strayed in life. Which one among us has not strayed along the path of life?"

The woman looked up at Harve, her dirty cheeks now stained from her tears.

"Are you a preacher?" she said.

"No, ma'am. Long ways from it. Maybe your husband done wrong by you, but this ain't no way to get even with him, hauling his carcass to a whore. Best let the good Lord sort out such matters. You've done about all you can for him."

"You're right," she said. "But I just couldn't scrape out a hole and drop him in it. You know what they say about a woman scorned. Me, I am right proper feeling scorned. Now Judiah's dead as last winter's skunk cabbage and I'm left alone out here in this god-damn' nowhere. All alone with naught but the wind to keep me company." She looked at the dead man and gave him a bitter stare. "You did me wrong, Judiah, and I shall never forgive you for it. May your soul burn in the lake of fire!"

They walked the mile or so back to the woman's homestead—a soddy in the middle of nowhere. A milch cow was staked nearby with not even a chicken or a horse to keep it company.

"If you'll bury him, I'll fix you men something to eat, if you don't mind eating corndodgers and slab pork, that is."

"No, ma'am, we don't mind eating anything," Harve said. "You got a spade?"

Teddy Green and John Henry Cole set to digging the grave, while Harve looked on, overseeing the burial. "Better go deep with him so the coyotes and wolves don't come along and dig him up," Harve said. "That poor woman probably couldn't take seeing him make an appearance again. I'm sure she's glad shet of him. Imagine how she'd be affected, was she to come out some morning and find him lying there, dug up by wolves, gnawed on and such."

"You want to dig this grave, you're welcome to it," Green said, a bit irritated at all the advice. "I've buried lots of men and I've never yet had to have anyone tell me how to do it."

Harve said: "I'd have a hard time digging a hole with having only this one arm. If I had two, I'd pitch in and help you boys. Someday I intend to go find my other arm, or what's left of it. I reckon the coyotes and wolves et everything but my arm bone, but, still, it would be good to have it, so when they bury me, I'll have all my parts. I'm a firm believer in departing this world with all that the good Lord gave you when you came into it."

"You think having all your parts in the hereafter is going to make a difference?" Green asked.

"Well, it can't hurt," Harve returned. "Suppose I have to end up wrestling the devil to fight my way into the pearly gates?"

When they finished planting the man, they washed up in a barrel of rainwater before going inside and eating the corndodgers and slab pork she'd prepared for them. They sat at a small handmade table in the dim light and ate ravenously while the woman sat and watched in stony silence. Finally they finished what had been set before them, then shoved back from the table, feeling as though they'd just dined at the finest establishment in seven states.

"There's some cider," she said, pointing to a jug. "You boys might as well have at it. Judiah sure ain't going to be missing it, and I'm a teetotaler and would never allow hard liquor to pass my lips. Whiskey steals a body's brains. The raw frontier has stolen about everything from me there is to steal, and I'll be hanged before I let my brains get stole, too."

Harve looked at Green and Cole and then, with a shrug, reached for the jug and pulled the cork with his teeth. "Well, let my brains get stole," he said, and took a long pull and smacked his lips.

"You gents look poorly," the woman said after they'd finished passing around the jug. "What happened to you and how come you're out here without so much as a horse among you?"

Cole explained to her about the storm.

"Oh, yes," she said. "I heard it howling a couple of nights ago after I hit Judiah with that shovel to get him off the cow. I thought for sure the wind was a sign from the Almighty and would blow all this dirt down on us and kill us. Maybe I'd be better off if it had. Least I wouldn't have to live with the shame of a straying man."

"I guess there'd be nobody to know that but you," Teddy Green said. "You're the first person we've seen for nearly two days."

"It's high lonesome, that's a fact," she said.

"We were trying to get to that town, Hump Dance," Green said. "Is that where you were headed with your husband?"

"Yes," she said. "The most sinful place in God's creation. Full of syphilitic whores and evil spirits. I hope that storm went through there and blew it to Kingdom Come. It is a blight of humanity and maybe, if it got blowed away, some decent folks would come through and build a new town where a woman could walk the streets without being molested by tramps and liquored-up men, and a husband could go without getting drawn into the lair of harlots."

"Well, we best get started," Green said. "We've a lot of ground to cover."

"Judiah's clothes are in that trunk yonder. You gents are free to help yourself to any that will fit you. What need do I have of a dead man's clothes?"

They thanked her for the offer but none of them really had need of a dead man's clothes, either. They headed for Hump Dance.

Harve kept an eye on the sky, saying he was watching out for more crows. "I reckon we'll be lucky if we don't see no more crows this trip."

"I see any more crows," Teddy Green said, "I'm going to chunk a rock at them."

"You'd have to have a pretty good arm to chunk a rock at a crow and hit it," Harve said.

"If you don't stop talking about crows, I might take a rock and chunk you with it," Green said. "My disposition is sour and all this talking about crows isn't improving it any."

Harve was about to reply, for there was little he liked better than arguing a point, when they heard the drum of hoofs and turned to see riders, bearing down on them.

"Hope they ain't road agents," Harve said. "We don't have even a stick to fight with."

"They're not road agents," Cole said. "That's Colorado Charley Utter and his bunch."

CHAPTER SIXTEEN

They sawed at their reins until they pulled their ponies up just short of where the three men stood. Colorado Charley Utter looked disdainfully at their condition and said: "You boys look like you been rode hard and put away wet. What happened, some road agents come by and rob you?"

Teddy Green glared at the man.

"Never seen me a bunch of barefooted stragglers out on these plains that lived to tell about it," Utter said. "Why, you boys would be easy prey for any yahoo with bad intentions!" This said, he looked at his crew and hooted like they had tickled his funny bone.

"You best ride on out of here, mister, and leave us alone," Teddy Green said.

Colorado Charley blinked like an owl. "Why, we could rope you boys and drag you around behind us like you was tree stumps. How'd that be?"

"Move along, Utter, before you talk your way into a fight," Cole said. He was feeling some of Teddy Green's wrath at being fooled with by a bunch of assassins.

One of Colorado Charley's sidekicks, the one with the batwing chaps and Walker Colt on his hip, leaned off to one side and spat and said: "Hell, Charley, let's just shoot the sons-of-bitches and be done with it. They'd be as easy to kill as prairie chickens."

He was right, of course. They were armed to the teeth and all the three men had was their pride and not much of that.

"Hold off, Miller," Utter ordered, raising his right hand. "No use wasting good bullets." Then he leaned forward, spat, and looked at John Henry Cole and said: "Why, it'd just be a good waste of bullets. I reckon these yahoos will plumb walk themselves to death." With that, he spurred his horse and rode away, the others close on his heels, except for Batwings.

"I ought to shoot you boys just for practice," Batwings said.

"Yeah, maybe you should," Cole agreed. "Hell, you'd be doing us a favor, I reckon. We don't find water and food soon, we'll die a hard death. A bullet would be a blessing."

Batwings seemed to like that, the fact they'd die a hard death. It caused him to smile like a mule eating briers and Cole thought: *If he doesn't shoot us, I'll find him and make him wish he had.*

"You gents have a good walk, hear." Then he rode off.

Harve whistled and said: "Thought the son-of-a-bitch was going to plug us with that big iron."

"I'll remember him," Teddy Green said.

"Yeah, me, too," Cole said.

They made Hump Dance in three hours—which is to say they limped on in. Their feet were bleeding, but their bellies were full of corndodgers and fatback the widow had fed them, so they probably weren't nearly as bad off as they appeared. However, they did see women grabbing up their children and ducking inside whatever door was nearest when they saw what looked like three disreputable range bums.

"They act like we're heathens," Harve said.

"We probably look worse," Cole said.

"I still got that twenty-dollar gold piece in my pocket," Harve said. "Let's stop in that whiskey den and have us a beer, and then I'll see if this burg has a telegraph and wire Denver for funds so we can buy some horses and outfit ourselves."

A spot along the bar cleared when they approached. It was either the sight or the smell of them, or maybe both. They drank their beers in silence, then

Harve ordered a second round, and they drank that.

"You boys look like you could use a whore," the bar dog said. "You ain't got no boots and no hats, but that don't mean you ain't got no need." He had his eye on Harve's double eagle lying atop the bar.

"We need a lot of things, mister," Teddy Green said. "Whores ain't one of them." Green's voice was rough and tired and mean from the long walk. He had said earlier that if he didn't get himself a hat and a horse soon, he might kill the next man who gave him any guff.

Harve wiped the foam from his lips and asked the bar dog if they had a telegraph in town. "Sure, sure," the man said, then told him how to get there.

"We might as well wait here for you," Cole said. "At a table near the back where we won't be a living spectacle for every yahoo in Kansas."

They took their beers and found a table where the light was dim. Cole and Green sat there about five minutes before Teddy Green said: "I've never been in such poor shape in my life, not even fighting Comanches in Texas."

"Well, a Comanche is one thing and a cyclone is another," Cole said. "We just had the misfortune to be in the wrong place at the wrong time."

"You ask me, this whole state is the wrong place."

"I won't disagree with you. What I've seen of it so far hasn't exactly made me want to go find a wife and move here."

"At the rate we're going," he said, lifting his glass of beer to his mouth, "we won't ever catch up with Ella and that man she's run off with. Either Charley Utter will, or that murderous fool, Gypsy Davy. I'm afraid it's too late for us, John Henry. I've got a down and dirty feeling about this mission."

"Well, maybe if we don't catch up with them, neither will Colorado Charley or Gypsy Davy."

"Those are long odds, John Henry. Leastways far as we know, they've got horses. We don't even have a single rusty pistol among us. I am thoroughly disgusted."

"You can give up," Cole said, "if you feel that way. Go back to Texas and forget Ella."

Green stared at Cole. Even in the shadows, Cole could see the light in his eyes. "Technically she is still my wife. What kind of man would I be to quit and go back to Texas and forget about her? Worse comes to worst, I'll give her a decent burial."

"I understand," Cole commented.

"I try not to think about it, but my mind keeps turning it over, what they'll do to her if they find her first."

Cole let his own thoughts push aside his weariness. If they were going to stop Utter and his bunch, they'd just as soon do it sooner rather than later. Cole knew that, and he believed Teddy Green knew it as well. "We'll have to kill him."

"Who?"

"Utter, most of his men, next time we run into them."

"I know."

"You up for that?"

"I never killed a man who hadn't yet committed a transgression," he said, "or hadn't cornered me in a fight."

"You killed Comanches."

"That was different."

"Maybe not as much as you think."

"Don't tell me what I think, John Henry."

"I'm just saying, if we take on Utter and his bunch after the fact, it will be a little too late, don't you think?"

He bobbed his head. "Yeah, way too late."

"Then we stop them the next time we run into them."

"I'll do whatever it takes," he said. "You?"

"I didn't walk halfway across Kansas just to get faint-hearted now."

"Well, if your friend doesn't get the money wired here, we might have to chunk rocks at them."

"Like David slew Goliath," Cole said.

"Our aim will need to be true," Green said.

"Let me ask you something. You ever wish now that you hadn't chased Comanches and run them to ground?"

There was a moment of thoughtful silence between them before Green answered. "Yes, many times. They were a noble people, but sometimes they committed wrongful acts … that's why I did it. But I miss not having them as adversaries. They were a worthy breed … not at all like Colorado Charley Utter and those pistoleers that ride with him, or that ear-wearing maniac, Gypsy Davy. Such men don't compare with the Comanches."

"Does it feel a little odd to you?"

"What's that?" he said.

"That we both love the same woman."

"Not so odd. Ella's an easy woman to love."

"I guess the strange part is," Cole said, "neither one of us seems to know her as well as we thought we did."

"Do we ever really know another person?" Green said.

"No, I guess not."

They sat and nursed their beers for half an hour more before Harve returned, looking like the cat that had swallowed the canary.

"We're fixed up boys … got us a line of credit at the bank," he said, waving a telegram. "Had my bank in Denver send a confirmation of my resources. We're back in tall cotton, boys. We can walk over to the mercantile, get us some duds, pistols, boots, and a new hat for you, Mister Green. Then we'll take a walk down the street where I'm told there's an Injun who has horses for sale."

"Well, things are looking up again," Teddy Green remarked. "Maybe we will find Ella yet, before the others do."

They bought the clothes they needed. Teddy Green selected a broad-brimmed hat the color of a dove. When Harve asked why didn't he want another bowler—there were several on display—Teddy Green replied: "No, sir, I think that fancy bowler was nothing but bad luck to me. And besides, I probably looked foolish in it. It was a vanity on my part. This one will do just fine." And he set it squarely down on his head.

"Well, at least now you look like a Ranger and not some fancy-Dan," Harve said approvingly.

They each bought weapons. Cole chose a .45 Schofield because he liked the heft of it. Teddy Green favored a Russian model .44 Smith & Wesson, and Harve picked out a double-action .45 Colt with bird's-eye grips. They also bought Winchester repeating rifles and plenty of shells, boots, saddles, and blankets.

"Throw in a few cans of those peaches, too," Harve told the clerk. "I got a sweet tooth for peaches."

They walked out of the mercantile different men, dressed and armed and looking dangerous.

"I don't feel naked now," Teddy Green said, shifting the .44's weight in the scabbard of his gun belt. He wore it crossed over on his left hip, butt forward.

"We'll go down there and see that Kiowa the man told me had the horses," Harve said. "Then we'll find us a bathhouse, scrub off this prairie, and get the nits washed out of our hair. Afterward, we'll eat like hogs and get a fresh start in the morning."

No one disagreed with the plan.

That night, as they sat in the saloon, having filled their bellies with steaks, fried onions, potatoes, and cornbread, Cole couldn't help but feel guilty that they had been delayed in the pursuit of Ella Mims. Outside, the wind was whistling and rattling the windows and they were sitting around, cozy and content. Who knew what depredation Ella might be suffering at that very moment? Cole feared that with every passing hour, their chances of finding her before the others did grew slimmer and slimmer. He saw the distant stare in Teddy Green's gaze and knew he was thinking the same thing. Men in love, Cole thought. They were willing to do anything to save the woman they both loved. It occurred to Cole that, if things turned out badly, this might be the last trail for all of them. He drank his liquor and listened to the wind and rolled himself a shuck. The wind sounded like a woman moaning—like Ella crying to them from the grave—and a chill ran down his spine. For the first time since they'd begun the journey to find her, Cole was afraid that maybe they were already too late, that maybe Teddy Green's earlier premonition was right.

CHAPTER SEVENTEEN

They continued south for several more days without any change in scenery. The prairie seemed as endless as an ocean, the grasses stirred by constant winds. Large white clouds drifted overhead and every so often they would see herds of grazing antelope in the distance but could never get within rifle range to bring one down. The meager supplies they'd purchased in Hump Dance were again running low, and so were their spirits, since they hadn't yet come across any sign of Ella Mims and Tom Feathers. Cole was even starting to doubt that they were on the right trail. The fugitives could have gone off in any direction at any time. But if the information they'd received was correct, the fugitives were heading for Gonzales, Texas, and that put them on the right road.

Night found them camped along a tributary twenty miles north of Dodge City, according to Harve, who claimed he was now familiar with the country.

"This here is Pawnee Creek," he said as they unsaddled the horses.

"Looks more like a river than a creek to me," Teddy Green said. "Why, a man could drown in this river you call a creek."

"A man did drown in it," Harve said. "His name was Jim Bones, and he drowned right in this very creek whilst trying to ride a paint horse across it.

Paint horses ain't very good swimmers. I'd never ride a paint horse across no creek, or no river, either."

"I've never known paint horses to be worse swimmers than any other horse," Teddy Green said. "Whatever gave you such an idea?"

"Having to write a letter to poor Jim's folks back in Missouri is what gave me that idea," Harve said. "Why, if he had been riding any other color horse than a paint, he might be alive today. And so might the horse. As it was, we never found either of them."

Teddy Green waggled his head as he shook out his blanket and placed it on the ground. He and Harve Ledbettor seemed made for each other; they bickered like two old maids on just about every subject that struck their fancy. But Cole had a feeling that they genuinely liked each other and would have missed the company and the chance to argue if one or the other wasn't there.

"What do you say, John Henry?" Harve asked, not content to let the matter drop. "Ain't a paint horse just about the worst swimming horse there is?"

"I guess a paint horse can swim just as good as any other color horse," Cole said. "And Jim Bones might have drowned no matter what he was riding. River crossings are always iffy and come tomorrow, we'll have to find ourselves a place to cross this one."

"I know one thing," Teddy Green said, wrapped up in his blanket now. "A mule will never put itself in harm's way. If Jim Bones had been riding a mule, he might not have drowned at all because no mule will cross deep water."

"Well, I have heard that mules are smarter than horses," Harve said. "But it is unseemly for a man to go about on a mule. Anybody want to share this last can of peaches?"

"Not me," said Teddy Green. "I'm not partial to peaches."

"*Humph,*" Harve muttered. "I never met anybody who wasn't partial to peaches."

"Well, you have now."

"I guess you two will argue until the stars fall out of the sky," Cole said. "Maybe we ought to get some shut-eye."

Harve looked up at the sky as though he expected to see the stars falling, then chuckled and ate his peaches, making slurping sounds before tossing the can aside and rolling up in his blanket. They could hear the river slipping its banks and it seemed like just one more obstacle to finding Ella Mims.

* * * * *

The next day, they found a place to cross and came out on the other side in fine shape and by midmorning they rode into Dodge City.

"Let's go check in with the law and see if we can learn anything about strangers passing through in the last few days," Cole suggested.

"I'll catch up with you," Harve said. "I've got to get me a refill on this flask and buy some more peaches."

Cole asked a kid with a spotted dog where the city marshal's office was and he pointed and said: "Yonder is Mister Earp's office."

They tied off in front of the office. Cole wondered whether or not Earp knew anything about Ella Mims or Tom Feathers having passed through, or about seeing any of the others—Charley Utter or Gypsy Davy. He was a much bigger man than Cole had supposed him to be. He was sitting behind a desk, writing something on a piece of paper when the two walked in. Another man sat in the corner, reading an issue of the *Police Gazette*. Both men wore black frock coats and city marshals' badges and both looked up.

"Help you gents?" the one behind the desk said.

"You Earp?" Teddy Green said.

"Yes, sir," he said, and Cole could see the instant precaution in his gaze. "Who's asking?"

"I'm a Texas Ranger and this man's accompanying me. We're looking for a woman who might have passed through here a few days ago traveling by hack. She'd be with two men, one of them a colored."

Earp had a sandy mustache that drooped below his chin and slate-gray eyes. The other man reading the *Gazette* could have been his twin.

"No, sir, I haven't seen anyone of that description, but you might ask my brother, Wyatt."

"I thought you said you were Wyatt?" Teddy Green said.

"No, sir, you asked me if I was Earp, and I am an Earp, but I'm Morgan Earp. That 'un in the corner is Virgil. Wyatt is running a faro game over at the Alhambra."

"Which way is that?" Cole asked.

Morgan Earp looked at him as he said: "Out the door, turn right on Front Street, take it to First, and take a left. You can't miss it … Kelly's Opera House is upstairs, Hungerford's meat market is right across the street, and George Dieter's Centennial Barbershop is two doors down, same side, in case you're thinking of getting a haircut whilst in the city."

It was a little more information than they needed, but they took it and left. Cole could feel Morgan Earp's gaze on them.

"Looks like the Earps are the entire police force," Teddy Green said.

"They usually are, from what I've heard about them," Cole said.

They found the third brother dealing faro.

"I'd like a word with you, Marshal," Teddy Green said, interrupting the game. Several players grew scowls and one started to protest the interruption, but Teddy Green cut him off with a hard stare. Earp, on the other hand, shuffled the deck between the fingers of one hand; the other hand, Cole suspected, was holding a self-cocker somewhere below the table.

"I'm off duty," Earp said. "Come see me in my office tomorrow if you want to talk."

"I'm a Texas Ranger, looking for someone," Teddy Green persisted. "I'd appreciate your co-operation as a fellow lawman."

Cole saw a half smile on Wyatt Earp's lips.

"This is Kansas, son. Texas is two states down."

"I know where Texas is," Teddy Green said. "I'll ask you again for your co-operation, then I won't ask a third time."

Earp's gray-eyed stare was cold and calculating. Cole could see he was taking the measure of Teddy Green, just as Green had already taken the measure of him. Cole knew by reputation that Earp wasn't a shooter. He was known for striking men across the head with the barrel of his Peacemaker, what they called buffaloing a man. Cole thought he knew after a moment of contemplation that Earp wasn't going to buffalo Teddy

Green without paying a heavy price for the trying.

"All right," Earp said. "Charley, take over."

A man with a patch over his left eye and garters on his sleeves took Earp's place and the three of them walked over to the bar where Earp ordered whiskey and branch water.

"So, what's so all-important you need me to leave my business?" Earp asked after tossing back half the glass of liquor.

Green said: "We're looking for a woman and two men who might have passed through here two, three days ago. One of the men is a colored. They would be driving a hack, maybe the colored on a horse outriding, a bodyguard. You seen anybody fit that description?"

"Yeah, I saw them. They came in a few nights ago, stayed at the Dodge House, except for the Negro, who stood watch out front. Left first light the next morning."

"Which direction?" Cole asked.

Earp looked at him. "We met?" he said.

"No," Cole said.

"What's your name?" he said.

"John Henry Cole."

"The name sounds familiar," he said, "but I can't place where I've heard it."

"Wyatt," Mattie Blaylock said as she approached. She glanced at Cole and smiled. "John Henry, how have you been?"

Earp gave her a hard look.

"Wyatt, this is John Henry Cole, a second cousin of mine from back in Illinois."

Earp's jaw muscle twitched.

Cole showed no reaction to the lie. He knew her, yes, but not as a second cousin. She had nursed him back to health after a colored prostitute had shot him, thus trying to prevent him from taking a man to jail. Cole remembered Mattie telling him how the man who he assumed was her husband had run out on her and left her alone on the frontier. Now, here she was.

"I'd heard you'd gotten married, Mattie," Cole said, going along with the fabrication.

"Yes, Wyatt and I have been married for quite some time."

Teddy Green was getting restless with all this small talk. "We've got work to do, John Henry." He turned his attention back to Earp. "Which way did they go when they left here?"

"South road," Earp said without taking his gaze from Cole.

"You see anybody else come through here, a lone man wearing a string of ears around his neck?" Green asked.

"Ears?" Earp said.

"I guess you haven't, or it wouldn't surprise you. How about a bunch of riders got their hats pinned up, you see them?"

"Saw some riders, yesterday … United States deputy marshals."

"Hats pinned up?" Teddy Green repeated.

"Yeah, hats pinned up. What about them?"

"They're not lawmen," Cole said.

"They had the papers and badges to prove it," Earp replied. "I checked."

Cole exchanged looks with Teddy Green.

"Judge Beam made them official by deputizing them," Green said. "To make it look like less than a squad of assassins."

"What the hell is this all about?" Earp demanded.

"Nothing," Teddy Green said. "Leastways, nothing that should concern you."

Earp was getting red around the gills.

"I hope you are taking good care of my cousin, Marshal," Cole said. "I wouldn't want to think that she's not well cared for here on this rough frontier."

Earp's gaze narrowed, uncertain what Cole might know or not know about Mattie and him.

"Blood runs thick in our families," Cole added. "Always did, always will. One thing … we take care of our own."

Mattie gave a light-hearted laugh and touched Cole's wrist.

"Did I ever mention, dear Wyatt, how serious some of my cousins can be about family?"

"You gents ought to get moving if you're after that woman and her friends," Earp said. "They got a good three, four days jump on you."

"You're right," Teddy Green agreed, and turned to leave. Then he paused and said: "You coming, John Henry?"

Cole gave it one more second to see if Earp wanted to take it further, but nothing happened, and Mattie kissed Cole's cheek and said: "Tell the folks hello for me when you get back home, John Henry. Tell them everything is fine and that I miss them." The look in her eyes appealed to Cole to let the matter drop and so he did.

"You take care of yourself, Mattie, you know how we all worry about you."

"I will," she assured.

Teddy Green was already tightening the cinch on his saddle when Cole caught up with him.

"Well, did you get all your good byes said?" he asked. "And where is Grumpy?"

Harve was just coming out of the Long Branch, carrying several bottles of liquor.

"We leaving?" he asked.

"What's it look like?" Teddy Green said.

"Looks like we're leaving."

As they rode past the Alhambra, Cole saw Mattie and Wyatt and Wyatt's two brothers, standing on the walk, and thought to himself that someday Wyatt Earp was going to give her untold heartbreak.

"You boys learn anything?" Harve wondered.

"Yeah," Teddy Green said.

"I learned something, too," Harve said.

"What's that?" Green snapped.

"That a man can't hold his hand against a glass jar that has a rattlesnake in it when the snake strikes."

"What on earth are you talking about?"

"In that saloon they had a rattlesnake thick as your arm in a glass jar and the bartender was taking bets you couldn't hold your hand against it and not jerk it away when the snake struck the glass. I bet him a dollar I could. I lost."

"Next time you want to throw a dollar away," Teddy Green said, "throw it my way."

"I could have won five," Harve said. "Seemed like good odds at the time."

"Men who fool around with rattlesnakes are foolish, indeed," Teddy Green said. "I knew a preacher down in Tascosa who believed you could let a rattlesnake bite you and not kill you if you had enough faith in the Lord. To prove it, he let one bite him one day in a church full of women and children and died on the spot."

"That's foolish!" Harve said. "Do not tempt the Lord, the Bible says."

"I guess maybe that preacher didn't read that part. After that he never got another chance," Teddy Green opined.

"Maybe, if we spent less time talking about paint horses and rattlesnakes and preachers," Cole said, "we might concentrate better on the task ahead of us."

"He's a mite touchy," Harve remarked to Teddy Green.

"He found out his cousin is married to Wyatt Earp."

"*Hmmm* … I saw Earp bust a cowboy's skull in Abilene once with his pistol. Then he horsewhipped him."

"I doubt he'd horsewhip a woman," Teddy Green said.

"I'd almost as soon be horsewhipped or snake-bitten than to listen to the two of you jabber all the way to Texas," Cole said, and put the spurs to his mount.

Harve was right. John Henry Cole was definitely a mite touchy.

CHAPTER EIGHTEEN

The bodies were found an hour after breakfast. They were lying in a circle around a cold fire of buffalo chips—eight, maybe ten men sprawled out.

"Christ and Jesus!" Harve said.

"Massacre," Teddy Green said, "is what it looks like."

"You notice?" Cole said.

"Yeah," the Ranger said. "I noticed first thing."

"Their ears are cut off," Harve said.

Cole dismounted and took a closer look. "That's not what killed them," he said. "These men were shot."

"How could one man shoot this many men without himself getting killed?" Teddy Green asked. Gypsy Davy wasn't among the lot.

Turkey vultures wheeled in the sky above.

"A smart piece of shooting, if one man did it," Harve said.

"Looks like perdition," Teddy Green said. "Like Armageddon, like these men were smote by the hand of God."

"Or the devil," Cole said.

One of them had a tintype clutched in his hand. It showed the picture of a woman with dark ringlets of hair, her eyes staring into the camera.

"They won't meet in this world again," Teddy Green said, taking the tintype and looking at it before placing it back in the dead man's hand.

Then they heard a moan.

Harve jumped two feet and stared at the bodies. "Which one said that?"

A hand twitched and Cole rolled the man over. Harve took his canteen and spilled water over the man's lips. His head was bloody; one of his ears had been sliced off; his face was black from gunpowder.

He rolled his eyes when the water touched his lips and he moaned again. There was a knot in the middle of his forehead the size of a turkey egg.

"This boy's been cold-cocked, it looks like," Harve said. "Look at the size of that knot on his head."

"Cold-cocked and cut," Teddy Green said, "but I don't see a bullet hole in him."

"Then he's lucky," Harve said.

"What's your name, son?" Cole asked. He looked young—eighteen, maybe not even that old.

He blinked several times, licked his lips, and stared up at them.

"They call me the Cincinnati Kid," he said. "But my true name is Joe McCarty."

"The Cincinnati Kid, huh?" Green repeated.

He nodded.

"What happened here?" Cole said.

"Turrible bad fight, mister."

"We can see that, boy," Green said. "How'd it come about?"

"Was camped," he said. "That's all. Then these fellers rode down on us like blue hell and started shooting us to ribbons. We didn't stand a chance."

"Why did they shoot you to ribbons?" Harve asked.

The boy waggled his head. "I guess they thought we were the Canadian River boys done all that bank robbing and killing. We figgered they was the law come to do us in."

"Canadian River boys?"

"Yes," the Kid said. He looked around, saw the dead, and added: "God, they're all kilt but me."

Harve snorted, looked around at the gaggle of dead men, and said: "You boys sure as hell don't look like no serious outlaws. Why, take a gander … there ain't one among the bunch looks like he's old enough to shave."

The boy looked at Cole, blinked again, sat up, let out a groan, and felt the knot on his head.

"Yes, sir, I'm admitting it, that's who we were … the Canadian River boys, worst bunch of outlaws in three states. Robbed and killed everybody we could … shot em, stabbed 'em, dragged 'em, even run over some with our horses. We were mean, mean, mean. Wasn't nobody or nothing that we ever feared until yesterday." Then he rolled his eyes and groaned.

"You don't look like a yahoo that could even kill time," Harve said. "Why you can't be more'n a dang' child."

"Well, sir, I was part of these here dead boys, all right. I may have even been the worst of the bunch, truth be told. I've done things I'm nearly shamed to admit."

"I ain't buying it," Harve said. "You don't look like you could whip a schoolgirl, much less rob and murder folks."

The boy looked contrite.

"I don't know," Teddy Green said. "It's been my experience that killers and thieving trash come in all ages and stripes. Maybe we ought to take this boy to the nearest town and see him hanged for his crimes."

The boy nodded. "Yes, sir, you'd be right in doing it. I deserve to hang for what I've done."

"Hell, maybe we ought to just shoot him and leave him here for those turkey vultures," Cole said.

Harve looked up, saw the swarm of dark-winged birds circling overhead. "First they pluck out your eyes," he said. "And you don't even have to be dead yet. Birds like that find eyes to be the tastiest of morsels. Then the wolves come and tear open your guts and eat them."

Green said: "Seems to me, that's a better fate for a killing, thieving, no-account rascal such as yourself."

"They'll probably chew off your other ear, too," Harve added.

The boy reached up and felt the ragged fringe where his ear had been, winced, and pulled away bloody fingers. "I thought it was a dream I was having," he said, his eyes wide with astonishment. "I thought I was only dreaming that a feller was cutting off my ear. Oh, Lord, I'm violated!"

"That's nothing compared to what's going to happen to you," Teddy Green said. "Let's go."

They turned to mount their horses when the Kid shouted. "Don't leave me for the buzzards to pluck out my eyes and the wolves to eat my guts!"

"You said it yourself, boy," Green said, putting a foot to the stirrup. "You are the worst kind of breed there is. Best you die hard … maybe you'll get your reward in heaven but not here on this earth."

"I was lying!" the boy shouted. "I ain't no killer. Why, I ain't hardly fired my pistol at nothing but jack rabbits, and even then I didn't hit nothing."

Teddy Green strolled over to the boy and looked down at him.

"Honest, mister. I just joined up with these fellers yesterday, ran across their camp here, and asked could I stay for some coffee and hardtack. I just happened to be in the wrong place at the wrong time, that's all."

"Why'd you make up that story then?"

The boy dipped his head, moaned, looked up again. "Me and my brother Henry come two thousand miles with our ma," he said. "She died and Henry went to New Mexico to seek his fortune. Me, I stayed right here in Kansas, seeking my own. Henry's made a big name for himself as an outlaw and I wanted to be wild and wooly just like him. So when these boys told me who they were and what all they'd done and asked me to throw in with them, I couldn't hardly say no. That 'un there … the one with the greasy pants … he was the leader. Called himself Sunny Jim. He's the one said I could either throw in with them or taste lead, meaning he'd shoot me down like a yellow dog if I didn't. That 'un next to him is Muddy Water Bill. Those others I hardly remember their names."

"These riders that sent you boys to perdition," Harve said, "what'd they look like?"

"Hats pinned back," the Kid said. "That's about all I remember … that, and they could shoot awful good. Killed us all in about ten minutes, except for me."

"How come they left you?" Green asked.

"I guess they thought I was kilt like all the others. How it happened was, Muddy Water Bill swung about to shoot one of them and knocked me senseless with the barrel of his Winchester. I reckon I was standing too close behind him. Next thing I know I'm dreaming of some yahoo leaning over me with a knife."

"One of the pinned hats?" Cole asked.

"Uhn-uh," the Kid said. "This feller wasn't wearing a hat. Fact is, he had long dark hair. And another thing. He was wearing a ..."—his eyes grew wide—"a string of ears around his neck."

"No pinned hat?" Harve repeated.

"No hat."

"Gypsy Davy," Cole said. "And the others were Colorado Charley Utter and his bunch."

"Why you reckon they shot us?" the Kid asked.

"Practice," Teddy Green said.

"Practice?"

"There was no way they could have known you were outlaws. My guess is they just got restless to shoot someone and you boys were it. You are a lucky man, Kid," Green concluded.

"Well, why'd that feller come along and cut off my ear, you reckon?" The Kid had buckteeth and his eyes were slightly crossed. He again touched the side of his head gingerly. "What'd make a body do something like that?"

"Souvenir," Harve said. "He's got a thing for ears. Be glad he didn't cut off both your ears or you wouldn't have no way to hold your hat. As it is, it will fall to one side more'n the other, but that's not so bad. Lots of men with two ears wear their sombreros like that."

"Well, I'm mighty mad I was violated in such a manner," the Kid declared. "I intend to find that man and get my ear back and teach him a lesson in the doing."

"You best hie on back to Cincinnati or wherever it was you said you were from," Teddy Green said. "The frontier is no place for a tenderfoot to be, as you can plainly see if you were to look into a mirror. That ear will be a long time growing back, but if those fellows had shot you full of lead like your *compadres*, you'd be a lot sooner dead."

"No, sir," the Kid said, standing up, then wobbling like a newborn colt. "I intend to track that bastard down and get my ear back."

"Well, good luck to you, boy," Teddy Green said, and mounted his horse.

"We can't just leave him here," Cole said.

The Ranger gave him a flat stare. "We're closing ground on them," he said. "You want to slow us down by hauling this yahoo along?"

"Well, then, at least have the decency to shoot him," Cole said. "It'd be a more generous act than leaving him out here alone on foot, him leaking a blood trail the wolves can follow."

Teddy Green looked thoroughly disgusted at the suggestion. "OK," he growled, kicking a foot free from his stirrup. "We'll ride him double to the next town."

"Dodge is back yonder," young Joe said as they started out on the south road again.

"We ain't going to Dodge," Teddy Green said.

"Why ain't we? It's the closest town."

"Because we've already been there. Now stop yapping."

In spite of Cole's concern for the boy's welfare, Teddy Green was right, even if he was as hard as nails about it. Having to ride the boy double would slow them down considerably. Each hour, each day that passed without them catching up to Ella Mims and Tom Feathers only decreased the chance of finding them alive. Colorado Charley Utter and his bunch, along with Gypsy Davy, were leaving a bloody wake across the landscape. It seemed all they were doing was following after them and cleaning up the mess.

CHAPTER NINETEEN

There wasn't spit for the next two days and riding an extra man, even one as light and slender as the Kid, made the going slower than it should have been. The landscape was more of the same, except the country became a little more hilly, the soil turned reddish, and the rivers and creeks more muddy. They were even seeing more trees, scrub oaks and blackjack trees.

"I know this land," Harve said. "Crossed it many times droving. What they call no man's land, Oklahoma Territory. Bad place to be unless you're an outlaw. Hide-out of killers, thieves, rapists, and every sort of bad actor you can imagine." He turned and looked at Joe, who was riding behind Cole. "Why, you ought to be right at home here, Kid. You being the cold-eyed, one-eared, only surviving member of the Canadian River boys." Harve took great delight in japing the Kid about aliases and falsified reputations.

"Why would any thieves or killers want to come here?" the Kid said, looking about. "We ain't seen nary a mercantile or even a drummer to rob or kill."

"They come here because the law is afraid to," Harve explained. "Those federal marshals sent out of Judge Parker's court over in Arkansas won't come this far. No fool in his right mind who wears a badge would come to such a hellish place."

Teddy Green's eyes snapped. "I'm wearing a badge and I came here," he said sourly.

"Well, I must admit," Harve said, "you're a rather odd duck to begin with."

"What do you mean by that statement, Mister Ledbettor?"

"Just meant that there ain't many men who'd go clear to hell to find an ex-wife. In fact, most men would head in the *opposite* direction when it comes to ex-wives."

"Well, I ain't most men," Green said.

"That's sure enough plain as paint." Then Harve, who was riding slightly in the lead, drew up short.

"What is it?" Cole asked.

"Look," he said. "Ain't that the biggest rattlesnake you ever saw in your life?"

A diamondback rattler was stretched out on a rock in the warm sun near the road; its body was the thickness of a man's arm, its length well over six feet.

Before Cole knew it, the Kid leaped off the back of the horse and quickly grabbed up the big snake by the tail and cracked it like a whip, snapping off the head.

"Dinner!" the Kid said, holding it up proudly.

"Dinner?" Teddy Green said. "What sort of fool would eat a snake?"

"You ever et one, Mister Green?"

"No, and I ain't never going to eat one, either."

"Tastes like chicken, you fry 'em right."

"I'd just as soon eat a real chicken if I wanted something to taste like chicken."

"How about you, Mister Ledbettor? Mister Cole?"

"No thanks, Kid," they said in unison.

He shrugged and said: "Suit yourself."

The horses needed a blow and there was a small, meandering, muddy stream nearby, so they made noon camp and smoked cigarettes, except for Teddy Green, who said he preferred cigars but had forgotten to purchase any in Hump Dance. Harve produced one of the bottles of $20 whiskey from his saddlebags and offered it around while they sat and watched the

Kid skin and cook his snake over a mesquite fire.

"You know it was the devil in the form of a serpent who tempted Adam and Eve in the garden," Teddy Green said. "It's why God didn't give legs to a snake."

"Imagine if He had," Harve said. "What terrible creatures they'd be. Why suppose a big old rattler like that 'un had legs and could run as fast as a horse? Wouldn't this be a mighty dangerous world?"

Green seemed to think about that for a while. Cole's thoughts were on Ella Mims. Thinking about her and the things that had transpired since he'd last seen her, he could only wonder how different their fate would have been if he had asked her to marry him when he had the chance. Just those few words could have changed everything for them.

It was easy for a man to imagine all sorts of things, given the time and inclination. Lately Cole had been doing a lot of thinking about life, what lay ahead for him, given the fact that he was a year older than Bill Hickok who, like most of Cole's contemporaries, had already been sent to the grave. A man Cole's age and with his past, surviving on the frontier, gave him cause to think. But if he did have many more years ahead of him, he would like them to be in the company of a woman like Ella Mims.

Cole watched the Kid, squatting before the fire, content, he supposed, to be alive, the prospect of a full belly, and all the world yet ahead of him. Some of the pain had probably healed already. It seemed like only yesterday that Cole was as young and foolish as Joe McCarty, a jug-eared cowboy hardly green broke, chasing the rear-end of longhorns and eating their dust up trails like the Chisholm, the Bandera, the Good-night-Loving, and a lot of others. In a way, it seemed like it had never happened, like a dusty dream. But it had happened and he'd grown long in the tooth and he knew that his gun hand was slower than it once had been, and that he couldn't stay in the saddle forever. Sooner or later, he would have to find a place to light and take root or end up dead, maybe on some sawdust floor like Hickok. The taste of lost opportunity turned bitter in his mouth.

The Kid pulled smoldering chunks of the rattler off his roasting stick and ate them, seeming delighted with his repast while the rest squatted on their heels and watched.

"You fellers don't know what you're missing," he said.

Finally it got the best of Harve and he said he'd try it.

"Damn, the Kid's right," Harve said, tentatively chewing on a piece of the snake. "Does taste like chicken … sorta. Let me have another piece of that serpent, Kid."

Cole thought: *What the hell?* His belly was starting to scrape his backbone and he was hungry enough to eat cactus. It wasn't so bad—fried snake— once you got over the thought of it.

But Teddy Green would have none of it. "Some things are just too vile for a man to put in his mouth," he said. "You'll not catch me eating a creature that crawls on its belly … and that includes horny toads and Gila monsters."

"Horny toads and Gila monsters got legs," Harve said.

"Little bitty ones," Teddy Green said. "Not enough to count. They are just serpents with little bitty legs."

They rode the rest of the day, and as dusk started to overtake them, they saw some lights off in the distance. "Could be a town," Harve said.

"Don't care what it is as long as we can buy a meal, something other than serpent to eat," Teddy Green said.

Actually it wasn't a town, but a collection of shacks built around a large garden.

"We'd best be cautious in our approach," Teddy Green said. "What Mister Ledbettor says is true about this territory … it's a refuge for bad actors. Decent folks will be jumpy about the approach of strangers."

But they'd already been noticed. Several men stepped out of the shadows, each had a shotgun cradled in his hands. These were the dark faces of Negroes.

"What you men want?" one of them said. He was an older man with a cotton-gray fringe of hair.

"Meal, if we can get it," Cole said. "That and a place to water our horses."

"Be hard pressed to get a meal 'round here," the man said.

"Why's that?" Green asked.

"Look at you," the man said, then glanced at the others who stood spread out.

"What about us?" Green said.

"You white," the man said.

"I'm also a lawman," Green said. "Texas Ranger."

"This here ain't Texas, mister, and all the law that exists is these." He waggled the barrels of his shotgun.

"If I had a dollar for everyone who's told me this wasn't Texas, I'd be a rich man," Teddy Green replied. "I *know* it ain't Texas. Fact is, I'm dang' glad it *ain't* Texas, for, if it was, I'd be ashamed to be a Texan."

"Insults ain't gonna buy you much except trouble, mister," the man said.

"Not trying to insult anybody, trying to buy a meal," Green said.

Harve spurred his horse a little ahead and said: "The color of gold matter to you gents, whether it's a white man's gold or not?"

The men looked at each other.

"Gold money?"

"Double eagle. Give you one for a meal for my friends and me and some grain and water for our mounts, how will that be?"

"That'd be just fine, but I'd like to see the money afore I feed you."

Harve flipped the man a coin, and he caught it and examined it before slipping it into his pocket and lowering the scatter-gun. The others were slow to lower theirs until the old man said: "Welcome to Nowhere."

"That what they call this place?" Cole said. "Nowhere?"

"That's what it is," the man said. "So that's what we call it."

He told them where they could wash up and water their horses and had one of the younger men pour out some grain in nose bags for their mounts. Inside the shack, the old man sat at the head of the table. Up and down both sides, sitting on benches, were children. Cole counted twelve.

"These are my young 'uns," the older man said, and named them, each and every one. "And that's my wife, Hattie, doing the cooking." A large black woman stood at the stove with her back them and only every now and then glanced over her shoulder. The room was filled with the smell of fatback and beans and cornbread. It was a good smell.

"What happen'd ta your arm, mister?" a youngster about halfway down the right hand row of children said. He was maybe five or six years old, wide-eyed and curious.

The older man spoke up, told the boy to mind his manners, but Harve grinned and said it was OK, he'd been asked the same question lots of times. It was plain, however, that the loss of an arm was not fit conversation around a supper table, so Harve didn't go into the grisly tale.

After supper, the older man, who said his name was Israel, asked them to join him out of doors, which they did. The sky was just turning a dark shade of plum against a dark-silver background and some of the other men were standing around a large fire of blackjack stumps, the flames trapped in their eyes.

Israel introduced them all around and told them this was all one family, cousins and brothers of his, nephews, men who'd brought their wives and children to this far end of the settlements to be shed of the troubles that still existed for a colored man closer in. He told them that he and some of the older men had fought the Cheyennes, Sioux, and Apaches as buffalo soldiers in the 9th and 10th Calvary regiments; how after they'd all been blooded and after the fighting was over, they went home to the same hard conditions they had left.

"Don't seem to matter none what you did or didn't do for this country," he said, looking sharply into the flames, the stem of a corncob pipe clenched between his teeth. "You a black man, you still just a slave in most white men's eyes. That's why we came out this far, figgered no white men here to contend with. Ain't, either, except the occasional dodger. You see now why we carry shotguns and take notice of strangers."

"Pays to be alert," Cole said. "No matter whether you're white or black or red in this country."

"Got that right, mister."

They talked at length about the war, about crops and rain and outlaws while Harve produced a fresh bottle from his saddlebags and passed it around. Then the conversation turned to what their business was this far from anything and Teddy Green told them. The mention of Ella Mims and Tom Feathers brought a pall over the talk.

"You seen these folks?" Cole asked. "It's important we find them before some others do."

"Ain't seen nobody," Israel said. "Nobody's been through here in a month."

Logic said that was hard to believe, considering that they'd been traveling the same road since Dodge, which lay just a hundred yards to the north of the settlement.

"You sure?" Teddy Green said. "I don't see how you could have missed seeing them."

"Ain't seen nobody like you described or like you ain't described, either. I guess we best be turning in … getting late, lot of planting to do tomorrow."

It was a signal to the others to slip off into the shadows and head toward their homes. Israel said the newcomers could camp the night but would appreciate it if they were gone by daylight. "Nothing against you," he said. "Jus' that, well …."

"We'll be gone," Teddy Green said. After the men left, he said: "They saw them."

"I agree," Harve said. "Clammed right up when you asked them."

"I'm sure they've got their reason," Cole said. "Out here, middle of nowhere, man's best to keep to himself."

"They seemed like honest enough men," Harve said.

"Honest to a point," Teddy Green said.

"The outrider," Cole said. "Bittercreek Newcomb said he was a black man."

"Then that's it," Teddy Green said. "They wouldn't say anything against him because he's one of their own."

"Makes sense," Harve said. "Feathers's man could have told them they were being chased by a pack of white devils … don't we look it, truth be told?"

"Maybe the lack of an answer is our answer," Cole said.

The boy, Joe, strolled back into the fire's light.

"Where you been, Kid?" Harve said.

"Relieving myself."

"Of what?"

Joe grinned sheepishly.

"Say you didn't?"

"Didn't what?"

"Wander off into the bushes with one of those young gals."

"I might have taken a stroll down by the creek out yonder," he said. "And maybe one of them young gals happened to come down there for a pail of water. And maybe we even exchanged a few pleasantries."

"Jesus, Kid, you want to get us shotgunned by some outraged daddy?"

"Didn't do anything, me and her, just exchanged some pleasantries."

Teddy Green warmed his hands in front of the dying flames and stared into them. A knot worked along his jaw line.

"From now on," Cole said, "stay close to camp, understood?"

The Kid looked at him, lowered his gaze to the flames. "Yes, sir."

"Was she sweet?" Harve asked. "'Cause if you are going to die over a gal, she ought to at least be pretty and sweet."

The Kid blushed, the fire sputtered and crackled, and a thousand stars were flung across the sky. Among them, only the Kid seemed to be enjoying the moment.

CHAPTER TWENTY

John Henry Cole thought Bill Cody and others like him had wiped out all the great herds of buffalo on the plains. If you ever been to places like Fort Griffin and Dodge and seen the mammoth pile of buffalo skulls and bones, smelled the stink of hides waiting to be shipped east, you'd know what was meant about the eradication of the beasts. Once was a time you could see herds so vast that you could practically walk from Texas to the Canadian border atop their backs without ever setting foot on the ground, or top a rise and see before you a carpet of dusty brown hides, humps, and horns that went from horizon to horizon. So many, a crew of hide hunters could set up shop half a mile downwind and melt the barrels of their Sharps rifles, trying to kill them and still not make a dent. So many, the land became littered with their rotting carcasses after the slaughter, and if the wind was right, you could smell death twenty miles away. So many, the wolves got so fat and lazy trying to eat up all that meat, you could walk up and club them. As one old Cheyenne who'd remembered put it: "The white man has emptied the prairies of the buffalo."

So when Cole first felt, then heard the rumble, and jumped from his blankets in time to see a large herd of the shaggy beasts coming directly out of the gray dawn at full charge, bearing straight down on them and the

126

settlement, he thought he was dreaming. Teddy Green and Harve Ledbettor leaped from their blankets, too, their Winchesters at the ready. The people of Nowhere came tumbling out of their shacks, the men carrying their shotguns. The charging herd seemed an implausible sight to behold, and for a full few moments they were all mesmerized by it.

"Holy shit!" Harve squawked.

"They're coming straight for us!" Teddy Green said in disbelief. For the first time, he looked uncertain.

Cole saw the people of the settlement—the men, the women, and children—and saw destruction and death if the herd continued their course and overran them.

"Get inside!" Cole shouted. "Get in and stay there!"

Israel looked at him, his eyes keen, a hard-eyed stare as though their presence, the presence of white men, had brought this misfortune with them.

"Take your families inside!" Cole yelled.

"I ain't never seen nothing like it!" the Kid cawed. "Why, there must be a hundred of them!"

"More like several thousand," Cole said. "Mount your ponies and we'll try and turn them before they reach the settlement."

"Huh!"

"Hell, yes!" Harve shouted. "Like in the old days before Cody killed them all! Hell, yes!" He was the first to run for the horses. "Get inside with the others, Kid, and stay there!" Harve paused to look at Cole, then continued to run for all he was worth.

"We don't stand a chance in Hades of turning that herd!" Teddy Green said as he and Cole ran for their mounts.

"No, but we have to do something or else they'll run right over us!" Cole insisted.

They stepped into leather and wheeled the horses about and slapped their flanks with the barrels of their Winchesters. The horses were balky about charging ahead at a thundering herd of buffalo, and who could blame them?

"Try and shoot the leaders!" Cole shouted. "Come at them from the flank and knock as many down as you can!"

It was risky business. It was always risky business when you shot buffalo from a galloping horse. One misstep and you were under their hoofs. One quick turn and they had their horns up in your pony's belly. They were five hundred yards from the settlement and they closed the gap quickly, then swung wide, and came alongside the leaders and commenced firing into them.

Harve had taken the reins between his teeth and was firing and jacking shells by levering the Winchester with his one hand after every shot. It was an amazing piece of shooting and horsemanship, and anyone who saw it knew he'd hunted buffalo before and knew his business. The roar of the thundering hoofs drowned out the crack of their rifles as they dropped several of the leaders by firing almost point blank into them. You had to shoot them just behind the front shoulder—shooting them in the skull was useless, the bullets would simply bounce off.

Cole was concentrating hard on one exceptionally large bull that had taken the lead when suddenly his horse stumbled, then caught itself just as he pulled the trigger. His shot struck the bull in his haunch, and in the quickness of a breath he turned suddenly, his horns goring into the ribs of Cole's mount and just barely missing his leg. The horse went wild with fear and pain; blood spouted in a pulsating stream as the big bull ripped and butted with its horns. Cole felt the horse rear, felt them going over backward, the thundering herd swarming around them, sweat stinging Cole's eyes, his mouth full of dust. Falling, falling ... No time to think, Cole braced himself for the pain of trampling hoofs as he was slammed onto the ground, his pony swept from under him by the goring bull. Cole's head struck something hard and his world went mercifully black.

* * * * *

John Henry Cole awakened to flames of pain in his ribs, back, and right knee. He tried to move and it hurt like hell. Harve and a black woman were leaning over him. The woman had a wet cloth she was pressing to his face.

"Back from the dead, John Henry ... how was it?"

"Preferable to what I'm feeling being alive," Cole said, every word like a dagger in his chest. He knew he was going to cough, tried not to, and, when he did, blood flecked the pan he'd grabbed from the nightstand.

Harve offered a look at the contents, then tried to smile it off. He was dusty and sweaty and so was Teddy Green.

"We turned them," Green said. "I don't know how we did, but we turned them."

Cole tried to sit up but it felt like a rockslide on his chest.

"Busted ribs, pardner," Harve said.

"Put a bullet in me," Cole rasped.

"You're lucky all you got was busted ribs," Teddy Green said. "I once met a man who was struck by lightning on two different occasions and lived to tell about it, but he wasn't half as lucky as you. I never heard of any man losing his saddle in a herd of charging buffalo who lived to tell about it."

"Fell into an arroyo," Harve said. "That's what saved you."

Lucky, Cole thought. He had been shot and hadn't felt as badly off.

"Thing is, John Henry," Green said, "it'll be some little time before you can even sit on a horse … and we can't wait around that long."

Cole wanted to argue, to crawl out of the bed and prove Green wrong, but just breathing was pure torture. He cursed silently.

"We'll go on ahead, try and catch up to Ella Mims and Tom Feathers," Harve placated. "We'll head on to Gonzales and see if we can locate this Feathers *ranchero*, see if the two are there."

Teddy Green shifted his weight and said: "We're leaving the Kid, too."

Cole nodded, too angry and in too much pain to argue.

"I'll park this with you," Harve said, placing a bottle of whiskey on the bed. Then he handed the woman a pair of $20 gold pieces and said it was for Cole's care and feeding. "Don't let him get too fat and lazy, miss."

They shook hands and Cole heard them ride off.

"You wants anything, mister?" the woman said.

"Yeah, some … ribs that ain't … busted."

She looked at him and shook her head before leaving the room.

The old man, Israel, came into the room and stood at the foot of the bed.

"Want to thank you gents for what you did," he said.

Cole didn't want to say what he was thinking, about how he'd maybe traded Ella's life for theirs by getting himself this stove-up.

"Least we got our homes left, our garden saved, and plenty of meat to eat," Israel said. "Guess misfortune brings fortune at times, don't it?"

"I don't see how," Cole replied.

Israel smiled knowingly, like he had secrets locked up inside his head only he was privy to. "You'll see," he said. "There's a silver lining in every cloud. You'll see."

"You don't mind, I'd like to drink about half this whiskey my *compadre* left me."

He nodded his head. "Lottie will take good care of you long as you here," he said, indicating the woman who'd just left the room. "She's a dandy cook as well. You up to some sweet buff hump for supper?"

Cole had had about all the buffalo he could stand for one day. "The whiskey will do me just fine." It was like he had to squeeze out every word.

"I'll look in on you after a time," he said. "You need anything, you tell Lottie."

Cole felt alone and useless. Ella Mims was somewhere on the run and he couldn't do a thing about it. The world for him at that moment was a very damnable place to be. And as far as silver linings in the clouds—well, all he could see, or think about, were rainstorms. He didn't know how things could get much worse. But being a fairly sensible man who'd seen his share of misery, he knew that they could, and they probably would.

He heard the happy laughter of the folks from the settlements as they sallied forth to the killing fields where they'd shot a number of the great beasts—maybe truly the last roving herd of buffalo anywhere on the plains. Taking with them their skinning knives and baskets for the meat, they were about to harvest the shaggy brown manna. Israel and his people's silver lining, not Cole's. Cole's was there in the form of a bottle of expensive whiskey. It seemed a far cry from deliverance.

Another knock at the door and the Kid ducked his head in.

"You doing OK, Mister Cole?"

"What's it look like?"

"I guess I must be some sort of bad-luck charm," he said. "First I join up with the Canadian River boys and they get themselves shot all to pieces, then I join up with you fellers and a dang' buffalo herd nearly runs us over. You ever heard of anybody with such bad luck?"

"Just me, Kid."

He blinked, half smiled. "Well, I guess I'll leave you be, go out and help 'em skin some of those buffs. You need anything, you just holler."

Cole nodded.

The Kid closed the door and Cole started looking for that silver lining Israel had spoken of in the bottom of the whiskey bottle.

CHAPTER TWENTY-ONE

Later that day, Israel and some of the men came into Cole's room.

"We got us enough meat to last the season," Israel said.

"You came here to tell me that?"

Israel offered Cole a benign look. "We need to wrap those ribs, that knee of your'n, too. Looks twisted."

"Not in my lifetime."

Israel shook his head. "Could be one or two a them ribs is busted clean in two. We don't wrap 'em, they could stab you in the heart, lungs maybe."

"There's not enough whiskey left in this bottle to kill the pain."

He eyed the bottle, nearly gone now. He looked at one of the men, a big, broad-chested man with thick brown arms. "You help lift him, Ezekiel, whilst I cut off his shirt and Lottie wraps his ribs."

"Leave me be," Cole said.

"'Fraid I can't."

Strong hands lifted Cole as gently as they knew how, but it still hurt like hell and he wanted to bite his tongue off against the pain. It was like being suddenly plunged into ice-cold water. It took what seemed like forever before the woman had Cole's ribs wrapped sufficiently to suit Israel. And when it was finished, Israel told her to go to work on Cole's right knee. Cole watched as she split the pants leg up the middle.

"Fat as a *mater*," Israel said. "Best not jump around too much on it."

"I'll keep that in mind," Cole said through clenched teeth, the sweat stinging his eyes.

"I'll have Lottie come later and give you a bath, get some of that dust and blood offen you."

"No, thanks … I'll do my own bathing."

Israel looked at Cole as though he had all the sympathy in the world for him. "Best let her do it," he said. "It won't hurt half as much."

Cole closed his eyes, tired from the pain and with no more energy to argue. He was lying on a featherbed and between it and the whiskey all he felt like doing was closing his eyes, and that's what he did. He remembered turning once in his sleep and having the pain shoot up through him like bolts of lightning, waking him up, the room black as pitch.

After that he slept fitfully, on and off, waking when someone would come in the room, waking when someone pressed a cool rag to his face or put water to his lips. He woke completely when he felt his clothes being removed and his skin being bathed. The whiskey had done its job only in part, not completely.

Finally he came out of the fog and the pain came full bore and he cursed it as hard as he did his bad luck. Lottie came into the room with a plate of mush and buffalo meat.

"You up to eating?"

Cole shook his head, no.

"Israel says best you eat."

"Can't, won't."

She set the plate down on a stand next to the bed, shrugged, turned, and started to leave.

"Where are my clothes, miss?"

"Getting warshed."

"I had some tobacco, papers, and matches in my shirt pocket."

"Right there," she said, pointing to a small shelf just above his head, then reached and handed them to him. "You want me to fashion you a cigarette?"

"I can do it."

"You sure are an independent and grumpy man."

"Thank you," Cole said, and waited until she had left the room before fumbling with the makings. He couldn't even roll a smoke.

He felt something stiff above his left eyebrow, reached a finger, and felt a ridge of dried blood. He knew he must be a sight.

* * * * *

It took three precious days for the pain to ease up enough so John Henry Cole could sit on the side of the bed, use the privy without Lottie sliding a chamber pot under him. Israel came in several times a day to check on him.

"Ribs look good, but that knee looks out of kilt," he said. "Looks like I might have to set it back in place."

"Let's get it done," Cole said.

"You won't be able to stand it."

"Hell, tell me something I don't know."

He took a pouch from his pocket, poured some of its contents—a whitish powder—into a tin cup of water that he took from the nightstand, then swirled it around, and told Cole to drink it.

"What is it?"

"Something to put you out of the misery I'm going to cause you."

Cole looked at him.

"*Mambuto*," he said. "It's more powerful than any whiskey or any drug."

"Never heard of it."

"It's from Africa, where my people come from, handed down. Comes from a certain plant found there. Nothing like it here on the frontier."

"You ever had the pleasure?" Cole asked, eyeing the contents. The powder had tinged the water yellow.

"Not me personal, but I've seen it taken."

"For what?"

"Cousin of mine was with us in the Apache campaign and got hisself shot in the nuts."

"It helped?"

"He died, but at least he died without knowing it."

"That's a comfort to know. How do you know it wasn't the *mambuto* that killed him and not the getting shot in the nuts?"

Israel shrugged his shoulders. "Couldn't say for certain. Least he didn't die miserable."

"I think I'll pass on the *mambuto*," Cole said.

Israel looked at him, then shook his head. "OK."

Then he called in the men and told them to hold Cole down. Cole nearly flew out of bed when Israel's hands took hold of his knee and began moving it around. Cole drank the *mambato* and waited. He didn't have to wait long. A soft hum began inside of his head and his blood felt thick in his veins. Everything seemed to slow down at the same time so that his entire body felt like it was floating off the bed. He tried to say something but couldn't be sure the words even came out or what they sounded like. The faces of the men above him became distorted. When Israel leaned in close to look at his eyes, Cole saw a green light surrounding the man. The first moments created fear in him, then he felt a deep calm, as peaceful as anything he'd ever experienced. If he was dying, he thought, he welcomed it, surrendered completely to it. He felt a mixture of sadness and joy, of surrender and triumph even as his mouth grew dry as grit and he had trouble swallowing. He floated up to the ceiling and looked down upon the men surrounding his bed. Amazingly he saw himself lying there on the bed and continued to watch as Israel went about manipulating his knee, aligning it, then binding it.

Cole heard Israel say to the others: "For a white man, he's tough as they come."

Then he watched as they left the room before his world went totally black.

* * * * *

John Henry Cole awakened to the sound of a harmonica and someone thumping on a guitar. Singing. The shuffling of feet and the clapping of hands. It was dark in the room, and through the only window he could see the night sky flung with stars. There was a flickering yellow light licking at the blackness. Instinctively he moved his right leg and was surprised that he felt no pain in his knee, just a bit of stiffness. The rest of him still hurt like he'd fallen off a cliff. His throat was parched and he reached for the tin cup and the pitcher of water that had been on the nightstand. He fumbled for it, only to knock it to the floor. The music stopped briefly, then started up again. Israel came in, holding a lamp, shined it in his eyes, and said: "You ain't dead."

"I could use a drink," Cole rasped.

Israel shone the light on the tin cup, then called some of the men and had them carry Cole outside and place him in a chair. Then he told Lottie to bring Cole some water and something to eat.

"Last time he wouldn't eat a thing," she said.

"Don't be quarrelsome, woman, bring this man some victuals."

Israel handed Cole a jug and said: "Drink some o' this."

"More *mambuto?*"

Israel grinned. "Cider … hard cider."

"What's the occasion?" Cole asked, taking up the jug and watching as couples danced to the music around a huge bonfire.

"It's Saturday night," Israel said. "End of the work week. Tomorrow's Lord's Day. But tonight, we celebrate."

"Celebrate what?"

"Lots of things," he said. "Our freedom, for one. Fact we ain't all killed or slaves or on the run from the law. Fact we got ourselves a place we can call home. Fact we got plenty o' meat and a mouth harp and an old guitar and somebody who can play them. You think of any more reasons to celebrate?"

"A good horse and healed ribs," Cole said, taking a hard pull from the jug.

Lottie brought him a plate covered with buffalo meat and red beans cooked in fat, and this time he was up to eating, and that's what he did. He licked his fingers when he'd finished.

"Here, I brought you this, too," she said, handing him the makings.

"Grateful," Cole said. "And I didn't mean to be grumpy with you before."

She was as plump as a laying hen and had a round dark face and wore a red kerchief around her head. And when she smiled, she looked like the happiest person in the world.

Cole leaned back and rolled himself a shuck and offered the makings to Israel. He declined, said he never took up the habit. Cole asked why and he said because of being a poor man. To let himself take pleasure in something he couldn't always afford, he reasoned, was just another road to more misery and he'd had enough misery in his life that he didn't want to give himself more by developing bad habits he could ill afford.

"How about the cider?" Cole said, holding forth the jug. "Isn't that a bad habit?"

"Cider's something a man can always make if he knows where to find apples or berries. A man needs seed for tobacco and the right weather. Seed costs money and the weather you can't ever count on. I hear back east, they make cigarettes you don't have to roll that come in a package you can buy for a nickel."

"It would take away half the pleasure of smoking," Cole said, "not being able to roll your own."

"That Kid," Israel said, watching Joe trying to dance to the music even though he didn't have a partner. "He's a lively boy. What happened to his ear?"

"It's a long story," Cole said. "You mind passing that jug again?"

They seemed happy, the lot of them. There wasn't anything around for miles, no sign of civilization, no towns to gamble or drink or whore in. No churches to pray in, no outsiders to mingle with or bargain with. It was just they, left to their own devices, dependent on one another for their survival and for their joy. They were not so different from their ancestors, the first people God had led into the wilderness in search of the Promised Land. Maybe *this* was the Promised Land, Cole reflected, and they'd found it. It certainly seemed that way as he sat and smoked and listened to the music and watched them dance. The happiness creased into their dark faces as they laughed and sang. Cole felt something he hadn't felt in a long time—envy.

CHAPTER TWENTY-TWO

Cole busied himself by watching the men and women plant and cultivate their large garden and talking to young Joe. The Kid related to him the story of his past with his brother Henry, who was making a name for himself down in New Mexico.

"Some call him Kid … some Billy the Kid," Joe said. "I guess he's shot some people down there. You said you were a lawman once in Texas, you ever hear of him?"

"No, he must do all his killing local," Cole said. "There's lots of bad men between Texas and the border."

"Our real name was McCarty. Mother moved from Cincinnati to Silver City and married a man there named Antrim. Thin-faced son-of-a-bitch, ugly as a boot. My mother was a handsome woman … beautiful Irish, with strawberry red hair and eyes with the green of Ireland in them. She married Antrim 'cause she was sick with the lung fever and desperate and wanted somebody who could take care of me and Henry … his true name … once she'd passed on. Trouble was, soon as she took her last breath, Antrim got shed of us quicker'n a dog tries to shed himself of fleas. Henry ended up stealing a Chinaman's clothes for a feller named Sombrero Jack. This Sombrero Jack offered him fifty cents to do it, and

Henry landed in jail for it. I helped bust him out … dug him out with one of Mother's old kitchen spoons. Why, that jail wasn't nothing but some mud slung up on some mesquite poles. That's the day our life of crime began. He fled to Arizona where he shot his first man, a blacksmith who was molesting him. I took out for Dodge City, where I heard there was plenty of opportunity. Ended up swamping out saloons, emptying the spit of men like Wyatt Earp and Bat Masterson. Wild Bill Hickok, too. I suppose you heard of them?"

Cole generally didn't go in for a lot of conversation, but since he didn't have much else to do while waiting for his ribs to heal but sit there and listen, he gave the Kid his head.

"I'll tell you something, Mister Cole, spit is spit, don't matter whose mouth it comes out of."

"I'll keep that in mind."

"I met a gal there in Dodge," he said. "It was the one good thing that came out of going there. Her name was Maggie and it didn't matter a lick to me that she was a whore."

"She break your heart?"

"When she drank poison and killed herself, she did. I wanted to marry her, asked her to, but she said I couldn't offer her much being nothing but a saloon swamper. She was right. I told her I wasn't always going to be swamping out other men's spit and she looked at me and said … 'Why, you're just a kid and I'm nearly twenty-three. Time you get around to a regular profession, I'll be old and ugly and worn out.' That was the saddest moment of both our lives, I believe. I think she loved me, but not enough to keep her from drinking mercury. You ever seen the look on someone's face that has drunk mercury?"

Cole shook his head negatively.

"That's when I decided to make something of myself. I wanted to go and become an outlaw because I didn't have no education or skills for nothing else. And I sure didn't want to end up drinking mercury."

"So you met the Canadian River boys and decided to join up with them."

"Truth be told, yes." He squinted into the glare of the slanting sun. "Well,

I didn't know who they were when I came into their camp. And once they told me and what all they'd done, I was a little afraid of getting mixed up with such bad ones. I mean, I wanted to be a regular *hombre*, a mean blood and all that, but I didn't take to killing innocent folks. Robbing banks seemed OK, for it's the rich man who owns the banks and I reckoned it wouldn't hurt them so much to 'share a little of the wealth,' as Henry used to say when we'd talk about becoming outlaws."

"So you've never committed any actual crimes?" Cole said.

"No, sir, never did get the chance. I was a member of that gang exactly three hours when we got shot all to pieces by those fellers with the pinned hats."

"That tell you anything about being an outlaw?"

"Tells me I'd better get a damn' sight better at it or find another occupation to take up."

"Now you want to ride the vengeance trail, find the man who cut off your ear, and do him in," Cole said.

"Well, what would you do, Mister Cole, was it your ear he'd cut off?"

"'An eye for an eye,' the Bible says."

"Exactly, only this time it's an ear for an ear."

"You're going to cut off his ear?"

"Cut off both of them, I get the chance."

"This man," Cole said, "he's a bad *hombre*. I'd cut my losses, so to speak, and find myself a steady job like clerking, find an honest woman to settle down with, raise some children, a garden. Take a look around you, Kid, what do you see?"

"Folks hoeing and planting."

"Exactly. That's the way we were meant to live … in harmony with one another, not killing and robbing and cutting off each other's ears."

"You sound like a preacher."

"I'm about as far from a preacher as this here place is from the moon, Kid."

"I miss Maggie," he said. "If she hadn't killed herself, I would be with her today, still have my ear, and maybe an honorable profession."

"Most likely she would have broken your heart one way or the other, Kid. Some women are like that. She sounds like she was doomed from the get-go."

"Maybe so."

"It smells like rain," Cole said.

"They could use it for their crops," Joe said.

"That gal you met down by the creek the other night. You still meeting her?"

"Some," he said.

"I'd be careful with that. These are good people here, but I don't think they'd take well to you courting one of their daughters."

"I know, 'cause I'm white. She's already said that. Still, we sort of are taken with each other."

"Then I'd go ask her folks was it OK with them that you meet her."

"I know I should."

"I ain't your daddy, Kid. You'll have to work it out however you work it out. Thing is, these folks are kind enough to let us hole up here until I can step into leather and ride out. I'd not want to abuse their kindness."

"I understand," he said.

* * * * *

The rain came that night, hard and slanting, and Cole could hear it ping off the tin roof and spill off the eaves. For some reason, it created a deep loneliness in him. The story Joe had told him about the prostitute who drank mercury crept into his thoughts. The wind picked up and turned into a low, mournful moan, like Ella Mims's voice calling for him to come find her before it became too late. He didn't want to think about her being dead.

CHAPTER TWENTY-THREE

Another ten days passed before John Henry Cole could stand on the injured knee and take a breath deep enough that he felt like he could ride a full day without falling out of the saddle. In the course of that time, he'd become impatient from sitting in the shade and staring at his toes and Gila monsters. The Kid had busied himself by pitching in with the hoeing and planting and tossing secretive looks at a light-skinned gal, who Cole learned was the daughter of one of Israel's cousins. Her name was Iris. Cole had oiled his pistol and practiced the art of rolling shucks and tried hard not to think of his *compadres*, of Ella Mims and Gypsy Davy, of Colorado Charley Utter and his assassins. Ten days was long enough, he figured. It was time to get back on the trail.

He was about to call the Kid over, tell him he was leaving, when he saw a rooster tail of dust in the distance. He whistled and the bent backs straightened from their hoeing. When Israel's gaze fell on Cole, Cole nodded toward the dust. Israel wiped his hands on the rump of his jeans, then pulled a green bandanna from his pocket and wiped the sweat from his brow as he watched the dust get bigger.

He told the men to go get their shotguns and told the women to take the youngsters into the house, then walked to where Cole sat and said: "Could be anybody, could be nobody. Best to be prepared for whoever it is." Then he disappeared into one of the shacks and came back out again with his shotgun, as did the other men.

"What should I do?" the Kid said. "I ain't got a pistol nor even a knife if it comes to a fight."

"Might not come to that," Cole said.

"Mister Israel and the others sure enough act like it might."

"They've a right to be cautious, Kid. Maybe it's better you wait inside."

"With the women and children?" The indignation in his voice was sharp, high-pitched.

"I've got my Winchester inside. You can go get that, if you want."

"Yes, sir."

Cole stayed seated, but fixed it so his pistol was handy on his left hip. Joe came out of the house and stood next to him, the long-barreled Winchester, nearly as tall as he was, clutched in his hands.

Israel took up a position a few feet away. "Looks like it might be half dozen riders," he said.

"Maybe them fellers that shot us Canadian River boys to bits," Joe said.

"Well, they come down around here shooting, they'll get all they want," the older man said, his eyes white with determination under the brim of his straw hat.

It didn't take long before they could make out several riders, their ponies lathered, the foam flecking off their chests and forelegs, their tongues lolling against the iron bits.

"Oh, no," Israel muttered, when the riders were still a hundred yards out. "Rufus." He said the name like it was a curse he hadn't meant to utter.

Ten feet from the shacks the riders jerked hard on their reins and the dust swirled up around them, then settled slowly, leaving a fine golden coating on their hats and clothes. The one in front had oily dark skin and eyes as black as obsidian that came to rest on John Henry Cole and the Kid.

"Rufus," Israel said. "What you doing this far west of the Territories?"

It took a long, slow moment for the dark eyes to swing from Cole and Joe to Israel. "Uncle," he said, "me and my boys need something to eat, a place to rest our horses."

Israel stood motionlessly for a second.

"You taking in white people?" Rufus said, jerking his head in the direction of Cole and the Kid. "Slaves, I hope."

"Don't be rude, boy."

"Well, can we or can't we rest our ponies and get some grub from you, Uncle?"

"Yes, you is welcome to squat and rest up. I'll have some of the women fix you something to eat. Anybody following you?"

The dark face turned in Cole's direction again, the stare as hard as flint. Cole counted seven of them—Indian, Negro, and a mixture of both, all of them bad news and on the dodge, judging by the way they were dressed and the side arms they carried. Not a one in the bunch looked much older than Joe. The one called Rufus might have been nineteen, if that.

"Them's some hard-looking *hombres*," Joe said in a low voice when the riders walked their ponies to the water tank, then dismounted, and took up places around the long table kept in the yard for purposes of community meals.

"Keep low now," Cole said. "Don't give them cause to start up trouble with you. The way I see it is that after they get through filling their bellies and watering their mounts, they'd probably like nothing better than to dust a white child such as yourself."

"What about you?" he said. "I'd say you're as white as me."

"They'd probably want to save me for dessert."

The Kid gave a nervous laugh.

Israel came over after a time of sitting with the bunch.

"That's my brother's boy, Rufus Buck," he said. "His mother was a Cherokee. He's got a bad spirit. I'm his goddaddy, else I'd tell him to keep riding."

"No need to explain," Cole said. "Kin is kin."

"Better I do," Israel said. "Thing is, he hates white people, any white people, and lawmen most especially."

"He wouldn't be the first to feel that way. You can tell him we're not the law."

"I told him not to start no trouble with you boys, but he's got a boil on his butt about seeing you here."

"It's your place," Cole reminded. "You want us to leave, we'll leave. You've already done more than your share."

Israel looked deeply at Cole. "You 'uns turned them buff', kept them from overrunning our settlement. I owe you for that."

"Let's just call it even, then. Me and the Kid will ride out, save everybody the trouble."

"Thing is, you do that, I won't be able to protect you if Rufus and his bunch decide to take up after you."

"What do you suggest then?" Cole said.

"I don't know, just trying to let you boys know that they could start some trouble with you."

"I don't mean to insult your family," Cole said. "But I won't be laid a hand upon by any man."

"Understood," Israel said. "I'll do my best to see Rufus don't kick up no sand 'round here."

"Appreciated."

"We in for a fight, you reckon?" Joe asked after Israel returned to the table.

"Could be. You think you can hit anything with that Winchester?"

"I'm a good shot," he said. "Me and Henry used to pop rabbits with Antrim's needle gun, though he wasn't aware of it or he'd have skinned us."

"Popping rabbits ain't nearly the same thing as popping a man."

"I'll do what needs doing, I reckon."

"Anything starts up, let me make the first move. Don't go shooting anybody over words. We walk away from this thing, if they give us half the chance. Understood?"

He nodded.

Cole wasn't convinced. Fear makes a man jumpy. Lots of fear makes a man very jumpy. Cole had known men in the war who had become so overwrought with fear and the battle raging around them, they'd forgotten to load their muskets. At least the Kid was holding a repeater and wouldn't have to reload. Cole just hoped, if shooting broke out, the Kid wouldn't shoot him by accident. He told the Kid to go inside and pack up their gear.

"Now?"

"Yeah, unless you're planning on sticking around and marrying that gal you're so sweet on."

He arched an eyebrow, then ducked back inside the house. Cole turned his attention back to the callow youths sitting at the table, hunched over, feeding their faces, and talking among themselves. Every so often, Rufus Buck would look over his shoulder at Cole. Cole made sure Rufus saw that Cole was watching him, too.

In a few minutes, Joe returned.

"All packed and ready to go when you are."

"Hold tight, Kid. Let's see how it plays out."

The Kid looked nervous, shifting his weight, stealing glances at the table, seeing them cast hard looks in their direction. "What do you think?" he said.

"I don't know."

"I ain't scared," he said, meaning that he was.

"Go ask Israel if I could speak to him a minute," Cole said.

Joe did as asked and Cole saw the hard look Rufus Buck gave the Kid as he stood at the table, talking to Israel—like an owl eyeing a field mouse.

"What can I do for you, Mistuh Henry?" Israel said, carrying the shotgun in the crook of his arm, his eyes weary because of the tight spot he found himself in.

"I'd like to buy a horse off somebody, a good one that will ride two men to the next town."

He gauged Cole's words. "Might be Mose would sell you that big bay o' his. He's talked about selling it 'cause he can't get it broke to a plow."

"Tell him I'll pay twenty dollars and throw in a good pistol to boot."

Israel weighed that, then said: "That bay ain't worth twenty and a good gun."

"Today it is."

Israel went off, toward where the other men had gathered, watching Rufus Buck and his gang eating up a good share of their buffalo meat and beans. These men were obviously not much more comfortable with the presence of Rufus Buck than was Israel. Cole saw Israel speak to the one of the men, a stump of a fellow with a straw sombrero. They palavered for a moment, then the man walked in Cole's direction, Israel following.

"Israel said you'd give me twenty dollars for my bay horse and throw in a pistol to boot. That it?" he said, looking at the self-cocker on Cole's left hip.

"Twenty and this pistol, that's the deal," Cole said, handing it to him.

"Done," he said.

"Time we parted company," Cole said to Israel.

"You sure?"

"I've burned too much time as it is," Cole said. "I've got something to do and I can't get it done, lying around here. Kid, go get and put my saddle on that big bay in the corral."

"I can't promise your safety once you're out of the settlement," Israel reminded.

"I can't promise I won't kill your godchild, either. Let's just hope they've got better things to do today."

"I'd feel mighty bad you was to kill him," Israel said. "Those others is just trash. Rufus might be trash, too, from the stories I've heard about the depredations those boys have caused in Indian Territory. But he's still my kin, still got my blood in his veins."

"Let's hope he's got some of your good sense, too."

"I sure enough hope it don't come to trouble, Mistuh Cole."

"I do, too, Israel." Cole offered his hand and he shook it.

Joe returned with the horse saddled and said: "I'm ready … you?" Cole said in a low voice: "You see one of those yahoos make a move, don't be slow in letting me know."

Cole grabbed the horn, and when he had swung, his ribs still bit into him, telling him he wasn't whole just yet. Once in the saddle, he left a stirrup for Joe to swing up behind him, and then put the bay into a fast walk until they hit the south road.

"I'm going to miss meeting Iris down by the creek," the Kid said.

"You'll get over it."

"Glad we didn't have to fight them fellers, Mister Cole."

"You might have to fight them yet, Kid. Best be on guard. Keep a check over your shoulder now and then."

They rode till the sky turned crimson and was banded by a long line of silver clouds.

"You think we're in Texas yet?" the Kid asked as they set up camp.

"Texas, Oklahoma Territory, what's the difference? We'll get there when we get there."

"Just that I ain't found nothing good about Oklahoma," he said, "'Cept Iris, and her I didn't have a Chinaman's chance with."

"There'll be plenty of others to strike your fancy. I'll take first watch. You grab some sleep. I'll wake you in four hours."

"'Cause of Rufus Buck?"

"He's one reason. There could be others."

He stared into the encroaching darkness.

CHAPTER TWENTY-FOUR

They came just past midnight.

Shadows in the moonlight, seven riders strung out in single file scouting for their camp. Cole clamped a hand over the Kid's mouth and shook him awake. "Don't say anything, don't cough, fart, or make a sound," Cole whispered.

There was a hunter's moon and Cole figured even half an Indian could find them in that much light. He already had the Winchester at the ready. With just one weapon, he'd have to wait until they came close enough, and by that time it might be too late. Seven hardcases against a busted-up rannihan and an unarmed kid wouldn't be too much of a fight—unless they weren't as hard as they thought, or as ready. Cole could hear the Kid breathing rapidly through his nose.

"Any I drop," Cole said, "you run and take his weapon and shoot anyone but me."

Cole could almost hear the sweat dropping off the Kid's brow. He did hear the snuffle of their ponies, the clink of iron bits, the creak of leather—sounds that grew louder as they closed the distance. Cole put a firm hand on the Kid's shoulder, indicating for him not to move. They were a good fifty paces from them—still not close enough to suit Cole.

"Fuckin' white men," Cole heard Rufus say. "We find them, we cut off their nuts." Some of the others grunted, a few laughed.

Cole waited as they walked their ponies through the sage, the shod hoofs snapping mesquite twigs. And waited.

One of them said: "I think maybe they'd be over there by that wash, where there's a little water. I think maybe I see something over there."

They turned their ponies, just fifteen paces away from where the Kid and Cole lay.

"Hey, I see their horse," one said.

"Shut your mouth!" Rufus said. "You want them knowing we're coming?"

"Too late," Cole said, and fired into them. Even with the moonlight, it was hard to tell which was which. Cole would have preferred to take out Rufus with his first shot. Maybe the rest would quail. He couldn't tell which of them he shot first, which was second, but two flopped off their ponies and hit the ground hard.

"Go get their weapons, Kid!"

Flashes of gunfire spewed from the muzzles of guns, but the shots went wild as they were caught up in the excitement of sudden gunfire. The Kid duck-walked to the nearest body and snatched the pistol from his belt, but was having trouble firing it.

"Shoot the god-damn thing!" Cole shouted as he fired two more rounds, one striking a rider but not unseating him, and the other missing its mark.

"I'm trying!" the Kid yelled.

Suddenly it was as though they'd figured it out, where the killing was coming from, and the ground around Cole exploded with their shots. Cole rolled behind a fallen blackjack tree and the lead from their pistols chewed up bark and whanged away at it. The Kid was fumbling with the bandit's pistol when one of the riders closed ground on him, the horse striking him before he could bring up the pistol and get a shot off. Cole snapped off a quick shot, then the next round jammed in the breech.

Cole broke open his Barlow knife and pried the shell loose and quickly jacked another round into the chamber. But not quickly enough. The rider had the hoofs of his pony thrashing the Kid, and, when Cole came up and drew a bead on him, he saw the man take aim and fire three quick shots into the Kid—three white flashes that lit up the Kid's frozen features. It was just enough for Cole to see, too, the oily face of Rufus Buck. He took aim and pulled the trigger and watched Rufus pitch from his horse and fall next to the Kid.

A flurry of rounds rained all around Cole. A splinter of wood stung his cheek and instantly he could taste blood. He rolled away, the lead from their guns chewing up ground. But the dance of their ponies threw off their aim enough for Cole to scramble to the Kid and the man who'd killed him. His rifle jammed again. He grabbed the pistol from Rufus Buck's still-warm fingers and rapid-fired into the remaining four riders. One pitched from the saddle and the others turned tail. The whole fight had lasted less than five minutes, but it had exhausted Cole, and for a moment it seemed like he could barely move. He swiped more blood from his face and lips with the back of his sleeve. His mouth was parched and his ribs ached like a broken jaw, but those things didn't seem to matter just then.

There in the paleness of moon, he saw Joe lying, face up, his mouth open, his eyes partly so, a bloody wound to the throat, two more to his chest. Rufus Buck lay next to him, face down, unmoving, the two joined in death. Cole felt sorry for the Kid. He'd wanted to be an outlaw. Now he was never going to be anything. Maybe the Almighty knew the Kid wasn't cut out for a criminal's life: the loneliness of a prison cell or a hangman's rope. Cole thought of a line he'd read in the Bible once: *Death comes like a thief in the night.*

Cole tucked Rufus Buck's pistol, a Colt Peacemaker, into his gun belt, grabbed his Deane Adams and Smith & Wesson, and then bladed out the jammed round from the breech of the Winchester. Then he used the rifle to help him to hobble to where he'd staked out the bay. By the time he'd gotten the saddle on him, he was too tired to take another step. Still, he pulled himself into leather. The remainder of Rufus Buck's gang had scattered off toward the west. Cole doubted they would return for an encore. If they knew how defeated Cole felt right then, they might be tempted, but Cole thought those boys had had about all the fight they wanted for one night. He well knew he had.

He would have liked to have buried the Kid, but he had no shovel and no time. What was done was done. And after all that, the rain came.

CHAPTER TWENTY-FIVE

The rain hammered the land with a vengeance and hammered John Henry Cole along with it. It rained so hard the water seemed to boil up from the ground—a cold, slanting rain that lasted until dawn before it let up. And with the dawn Cole could see the roiling gray clouds scudding low over the broken red earth. He thought of the Kid, lying back there among the dead, the coyotes and the wolves that would surely find the corpses if they hadn't already, and the circling vultures. There was nothing Cole could do for him; there was nothing anyone could do for him. Cole rode on, through the dull light to a destination unknown. His life, it seemed, had come full circle. Thirty years earlier, he'd ridden away from a farm in Indiana—from a widowed mother and three brothers—off to make his fortune, to find his glory, only to go bust in the gold fields and end up fighting in a war in such far-flung places as Cold Harbor and Gettysburg, where he saw lots of boys with the same frozen mask of death on their faces as that of young Joe McCarty. Just as with the Kid, Cole had been unable to do anything for those others, either, except leave them to the ages and the ravages of the land. At least with the boys on those battlefields, men would come later, scooping up their bones and skulls into wheelbarrows for burial in mass graves. No such honor would befall a restless young man who'd gone off wanting to be like his brother, an outlaw. Thinking this way, John Henry Cole was so certain about what he believed had happened, that it never once occurred to him that Joe McCarty, although severely wounded, seemingly dead, had in fact survived the attack and would be found by Israel and some of the others when they went in search of Rufus Buck and his gang, concerned about what might have happened to them as well as to Cole and Joe McCarty.

* * * * *

Cole must have dozed in the saddle, for when he awakened, his horse was standing still and a raven-haired woman stood in a yard before a small, whitewashed house with several children clinging to her skirts. She held a Sharps saddle gun in her hands.

"You there," she said, "better keep moving before my husband gets back."

Cole's eyes felt like they had grit in them and every bone in his torso ached. He certainly looked disreputable, his clothes still wet, the brim of his hat battered down by the rain, his pony slathered with red mud.

"I'm afraid you're just going to have to shoot me," he said.

"Why's that?"

"Because I don't believe either this pony or me can go another step without rest."

The children—three girls and a boy—all looked up at her, their eyes big with wonder.

"Ma, you gonna shoot that feller?" the boy said.

"I just might," she said.

They seemed to shrink back.

"You'd be doing me a favor," Cole said.

"What's wrong with you?"

"Nothing a change of dry clothes, some Arbuckle's, and hot grub wouldn't cure."

"You a thieving man?" she asked.

"If I am, you can see I'm poor at it."

154

"Killer, maybe?"

"Nobody who didn't deserve it."

"How come you to land in this far-flung place?"

"I didn't, my horse did. I just came along for the ride."

She looked uncertain what to do about him. What, indeed, do you do with a man who's shown up in your front yard looking like a bad version of death? That was the question behind her eyes. A rooster crowed, and one of the kids jumped.

"We ain't got nothing, if you came here to rob us," she said. "Just these kids and that rooster, two, three laying hens."

"I didn't come here to rob you or otherwise bring you harm," Cole said. "You mind if I step down?"

She motioned with the barrel of the Sharps and he eased himself out of leather and leaned against his pony to keep from falling.

"You hurt?"

"No, not really," Cole said. "Just a little stove-up. Place I can water my horse?"

Again she used the barrel of her rifle to indicate a water tank off to the side of the house. Cole led his mount there and let him drink his fill.

"I reckon you could stand something yourself," she said. "You wait out here. I'll go fetch you something."

"Suits me down to my heels," Cole said.

He took a seat on a stump that looked like someone had tried unsuccessfully to pull from the ground, then tried burning it out, and finally gave up on doing anything with it. It made a tolerable chair. He reached for the makings and found the papers and tobacco wet.

The children seemed fascinated by his presence. They stood around in a semicircle gawking at him. Cole said: "I'm not a circus elephant."

That made them laugh.

"You look like a mud puppy," the boy said, and that made them laugh again.

Cole looked at his clothing and said: "You're right, I must have gone to sleep and fallen off my horse."

There was more laughter.

The woman returned, carrying a plate of biscuits and fatback and a cup of coffee.

"It ain't much," she said apologetically.

"It'll do," Cole said. "Thank you."

The lot of them stood and watched him eat but he didn't mind. The biscuits were tasteless and the fatback greasy, but he licked his fingers when he'd finished and washed it down with the Arbuckle's, and felt as if he might live until noon.

"Much appreciated," he said.

"Your leg need mending?" she asked. "I saw you limping like a three-legged dog."

"Bum knee," Cole said. "Had an accident."

"What sorta accident?" the boy asked. He was maybe ten years old, with a mop of corn-silk hair freshly cut in the shape of a bowl and gaping teeth.

"Fell off my horse," Cole said.

"You fall offen your horse a lot," the boy said, making his sisters giggle.

"Good thing I came along," Cole said, "or you young 'uns wouldn't have anything to laugh about."

The girls giggled some more.

"You kids go on and finish your chores," the woman said, "and leave this feller be."

They scampered off, and Cole wondered what chores they could have, given the spare conditions of their existence. The roof on the house looked leaky and the front door was missing a hinge and a good, hard wind seemed like it might blow the whole shebang into the next county. It wasn't Cole's place to question, though. He was grateful to have a belly full of grub and a little coffee to ease the chill in his blood.

"You want," she said, "I could wash and dry your duds."

"Thank you, but I've already put you and your family out enough."

"No trouble," she said. "I'm fixing to do a wash now, anyway."

"How'd it look if your man come home and found you washing my duds?"

She brushed a sprig of her hair away from her eyes where the wind had worked it loose from the tortoise-shell combs. "Truth is," she said, "I don't believe you have to worry none about my man coming home."

Cole thought about that a moment, looked up at the foreboding sky. It didn't look like the sun would come out anytime soon. The thought of riding another fifty miles in wet clothes made his skin crawl.

"If you're sure it's no trouble ..." he ventured.

"None. You can take 'em off inside. Wrap yourself in that old green quilt I got hanging on the wall."

Time passed slowly, the children came and went, laughing, acting as children do. With no schooling to occupy them, they spent a lot of time chasing each other around and around the house until they tired of that, then took out after the rooster, causing it to squawk and flap its short red wings and run a jagged course. The woman called to them to leave off on the rooster lest they frighten it to death, which only made them laugh all the harder until her voice grew stern. Then they slunk off like cats to an old shed, where Cole supposed there was something equally interesting to occupy their minds.

She'd built a fire under a wash kettle and scrubbed the clothes with a bar of yellow soap, then rinsed and wrung them out by hand, and hung them on a single line of wire that ran from a nail in the side of the house out to a dying blackjack tree.

"They'll be forever drying without any sun," Cole said when at last she'd finished and sat on the top step of the porch next to him.

"Not with this wind," she said. "If it don't rain, those duds will be dry in less than an hour. One thing we got in this territory is lots of wind. It's good for drying clothes, but not much else."

"Your man," Cole said. "He run off, get killed, something like that?"

"Don't know," she said. "He went out hunting one day and never came back. I went looking for him for a month. I had an old mule. I rode out as far as I dared, looking for Albert. Never found him, never found a trace of him. Like as not, he got carried off by a bear, or he just grew tired of all the responsibility of a wife and young 'uns and trying to scratch out a living from this hardscrabble."

She brushed her forehead free from more sprigs of hair with the back of her wrist.

"Seems like a poor place to bring a family," Cole observed.

"Not if you're wanted by the law, it ain't."

"On the dodge, your man?"

"Albert used to rob banks in Missouri," she said. "Till it got to be unprofitable."

"How does robbing banks become unprofitable?"

"The Jameses, Jesse and Frank and their cousins, the Youngers," she said. "They were a lot better at robbing banks than Albert ever was and that got the Pinkertons and most of the law in Missouri down on bank robbers. Pretty soon, it got so you couldn't walk in a bank that didn't have at least one or two armed guards. Albert was a lot of things, but he wasn't a gun artist. The other thing was the new safes the banks installed. Albert said you couldn't blow one 'cause of the amount of dynamite a man would have to use … that the explosion would blow up the whole bank and all the people and money in it. Albert wasn't no murderer like those James boys. He had a good heart in him. Couldn't kill a sand flea. Those new banks and armed guards just put him right out of business."

She folded her arms against the chill wind and stared off toward the horizon.

"It's just as well," she said. "Sooner or later Albert was bound to be murdered." She turned her head just enough to look at Cole over her shoulder. Her eyes were the same color as the sky—smoky gray. "You ever know an outlaw who came to any good end?"

"Most die young," Cole said. "Least the ones I've known."

"Albert just never liked the thought of regular work. He had a good heart but was shy when it came to hard work. Still, I miss him something terrible, and so do the kids."

"Maybe if a bear didn't get him," Cole said, "he will change his mind once he's been gone long enough, and come back."

She sighed and stared at the horizon as though, if she watched it long enough, Albert might appear. "I wonder how long is long enough," she said. "He's been gone a year already."

"Why stay on if that's the case? Don't you have some family back in Missouri?"

"Sister," she said. "That's about it."

"That's something, anyway. A place to start."

"No," she said. "I best wait and see if Albert *does* come back. I light out, he might not know where to look for us."

"How long you reckon you can hold out?"

She shrugged her shoulders. "Maybe another six months, leastways up till winter."

"Then what?"

"Then ... well, I imagine I'll have to take the kids to an orphanage and find myself some work in the nearest town."

The wind blew steadily out of the northeast. "You down to just biscuits and fatback?" Cole asked.

She nodded and said: "And not much of that."

"There any sort of town near here that'd have a mercantile?"

"Jack Ass Flats," she said. "About twenty miles that way," pointing with her chin.

* * * * *

The woman proved accurate about the wind. In an hour Cole's clothes had dried, cold and stiff. He was still in pain, but at least he had clean clothes and a full belly. He thanked the woman for her kindness as he stepped into leather.

"My manners are poor," he said. "I never caught your name. Mine's John Henry Cole."

"Charity," she said. "And those wild 'uns are Minerva, Jessie, Laura, and Albert, Junior."

They grinned up at Cole like 'possums, and he tipped his hat to them.

"Hope your man comes back soon," he said. "If he's out there and got any good sense, he will."

She offered Cole a weak smile as though she knew there wasn't a chance she would ever see Albert again but still held to the slimmest of hopes.

Cole rode away, thinking that the reason the frontier was so vast was because of all the misery and heartbreak it had to hold.

Jack Ass Flats was west and would take him out of his way, but it was a trip that needed taking, so that was where he headed.

CHAPTER TWENTY-SIX

The first thing Cole noticed about Jack Ass Flats was the man hanging from the telegraph pole. The corpse twisted in the wind to the creak of the rope that held him. The streets were empty and he felt as if he had ridden straight into a bad dream. He saw a string of ponies tied up out front of a saloon. It seemed like the place to stop.

The bar was lined with men of all sizes and shapes. They were in a celebrant mood. A few threw looks Cole's way when he stepped up to the oak and ordered a whiskey. The bartender said: "Two bits."

Cole placed the coin on the oak next to the glass, then stood for a moment before knocking the drink back, and let its burn fan out in his blood.

"You Cecil?" the man next to him said.

"Cecil?"

"Why, yes," he said. "Cecil Trotter, the executioner from Tahlequah."

"Sorry," Cole said. "I'm neither from Tahlequah nor an executioner."

"Too bad," he said. "We was hoping you were."

"Why's that?"

He grinned wide enough to show that his incisors were gold-capped. "Just so's we'd have the pleasure of telling you old McTavish's already been hanged. Imagine you saw him when you rode in … feller what's hanging from the telegraph pole."

"Hard to miss," Cole said. "What was his crime?"

"Pony thief, adulterer, and murderer. Killed his lover's husband. The husband caught them in bed together."

"Sounds like a bad situation."

He nodded knowingly. "Was … for him." The man gave Cole the once-over, probably wondering if he looked like a pony thief or a murderous adulterer.

"So this Cecil from Tahlequah is going to be a bit disappointed," Cole said. "Riding all this way for nothing."

"It got boring waiting," the man said. "Town like this, you take your fun when you can get it."

Cole thought of Teddy Green and how he would think it was unseemly to leave a dead man hanging from a telegraph pole where the corpse could be seen by women and children. "There a reason you just left that fellow hanging?" he asked.

"Well, hell, we was to cut him down right away," the man said, turning to make sure he had the attention of his *compadres*, who by this time were all ears, "it'd just get boring again."

"Yeah," said the man next to him, a short fellow wearing a Navy Colt with ivory grips. "The Flats ain't exactly Saint Louis, in case you ain't noticed. Ain't much to do here but watch paint dry and listen to the wind blow."

"So hanging a man is a real big deal," Cole said, "like the Fourth of July. Which way to the mercantile?"

"Down the street to your right, stranger."

Cole was tempted to order another whiskey, but he wasn't up to the company of men who would leave another man hanging from a telegraph pole for the sport of it. He found the mercantile and told the man what he wanted: beans, flour, sugar, coffee, cured beef in tins, some hoarhound candy. Then he asked that the store deliver the supplies to Charity and gave him directions to the woman's holdings.

"I know you've got a telegraph in this town," he said. "I saw a man hanging from one of the poles. Which direction is it?"

"Cross the street, down two doors."

The telegraph office was closed, a sign on the door said:

Out to Lunch.
Back in Thirty Minutes.

Cole figured the telegrapher was among the men celebrating in the saloon. He started to cross the street to seek him out when he had to step back on the walk to keep from getting run over by a spring wagon pulled wildly by a pair of high-stepping Percherons. Holding the reins and trying to keep her seat was a female dressed in a buckskin shirt and leather breeches. Cole wasn't sure whether she had control of the team or not until she brought them to a hard stop just beneath the pole where the dead man hung.

He watched her for a moment, saw her stare up at the body, then lower her head until her shoulders shook once. Then she climbed into the back of the wagon and took a knife from her belt and began sawing away at the rope.

"Better let me help you," Cole said.

She looked down, saw him, said: "Who are you?"

"Just a stranger passing through," Cole said. "Better let me help you."

The dead man's size made her agreeable. Cole climbed in the back of the wagon and hefted the corpse while she cut the rope, then he laid him out in the back of the wagon.

"This your man?" he asked.

She had short-cropped red hair that was as glossy as a rooster's feathers and sea-green eyes and a splatter of freckles across her nose.

"He's my father," she said. "His name's Flea McTavish."

"I'm sorry for your loss."

"Why should you be, unless you are the one who hanged him up there and left him like that?"

"No, I had nothing to do with it."

"Then don't apologize for what you had no hand in. You want to feel sorry for someone, feel sorry for them who did this."

She jumped from the wagon, reached back in under the seat, and took out a shotgun with sawed-off barrels and a whittled-down stock—to fit her own diminutive size, Cole supposed—and headed across the street to the saloon.

Cole took hold of her elbow. "You planning on getting some justice?"

She looked at him hard.

"It's just that there's probably twenty or thirty yahoos inside and everyone of them is drinking and armed."

"I don't see where that's your concern," she said.

"You don't think they'd shoot a woman, liquored up and growing bored again?"

She pulled free from Cole's grip and started across the street.

Cole didn't know why he felt it was any of his affair what the people in this town did—it appeared like they were all hell-bent on killing one another—but he fell in step alongside her, and followed her through the double doors of the saloon.

All the celebrating that had been going on stopped at the sight of the two of them, most of the attention going to the woman and the shotgun she was carrying.

"Who did it?" she said. "Step away from the bar."

For a whole minute the men stood frozen, beer mugs and shot glasses held in their hands, disbelieving looks on their faces.

"Who're the ones who hanged him?" she demanded.

The man who had been so talkative to Cole earlier said: "Diana, that thing loaded?"

"You do it, Woodrow?"

He shook his head. Cole saw some of the others ease away from the man, snake out along the bar out of harm's way.

"How about you, Frank? You hang him?"

Frank, the one with the Navy Colt, lost his grin. "Every man in this room knows what your daddy did," he said. "Hanging was too good for him."

"Step away from the bar, unless you want your friends to die with you," she commanded.

"Ain't nobody dying today, Diana," a voice from behind said. "Put that greener down before you shoot somebody."

Cole turned enough to see a familiar face, only this time he was wearing a nickel badge and holding a pistol.

"Stay out of it, Bill," the woman said without taking her attention from Frank.

"Can't," the lawman said. "It's my town."

"If it's your town, where were you when they hanged my father?"

"Collecting taxes," he said. "A man can't be everywhere at once."

"You should have been here," she said.

"I'll see that things get righted," he said. "But you cut loose with that scatter-gun, you'll just end up making it worse." Then the lawman said to Cole: "You there, mister, step away." He had failed to recognize Cole. It had been a long time since they'd last run into each other. Bill Tilghman said to the men at the bar: "Put your irons on the oak and step away."

They did, quickly enough.

"Now," Tilghman said. "You shoot any of those men, Diana, unarmed like they are, it'll be the same thing as what they did to your daddy. Let me handle this, woman."

She took a deep breath, let it out, then turned to face him. "God damn you, Bill Tilghman, for letting them do it!"

"It was my responsibility," he said, "and my mistake of thinking it would be done legally. Cecil was on his way over from Tahlequah. I thought he'd be here by now."

Her eyes filled with a bitter pain. "I'm holding you and this whole town responsible for what happened here."

"You might hold your daddy a bit responsible, too," Tilghman said. "Trouble with one wrongful act is, it often leads to others. Wasn't for his crimes, none of us would be standing here now."

She looked at him for a long hard second, then strode out of the saloon, brushing past him and through the double doors.

Some of the men snorted until Tilghman told them to "shut their cakeholes." He eyed Cole for a moment. "Have we met?"

"Once," Cole said. "Long time back on the Chisholm Trail. You were ramrodding beeves and I was looking for work."

He stepped closer where the light was a bit better, then with what for him probably came as close to a smile as you would see on Bill Tilghman said: "John Henry Cole. You sure found your way to hell and gone."

"Looks like you did, too," Cole said.

"I've some work to do here," he said. "Maybe after I'm finished, we can meet up at the café and have some coffee and catch up on old times."

"I'd like that, Bill, but to tell the truth, I've got to keep moving."

"You on the dodge?"

"Not to worry. You'll find no papers on me."

"I heard sometime back you was wearing a badge down in Del Río. What happened with that?"

"Long story," Cole said. "I killed a bandit and had to quit."

"Why's that? They don't like lawmen killing bandits down along that border?"

"Not when the bandit is a cousin to most of the population," Cole said.

"I see."

Cole started to leave, then took a moment to say: "Glad you didn't shoot that woman, Bill."

"I'm glad I didn't shoot her, either," he said. "She's my fiancée."

"Well, then that would have made a rough start of it for the marriage."

"You're telling me."

Cole could hear him telling some of the men at the bar they were being placed under arrest as he walked out to the street again. The woman snapped the reins over the rumps of the Percherons, turning them around in the street, then, when she arrived at where Cole was standing, brought them to a halt.

"If you are seeking a long and prosperous life, this ain't the place," she said.

She snapped the reins again and drove away.

Cole made for the telegraph office and this time he found the telegrapher in.

"How much to send a wire to Gonzales?" he asked.

CHAPTER TWENTY-SEVEN

In Amarillo, John Henry Cole sold the bay, the saddle, and a few of the pistols he'd taken from the dead after the fight with Rufus Buck's gang. He needed money and he needed a quick way to Gonzales, so he bought a ticket for the stage to take him from Amarillo to San Antonio. From there he could easily make his way to Gonzales with hopes of hooking up with Teddy Green and Harve Ledbettor. He'd sent a wire from Jack Ass Flats to be delivered to whatever local law enforcement was to be had in Gonzales that explained the situation and asking him if those two riders were in the vicinity, and if they were to let them know Cole was coming. There was a man named Beaver Smith who ran a private stage line out of Amarillo, what he called a mud wagon, and there were two other passengers besides Cole—a gaunt-looking drummer with a large mole on the tip of his nose, and a woman.

The woman wore a green, tie-back dress with black trim and a Western hat with a large ostrich feather pinned to the crown. She had a long face with dark curious eyes, an unattractive woman whose silence was disturbing. The other thing that was disturbing about her was the single scabbard with the mother-of-pearl-handled pistol on her hip. It was highly unusual for a woman to wear a side arm. Most kept a Derringer or knuckle duster in their reticules, but few openly wore pistols. This one did and she fancied a small riding crop laced around her left wrist. She had a certain way of running her gaze over you that made you feel like prize livestock she was considering buying.

The drummer seated next to her seemed quite interested in this homely woman and for the first several hours of the ride out of Amarillo, he could not seem to take his eyes from her. She appeared not to notice, but when the mud wagon pulled into the first way station and they got out to stretch their legs, Cole heard her say to the drummer: "Something about me that's got you so all fired dumbstruck?"

The drummer flushed red and he adjusted his trousers by hiking them up over his narrow hips. They were baggy on him as were the rest of his clothes—baggy and dusty.

"No, ma'am, just that I couldn't help but notice that fancy piece you're wearing. Unusual for a lady to go about fixed with a pistol. You ever shoot anybody with that iron?"

"Only those who took liberties with me," she said, giving him a hard stare.

He grinned weakly. "You care for a dipper of water?" he said, nodding toward a well that stood in the sun twenty feet from the corral. "I'd be happy to fetch some for you."

"That would be pleasant of you," she said, after which the drummer then hurried off, perhaps grateful to be out of her glare.

Cole noticed, when she spoke, she had large, horsy teeth that did nothing to improve her looks. She looked his way. He was rolling a shuck and anticipating how long it would take to make a change of the team and get back on the road again. This Beaver Smith, the man who owned the line, said they'd make San Antonio in two, maybe three days, depending on the weather.

"What's weather have to do with it?" Cole had said.

"I mean whether or not they is any road agents, busted wheels, or other disasters that might befall us along the pike," he had said, then grinned foolishly like a man who'd just played a great joke purely for his own amusement.

The woman said now: "What about you, bub?"

Cole licked the edge of the paper and finished the roll before twisting off the ends and striking a lucifer off his heel. "What about me?" Cole said.

"You interested in why I carry this pistol proud on my hip?"

"Not really."

"Why ain't you? Most men are when they see a woman with a hog-leg strapped onto her skirts."

"I'm just not," Cole said. "Free country, you can wear what you want, it's none of my business."

"Now I like that in a feller."

"Like what?"

"His willingness to live and let live. That's the way my Sam is, too."

Cole really didn't want to engage her in conversation and was relieved when the drummer returned with a dipper of water, which he handed her. She placed it to her lips but did not drink genteelly. She drank more like a man would, spilling a good portion of it, then wiping her chin with the cuff of her sleeve, never once taking her gaze from Cole. Finished, she handed the dipper back to the drummer and asked if he might go inside the little way station and see if they had any hard candy.

"I'm partial to candy," she said. "The hard kind. I've got teeth like a squirrel's, you know what I mean." She gave the drummer a lascivious wink, which caused his knees to buckle.

"Yes, ma'am," the drummer said, and quick-stepped it to the way station.

"Amazing what a man will do just for the sniff of a woman," she said.

"Amazing," Cole replied, then strolled over to the corral to look at the horseflesh.

The next thing he knew she was right there beside him.

"Going to see my husband, Sam," she said. "Got him in jail in San Antonio."

Cole was silent.

"Planning on hanging him."

"That's too bad."

She breathed through her long nose; it was an audible sound. When Cole didn't say anything more, she added: "Sam was always a man with bad luck on his side."

"In my experience, it's usually more than just bad luck that gets a man hanged," Cole said.

She snorted, and Cole could smell the faint odor of sweat and rose water as she stepped in a little closer to him. "You're right," she said. "It's me that's the one with the bad luck. Every man I've ever had a thing to do with has come to a terrible end ... Sam's just one. I had a lover went to prison for twenty-five years, serving time this very moment in Illinois. Green Duck, you ever heard of him?"

"No." Cole was content simply to smoke his cigarette and watch the hands exchange teams, turn out the old ones, and round up four fresh mounts to put in the traces. One particular animal they were having trouble with—a stout gelding with a blazed face.

"I spent a little time myself in the calaboose down in Dallas once," she continued, as though Cole had encouraged her somehow. "They claimed I was fencing stolen horses. Can you imagine that?"

Cole could, but he didn't say anything. She had an irritating manner of speaking, her voice too loud, too sharp to the ear.

"Well, if you ain't never heard of Green Duck, you ever heard of Cole Younger?"

Cole nodded that he had.

"He was my first husband. It didn't work out, even though we had us a child. Cole was too restless. He was cousin to Jesse and Frank James, you know."

Cole didn't know why she was telling him all these things. Maybe she thought he had the same fetching interest in her as the drummer had. Or maybe, because he showed no outward interest, it was a challenge to her the way it is to some women. All Cole knew for sure was, he had no interest in this woman and her lovers or her life or her reasons for being on the mud wagon.

The drummer returned and said: "Sorry, my sweet, but they have no hard candy, not even a twist of licorice."

He was a ferret-faced little man, barely taller than the woman. Seeing as how Cole was taking no interest in her, she suddenly allowed herself to warm to the man, smiled, and said: "Why, that's OK. What'd you say your name was there, feller?"

"George," he said. "George Pepperstick."

"How do, George Pepperstick. I'm Belle … Belle Starr," she said, and offered him a fancy gauntleted hand.

Cole had heard the name now that she'd mentioned it. It was a name much bandied about the courthouse in Fort Smith, Arkansas, when he had worked there. Although he'd never encountered Belle Starr before, or any of her roost of outlaws, he'd heard plenty of stories, randy and otherwise, about her. And once, while he was in the employ of Judge Parker, he'd heard the judge had sentenced Belle Starr to six months in the Detroit House of Corrections for being in possession of stolen property, mainly missing nags with altered brands illegally gained from throughout the Nations.

The driver hawed them back into the mud wagon and off they went again, only this time Belle Starr not minding so much that the drummer's eyes were all over her and his hand was resting on her knee.

"You do well drumming, George?" she asked.

"Do fairly well," he said. "Peddle knifes, special-made, guaranteed not to dull even after a thousand uses … the secret is in the honing."

"Oh, now that's very interesting," she said. "But how much you reckon you make drumming knifes, say in a year?"

It went on like that for several hours, Belle Starr learning of the drummer's earnings and he more than happy to brag a bit, saying how in one year alone he made almost $5,000, to which she feigned great surprise and said: "No!"

His face shone like a new penny. "Sure, sure," he said. "Why, I expect to earn half as much again this year. Everyone has need of a good knife. Would you like to see an example of my wares?"

She laughed bawdily and said: "You show me yours. I'll show you mine."

After two more stops to change teams, they pulled into a jerkwater town that Beaver Smith said had a hotel and a whiskey den. The other three or four other buildings were closed at that hour of the evening.

"We'll rest the night, be back here at dawn," Smith said. "You want a bed, the Alamo's the only place that's got any. You want a drink, a sandwich … something like that … you'll find it at Dirty Alice's, that way." He pointed with his nose toward the saloon.

"I don't know about you," Belle said to knife drummer, "but I could stand me a drink and some pickled eggs. Care to buy a lady dinner?"

"Shore do," he said, and offered her his arm, which she dramatically took.

"You want to come along and join us?" Belle asked, casting a backward glance at Cole.

"Maybe later," Cole said, and headed toward the hotel.

A man with a milky eye cast it in Cole's direction when he entered and said: "You in on the mud wagon?"

"You have any rooms to let?"

"Sure, sure. You want one to share or by your lonesome?"

"Lonesome," Cole said, and signed the register and gave him the $2 he was asking for the room. Cole trudged upstairs and removed the pistols, the ones he hadn't sold that he'd taken from the Rufus Buck gang. Then he propped the Winchester in the corner before sitting on the bed to remove his boots. His ribs still hurt like hell but the rest of him was healing fine. He figured to forgo supper and grab some shut-eye. It'd be another long day tomorrow and with any luck—considering if the "weather" held—they'd arrive in San Antonio the next day. With even greater luck, Teddy Green and Harve Ledbettor would have found Ella Mims and have her in hand when Cole arrived. He had every confidence in both men.

He lay back on the bed, which sagged under his weight, and closed his eyes and soon drifted into a light sleep.

He awoke sometime later to the sounds of laughter on the other side of the wall, and it didn't take but an instant to recognize the bray of Belle Starr and the voice of the drummer. The one thing Cole had noticed earlier was the silver wedding band on the drummer's third finger, left hand. Somewhere he had a wife waiting for him to return; some men were fools. Cole rolled over and closed his eyes and tried to shut out the sounds of their revelry, which went from loud talk and laughter to whispers and the creak of bedsprings, with Belle every now and then screaming out an epithet that would make a frontier marshal blush.

Finally Cole couldn't take it any longer and pulled on his boots, re-armed himself, and went down the stairs, out the door, and over to Dirty Alice's saloon. A whiskey or two, supper, and maybe once he returned to his room, things would have quieted down. The drummer didn't look like he was up to an all-nighter with the likes of Belle Starr.

A sloe-eyed faded rose tried to join Cole while he stood at the bar. He thanked her for her offer, bought her a watered-down whiskey, then took his sandwich and drink glass to a table where he sat alone. He tried not to think at all beyond the moment and killed an hour at Alice's before returning to his room. It was quiet next door.

Cole arose at 5:00 the next morning, shaved, washed his face, and combed his hair, then armed himself again and headed out the door. That's when he noticed the door to the adjoining room ajar and saw the drummer sprawled on the bed, face down and dressed in just his socks. Cole knew right away what had happened. He shook the drummer until he moaned and his eyes fluttered.

"Well, at least she didn't kill you," Cole said.

The drummer muttered something, and Cole took the pitcher of water next to his bed and poured it over him. He came up with a start, spluttering and waving his hands. Cole noticed the silver wedding band was missing.

"She skinned you," he said.

"Huh?" The drummer fisted the sleep and water from his eyes.

"Belle Starr skinned you."

He blinked several times, noticed that he was naked, and quickly grabbed at the blanket to cover himself.

"What? What?"

"You damned fool, you got skinned, cleaned out, rolled for your poke … even your wedding ring."

He looked at his left hand. "Oh, Jesus."

"How much did you have on you?"

He glanced at the corner of the room, where a valise stood open, then scrambled off the bed to check it, his pale bare buttocks exposed.

"Oh, Jesus," he said again. "My wallet is gone." Then glancing about. "So are my knife samples!"

"How much in all?" Cole asked.

He slumped there on the floor, a sprig of hair like a long piece of seaweed hung from his otherwise bald scalp. He was calculating in his mind the losses.

"Two hundred in my wallet and the knives and case worth at least a hundred more."

"That's a lot for the pleasure of an ugly woman," Cole said. "You better get dressed, if you want to make the mud wagon."

Cole walked down to the city marshal's office, but the door was locked. He intended to report Belle Starr, not that it would do much good. She'd probably stolen a horse and cleared out. Cole sauntered back over to the way station and waited while the driver and his assistant harnessed up a fresh team of horses. He rolled a shuck and was lighting it when he saw Beaver Smith look beyond the team and say to his assistant: "Why, that drummer forgot his shoes."

Cole looked and saw the drummer walking toward them in his bare feet.

"She took my shoes, too," he said.

"Who took your shoes?" Beaver Smith asked.

"Why, that woman with the fancy pistol you sold a ticket to in Amarillo."

The driver grinned. "You figured Belle to show you a good time without her getting something out of it? Mister, what sort of fool are you?"

"The biggest this side of the Chisos," he said. "Maybe the biggest in the whole of Texas. The thing I don't get is why she'd steal my good shoes."

"Why, probably to take them to her husband, Sam Starr," Beaver Smith said. "Belle probably wants him to look his best when he goes to meet his Maker."

They had a good laugh over that—Beaver Smith and his assistant—as the drummer and Cole climbed into the mud wagon.

"This is the worst trip I've ever had," he said. "What will Wilamina say when I come home with no shoes on my feet?"

Cole said he didn't know and sat back for the rest of a long ride.

CHAPTER TWENTY-EIGHT

The mud wagon and the drummer pulled into San Antonio late on the third night. A busted wheel had delayed their trip by some six hours. They halted in front of a gentlemen's club, the Golden Spur.

Cole needed to stretch his legs and decided to stroll down to the Guadalupe River, less than a block away. It was late and most establishments—except for the drinking parlors, gambling halls, and bagnios—were closed for business, yet it was still too early to find a room.

The air was warm and carried with it the smell of the river. The gaslights of the bridge were reflected in the green water below. The odor was pungent—damp and fishy. Across the way, ghostly under a full moon, stood the stone chapel of the Alamo—all that was left from the battle decades earlier between a handful of Texans and Santa Anna's army of over a thousand men. The chapel was the last refuge of the Texans. But neither the chapel nor its holy walls could save them from death. Cole had read that after the last Texans, including Crockett, had been rounded up, they were executed—shot in the back of the head—and thrown on a pyre, the smoke of which could be seen for fifty miles. Men died for a lot of reasons, border disputes being just one.

Cole listened, half thinking if he listened hard enough he might still hear the clatter of musketry and the cries of the wounded. But all he really heard was the clatter of shod hoofs on cobblestones and the cries of children playing down by the river, the voices of old men telling them to hush or they would scare away the catfish that the old men were so patiently trying to catch.

One of the old men saw Cole standing on the bridge and called to him: "*¡Hola, amigo!*" Cole nodded and asked if he'd caught many fish this night and he said, yes, he'd caught a few, but that in the last hour he hadn't caught a single one. "I have brought too many of my children with me to do any real good," he said, his face oily brown in the dim yellow light from the bridge. "My little ones like to play too much and are not serious enough for fishing."

"*Sí*," Cole said, and moved on.

For some reason Cole felt a deep uneasiness, as though someone were watching him, causing the flesh on the back of his neck to prickle. The sense of Ella Mims was strongly in his mind, like she was nearby, maybe just around the next corner, waiting for him. He knew how foolish this was, but at one point he turned and looked behind him. It was a disturbing feeling and he knew that he was letting his mind play tricks on him, like a man on the desert who sees mirages of cool water that don't exist. While not a superstitious man, Cole did believe in trusting his instinct because it has saved his hide more than once.

He continued walking the streets, trying to pay attention to his intuition, going blindly where his feet took him. Around every corner, he expected to run into her—the feeling that she was close was that strong. After an hour or so he gave up. He drifted back toward the center of town. Nearing the hotel he'd decided to check into, a man approached him from the shadows and he prepared for whatever trouble was coming.

"Pardon me, sir, would you happen to have a match?" He was a well-dressed man, had a dark mustache, was slight of build, and wore a cape.

Cole reached in his pocket and handed him a lucifer, which he struck against the brass plate on the hotel's wall. It was then, when the light flared, that he saw the familiar face of Doc Holliday. He lit his cigar, then held the light for a moment before snapping it out. He inhaled and coughed, then inhaled again, as though he were trying to do battle with himself by smoking away the lung fever in him.

"You're a long way from Deadwood," Cole said.

Holliday cocked his head, trying to figure out who Cole was, but with the heavy shadows he couldn't tell. "Do we know each other, sir?"

"We met in Deadwood, Doc. John Henry Cole. Remember?"

"It is truly you?" he said, his voice unable to contain his surprise. "Why, I heard that you had been killed in Cheyenne … that a man had shot you in the back. I see now that was wrong, for here you are, walking around in my town."

"Oh, when did San Antonio become your town, Doc?"

"Why, every town is my town whilst I'm in it," he said, then coughed again, hard, and had to support himself against the wall, his hand braced against the brass plate.

"Well, I'm sorry to disappoint you about my demise," Cole said. "I'm not staying long, so you'll have the city all to yourself."

Cole started up the street and Holliday said: "Wait."

Cole turned, knowing that when he did, Holliday could be holding a Derringer on him, ready to pull the trigger and assure that he fulfilled the rumor of Cole's death. Instead, he held only the lit cigar, its tip burning red in the blackness.

"I'd appreciate it if I could buy you a drink, over there at the Golden Spur. I am a member of the club."

"It's late," Cole said.

"It's never too late for a drink, sir. If anyone would know, it would be me. I'm the self-appointed timekeeper of drinking."

Cole wasn't in the mood to drink, especially not with Doc Holliday. His reputation as a mean drunk who went out of his way to pick fights only made him doubly dangerous. Cole wondered if Doc Holliday didn't have some fanciful, morbid wish that someone would kill him outright in a gunfight and save him from the lingering death in his lungs. If that was his intention, Cole didn't want to be his foil.

"I'll pass," Cole said. "I've had a long ride and still got a ways to go."

"A man's life should not be reduced to having to drink alone," Holliday said. "Whatever I've done to offend you, I regret." He stood there, one hand extended to support himself against the wall, his voice a near rasp from the effort it had taken in coughing away his sickness. But it wasn't for those reasons that Cole agreed to walk with him to the club for a drink. Cole had a sudden thought, a question that Holliday might be able to answer because of the dark world in which he operated.

"OK, Doc, I'll sit and have a drink with you."

"Well, sir, what are we waiting for?" With that he seemed to regain his strength, and they crossed the street and entered the gaily lighted club.

Most of the patrons were well-dressed men, with frock coats, gray fedoras, and kidskin gloves. But none was dressed any finer than Doc Holliday himself, who sported a cravat with a diamond stickpin to set off his Prince Albert coat. Hanging from the pocket of his brocade vest was a gold fob. Cole could see the bulge of a pistol in Holliday's pocket. He carried in his left hand a silver-tipped cane. Except for the malevolent gaze, Doc Holliday looked no different from any of the other dandies standing at the oak or sitting in red, cushioned chairs.

The club itself was posh with Brussels carpeting, green velvet drapes over the tall windows, a bar that ran one length of the room, a mirrored backbar, and waiters in jackets and white aprons. Several paintings of fat nude women hung on the walls and a cloud of gray smoke from expensive cigars hung in the air. It reminded Cole a lot of the Inter-Ocean Hotel in Cheyenne, where Billy Cook was shot to death while taking a bubble bath with a married woman.

"Over there," Holliday said, pointing with his cane to a corner with two empty chairs. A waiter came to take their order. "Two tall whiskeys," Doc said. When they came, Holliday held his glass to the light as though to examine the quality of the liquor, then said: "Farewell to Deadwood and old loves, eh?" His reference to a woman that they'd both had an interest in, but one that neither of them had won, didn't escape John Henry Cole.

Under the light, Holliday's pallor was like that of aged candle wax, his eyes sunken into dark cavities. Still, he was a handsome man, even in his condition, and several of the women who were in attendance with their escorts cast longing looks in Doc's direction. Holliday didn't fail to acknowledge a single one of them, offering them a slight nod and a wan smile.

"To old times and new," he said, hoisting his glass in a salute before knocking it back and signaling the waiter to bring another round, even though Cole hadn't touched his. "Drink up, the night is yet young."

"I have to be honest with you, Doc. I didn't accept the invitation to be sociable."

Holliday looked at Cole, his brow slightly furrowed, dampened with sweat, even though it wasn't that warm in the room. "Oh?"

"I want to ask you about someone."

The waiter came with two more drinks, and Holliday paid him from a fold of cash he pulled from his wallet. "Keep these coming until I tell you not to," he said, and the waiter smiled knowingly. Doc took up one of the glasses and pressed it lightly to his cheeks, rolling it for a moment, then set it down again. "Would that I could absorb the demon rum through osmosis," he said. "It would save me the time of actually having to swallow it and trigger my paroxysms. Now who was it you wanted to inquire about, sir?"

"Do you know a man named Gypsy Davy? Have you ever heard of him in your travels?"

His gaze came to rest on Cole in a way that seemed as though he were trying to see into his soul. "He's a complete madman, a man without a scintilla of conscience," Holliday said in that whispery, liquor-ravaged voice. "He is also a highly intelligent individual, which therefore makes him even more dangerous than your average brute. Whatever would bring you to ask about such a man?"

"I'd like for you to tell me what you know about him, Doc."

He tasted some of his liquor, his eyes seeming darker, if that were possible. "My first encounter with Gypsy Davy was when we met in Baltimore, where I attended dental school. Young Davy was practicing to become a physician. I met him at the party of a mutual friend. He was quite charming, Davy was. In fact, he was the most charming individual I've ever met.

And most deadly, too, as it turned out. He would have made a fine doctor if he'd been so inclined to save lives rather than take them. A brilliant mind." Doc Holliday pulled a silk kerchief from his pocket and wiped his lips with it, delicately, like a woman. "But you see," he continued, "Davy was a man with a taste for blood and blooding, and it wasn't contained simply in the surgical theater or in the practice of medicine. He enjoyed cutting people with his scalpel whether they be patients or simply men to whom he took a dislike. It is what ultimately brought about his expulsion from medical school."

"Tell me about that," Cole said.

"He killed two men in a fight in some riverside bar one night, cut their throats just like that, nearly decapitated the one. Do you know how sharp a surgical steel scalpel is? There were varying stories as to how it began, who perpetrated the engagement. But because of the notoriety, Davy was given his walking papers from the school. Some say it left him embittered enough to murder his mentor, the chief of the medical staff, because of it."

"Did he?"

Holliday shrugged, dabbed at his lips some more, then smoothed his pitch-black mustache. "The man was found with his throat neatly cut and Davy nowhere to be found afterward … he'd simply dropped out of sight. They say that one of the poor man's ears had been neatly sliced off as well, some sort of mark of Gypsy's vendetta. Nothing was ever proven and the murder went unsolved." Holliday finished his drink, then started to order another when Cole pushed one of his across the table.

"I need to stay sober," he said.

"Good Lord, whatever for? Sobriety only clouds the mind."

Holliday downed half of Cole's glass. The gleam in his dark eyes told Cole he was well on the verge of changing moods. "I later ran into Gypsy Davy in San Francisco, where he had become the fair-haired child of Nob Hill's effete and wealthy, regaling them with tales of his exploits on the frontier. He was written up in the *Police Gazette*, you know, several times … a regular Wild Bill." Doc spoke as if he were envious of Gypsy Davy's reputation, practically snorting the words. "It was in that yellow journalistic tome that

I first read that Gypsy's trademark for killing was slicing off the ears of his victims … claimed to the reporter that he had a collection of them. Thus, I assumed that he had indeed committed the murder in Baltimore."

Cole reached for his remaining drink and knocked it back.

"So what is your interest in this mad-hatter, John Henry?"

"It's a private matter, Doc, that's all I care to say about it."

"I can tell you this about Davy Devereaux," Holliday said. "You'd be wise to shoot him on sight like a rabid dog than allow him to charm you into revealing your throat to him."

The name struck a chord. "You certain about his last name being Devereaux?"

"Why, yes, I believe it was. I remember, because of its alliteration … Davy Devereaux."

Cole could feel his blood ticking in his wrist.

"Practically rolls off the tongue, doesn't it?" Doc said, his gaze gone flat now. He seemed to be staring at a porcine man sitting a number of tables away.

"Thanks for the drink, Doc, but I've got places to go."

"I would enjoy watching the encounter if you find him," Doc said. "Beware, John Henry, his blade is quick and sharp." Doc ran a finger across his throat.

But Cole was already on his way out. Something cold, like iron, pressed at the back of his skull. The questions hammered away: *Were Gypsy Davy and Ella married?* Colorado Charley Utter had called her Ella Devereaux. It might explain why she had been involved with Gypsy Davy, but it wouldn't explain why she'd be running from him. Had she loved him enough to be part of a murder? Cole had to get to Gonzales, find Teddy Green and Harve. Most of all, he had to find Ella.

CHAPTER TWENTY-NINE

A hard ride brought John Henry Cole into Gonzales late in the day. The sky was a bled-white and Gonzales seemed nothing more than a sleepy little village with plenty of natives in their cotton shirts and trousers and wide sombreros. He asked one of them where the marshal's office was and he told Cole in Spanish that it was above the *farmacia*, which stood at the east end of the main street. Cole thanked him and walked the horse he'd rented in San Antonio in that direction. He dismounted and knocked dust from his hat and ascended a set of outside stairs that led to an office above the drugstore. It was a warm day and the door stood open. A fat-bellied man with skin as brown as saddle leather sat hunched over a desk, eating tortillas filled with beans; a bottle of mescal stood near his right hand. He had a round face and pitch-black hair cut straight across his forehead and wore a leather vest with silver conchos for buttons. Grease ran down his fingers and smeared his chin and slicked his mustache. He didn't seem happy to have his supper interrupted.

"You John Law?" Cole asked.

"Juan Law?" he said in a heavy accent. "No, no, *señor*, you got me mistaken for somebody else, eh. I am Carlos. Carlos Delgado. I am the sheriff." Some beans dropped out of his greasy sandwich and he scooped them off the butcher paper they'd been wrapped in and fingered them into his mouth.

"That's what I meant," Cole said. "My name's John Henry Cole and I sent a wire to you a few days ago, asking about my friends … men named Teddy Green and Harve Ledbettor."

"Oh, *sí*, I got your telegram. What you want me to do with it, go find them, these men you talk about?"

It was clear this man wasn't going to be of much help unless Cole wanted to raid a restaurant. "So you haven't seen these men?"

He shook his head. "I wasn't looking for them, they wasn't looking for me, so I guess I haven't seen them."

"You know a man named Feathers, owns a cattle spread around here?"

He suddenly stopped eating. "Why you want to know?"

"This is important, Sheriff."

"So is my supper, *señor*. You tell me why you want to know about *Señor* Feathers, maybe I tell you where he lives."

"His boy," Cole said. "He's headed this way with a friend of mine, and I want to meet up with him."

"Oh, so if you are his friend, how come you don't know where he lives?"

Cole didn't care for the way the conversation was going. It was simply more time wasted. "Skip it. I'll find the place on my own."

"*Sí, sí*, you do that, *señor*, leave me to my meal, eh."

Cole started to leave, paused in the door, and said: "One more thing, there are some men coming, ten of them riding together, hats pinned up. They'll be asking questions, too, only they'll not fool with you … they'll shoot you in the guts for answers. If I find Feathers's boy before they do, I might save you and this town *mucho* trouble."

Some more beans dropped from his tortilla and his eyes narrowed with concern.

"*Señor* Feathers lives south of town … three, four miles … you'll know it by the big water tower he's got there. Who are these men who might come shoot me in the guts?"

Cole was already descending the stairs. He followed the south road until he spotted the water tower of which the Mexican sheriff had spoken. The sky was by then a dusty rose as twilight encroached; in the weeds crickets could be heard, beginning their night song.

A trace angled off from the main road toward the tower, and Cole followed it, pulling the Winchester from its scabbard as he went. Whoever or whatever might await him at the house, he wanted to be prepared. His heartbeat quickened when he topped a slight rise and there below stood a long house in need of some fresh whitewash. The house was topped by a cedar shake roof and three chimneys. Panes of window glass reflected the ocher sky and the rockers on the front porch sat empty. There was no sign of life, no livestock, no horses tied up out front.

Cole spurred his pony forward, the rifle balanced across the pommel of his saddle. Except for the state of disrepair of the main house, everything appeared to be normal. He pulled up and sat the horse.

Then a voice called from behind and above him. "John Henry Cole!"

He turned about slowly, not knowing if the man behind the voice was armed and dangerous. Standing on top of the tower was Teddy Green. Harve Ledbettor stepped out from within the shadows of one of the outbuildings.

"In the living flesh!" Harve cawed. "I see you finally decided to haul your bacon out of that featherbed and come join us."

Cole waited for Teddy Green to climb down from the tower while Harve summed up what had happened since they had parted company. "We ain't seen hide nor hair of any of them," he said. "I don't know how we could have missed them or got ahead of them."

"Unless," Teddy Green said, coming up, "they got waylaid somewhere along the road. Or changed their minds about coming here."

"You didn't backtrack?"

"We was waiting for you," Harve said. "Waiting for them and you. If we left, you might not find us. We figured it best to hang close a few more days, wait and see if they showed, if you showed and they did."

"The Mexican sheriff didn't deliver my wire?"

Teddy Green shook his head negatively. "Delgado don't leave that office or get more than a stone's throw from a dinner plate, if he can help it. I've had previous dealings with him … once came here to arrest a man who turned out to be Delgado's cousin. Never found the cousin, even though I suspect to this day Delgado was hiding him. I wouldn't count on him to spit."

"What now, John Henry?" Harve said. "We wait it out?"

"No. We backtrack."

"Let's get to riding then," Teddy Green said.

Harve squinted into the setting sun. "So late in the day, we won't get far."

"He's right, John Henry, may be best to spend the night and head out first light," Teddy Green said.

Cole sheathed the Winchester. "Stay if you want," he said.

They rode until dark.

* * * * *

That night, they could hear thunder in the distance. Harve looked across the campfire and said: "I hope it ain't another cyclone headed our way."

"You see any more crows today?" Teddy Green asked.

"Not a single one."

"Well, at least that's a piece of good news."

They sat in silence for a while before Teddy Green said: "We have to face the possibility that she's dead, John Henry."

"Then let us find her and bury her," Cole said.

He nodded. Harve passed around a bottle. They drank.

Stars smeared the sky above them while off to the west heat lightning flashed and occasionally they could hear the rumble of thunder. From off in the distance a coyote called, then another and another. Finally more silence.

They rolled up in their soogans and tried to sleep. Then Cole heard the crack of a twig from outside the light of the campfire. He slid one of the pistols from under his blanket and heard the others doing the same. The distinct double click of cocking double-action pistols—hammers being thumbed back and the single rotation of the cylinders—had the same effect as the rattle of a snake.

More silence.

"Maybe nothing," whispered Harve.

They waited, then heard a groan, and a shadowy figure stumbled into the firelight, dropped to his knees, and said: "Lord, mercy!"

He was a black man and bleeding from a head wound, a red stripe that scored his scalp, his clothes torn.

"Who are you?" Teddy Green demanded, jumping from his blankets with the barrel of his revolver aimed at the man.

"Isom," the man said. "Isom Dart."

"What happened to you, Mister Dart?"

"Was ambushed, two, maybe three days ago, maybe a day before that, I ... I sorta lost track of time."

He looked old.

"Why?" Teddy Green said.

The man blinked several times as though trying to understand the question.

"Give him a drink of whiskey," Cole said to Harve. "See if we got something we can patch up his ..."

That's when they all saw the missing ear—when the black man turned his head toward the light—the blood dark red, dried to a crust around what was left of the ear.

"Jesus," Harve said, "this feller must be ..."

"Tom Feathers's man," Cole said.

The mention of Feathers's name caused the black man to stare, wide-eyed.

Harve retrieved the bottle of liquor and pressed it into the man's hand.

"No, suh," he said. "I'm a temperate man."

"Don't be a god-damn' fool," Harve said. "Drink some of that red devil, it'll bring you to your senses."

Reluctantly Isom Dart did as ordered and didn't stop until he'd drunk a third of the contents.

"Where'd this ambush take place?" Cole asked once he'd revived.

"In a small cañon," he said. "Somewhere back up that way."

"Come daylight, you'll show us where," Teddy Green said.

"Yes, suh."

Teddy Green looked at Cole and said: "We're close."

* * * * *

They rode out at dawn, Isom Dart doubling with Harve, the black man indicating the direction.

"How can you be sure, you walking in the dark like you done?" Harve questioned.

"I can see good in the dark," he said.

"Oh, yeah, I remember Bittercreek Newcomb telling how you could see well enough in the dark to shoot a man."

"He's a fool," Dart said. "Damn' ugly one, too."

They burned three quarters of the day before Isom Dart said: "Turn off here. Up in there is where the cañon is."

Teddy Green eyed the sky, saw a wheel of buzzards, some of them dropping below a ridge of rock.

No cañon could be seen from the road, but as they cut through a stand of mesquite, they came upon an arroyo that snaked back into a small box-like cañon. There they found the abandoned hack, the horse dead in its traces, bloated and half-eaten—the big ugly birds flapped their wings and took flight at their approach.

"Looks like he killed everything," Harve said.

"Tell us what happened here?" Cole said.

"We was camped, pulled in here figgering to be safe. Mistuh Feathers say we soon be to his daddy's ranch, best we not tarry along the road." Dart slid off the back of Harve's mount and walked to the buggy, then cast his gaze upon the dead horse and shook his head. "He come outta nowhere ..."

"Who?"

"The Gypsy man, the one Miss Ella say be after her."

"What happened then?" Teddy Green asked.

"He killed Mistuh Tom. Slipped up on him and put a knife to him and cut his throat with it before I could get my sights on him. Then he shot me in the head, probably thought he killed me. That's all I know. I come to, bleeding, thinking maybe my brains be spilling out, but they ain't ... that bullet just run a track over my skull. It don't hurt so bad as this here," he said. "When I feel my ear ain't there any more." The story seemed to sap all the strength from him.

"The woman?" Cole said.

Dart shook his head. He didn't know.

Teddy Green said: "Where's Feathers's body?"

It wasn't there.

They followed a blood trail that climbed a rocky slope of the cañon's west wall and found Tom Feathers's body, lying among the cacti at the top.

"He didn't die right away," Teddy Green said.

"Look at the way he was cut," Cole said, more closely examining the corpse. "Just enough to let him bleed out."

"Davy wanted him to know he was dying," said Green.

"Pay back for taking Ella," Cole said.

"Pay back," Teddy Green said. "This is one mean son-of-a-bitch."

"What now?" Harve said.

"We read the signs, see which way they went," said Cole.

"What about him?" Harve indicated the black man, still kneeling by the dead horse.

"You take him back to Gonzales, wait for us there," Cole said.

"I came to fight."

"We can't just leave him, Harve."

"I hate splitting off from you boys."

"You might not have to," Teddy Green said. "Look."

A cloud of dust in the distance indicated riders headed their way.

"Colorado Charley?" Harve asked.

"That's my guess," said Green.

"Then let's make a stand here and now," Cole said.

"God damn right," Harve said. "I'm tired of playing behind the eight ball."

"So am I," Teddy Green said.

CHAPTER THIRTY

"You up to shooting?" Cole asked Isom Dart when they reached him in the bottom of the cañon.

He looked at Cole with eyes that spoke of regret. "I'll do what needs doing. Who you want me to shoot, anyway?"

"There's riders coming," Harve said. "Gypsy Davy wasn't the only one after Miss Ella."

They set up their positions behind rocks—Teddy Green and Harve to the right, the black man and Cole to the left—partway up the cañon's neck.

"We just gonna ambush 'em?" Isom Dart said. "Just gonna shoot 'em out from under their hats?"

"We'll give them a chance to ride away," Cole said. "But only if they prove to be agreeable."

He didn't ask anything more, simply wetted his thumb, wiped it over the front blade sight of the Winchester, then settled in.

"Let me ask you something that's troubling me," Cole said.

He didn't take his eye from the sights.

"How come you and Feathers are just now getting this far south? You should have been here at least a week or two ago."

"Miss Ella turned sick, had to find her a doctor. She was laid up for a time, thought she might die. Delayed us coming."

"What kind of sick?" Cole asked. "What was wrong with her?"

"Don't know. Just sick is all."

"How was she when Gypsy Davy waylaid you?"

"Still weak as a kitten," he said. "All the color washed out o' her, but well enough."

For that, Cole was relieved. If Gypsy Davy had meant to kill Ella, they would have found her body. It was a two-edged sword, that thought. Cole was glad she was alive, but the knot in his belly that she was in the company of a madman was little comfort.

They could hear the clatter of shod hoofs coming down the cañon. Cole signaled for the others to get ready, but to wait for his play.

They could hear the echoes of voices from Charley's bunch, glancing off the cañon's walls.

"Something's dead up in here, see those buzzards circling?"

"Might be we lucked out and they all perished on their own," Cole heard Charley say. They were close, just around the bend.

"Be our bad luck, I was counting on having a little time with the woman before we finished her." This sounded like Batwings, Charley's sidekick.

"Hell, we all were!" another cawed.

"You boys, shut them cake-holes. Why, if there is dead up in here, you'll wake them up."

They came into view, two abreast, Charley and Batwings in the lead. The ambushers waited until they'd all cleared the bend before Cole said: "End of the trail, Utter. Don't even think about it. We've got you nailed. You do anything, this is where you'll stay, where they'll find your bodies."

Surprise crawled all over Utter's face as he jerked hard on the reins.

"John Henry Cole?"

"You still want to shoot us like prairie chickens?" Teddy Green called down from his position. "Go ahead."

Batwings turned his attention to the rocks on that side of the cañon.

"Yes, sir!" Harve shouted. "Hell, it'd be my pleasure blasting you yahoos!"

"I wanna know what's your stake in all this?" Charley said.

"We're not here to talk, Charley," Cole snapped. "Drop your irons on the ground and dismount."

Some of the horses snuffled and pawed the ground—they smelled the death.

"Then what, we do that?" Charley said. "You planning on leaving us afoot, something like that?"

"Something like that, but only on the condition that you hoof it back to Denver and tell the judge you failed in your mission."

"No can do. Why, I ain't never failed in my mission, ain't about to now. We got ten guns to however many you got in them rocks and my suspicion is you ain't got much but them two others was with you last time we met … that feisty Ranger and the one missing an arm." Charley was full of himself, considering the position he was in.

Cole said: "We got you in our sights, that's all you need to be concerned with. You can go tell the judge yourself or he can read about it in the papers. Makes no never mind to me, Utter."

"The hell you say!" he shouted, jerking his pistol.

Cole shot him out of the saddle. It was too late to do any more talking. Guns jerked from their holsters, rifles and pistols cracking, bullets ricocheting off the rocks, scattering dust and riders, men pitching from their saddles. The ambushers shot into Utter's posse with a fury, and some of them scattered back up the cañon, while the rest lay dead or dying. Batwings was one who scattered at the first shot and Teddy Green shouted that he was going after him. Cole called out to let him go, but Green was already stepping into leather.

"Jesus," Cole muttered, and went for his own horse. There was nothing like a bull-headed, right-minded, never-forget-an-insult Texas lawman not to let a fight come to a quick end. Teddy Green was spurring his horse up the cañon by the time Cole hit leather.

"You want me to stay here or what?" Harve shouted.

"Stay here!"

Cole was eating Teddy Green's dust when the *pop! pop!* of pistol shots opened up ahead of him. Teddy Green had caught up with someone, or someone had caught up with him.

By the time Cole rounded the next bend in the cañon, where it began to open up, Teddy Green was down on his knees, his horse shot from under him, struggling to rise. Blood stained his shirt—he'd been caught in a crossfire. The bastards had made a stand instead of running, instead of going back to Denver.

Teddy Green was firing his pistol toward a rock outcropping. Then Cole saw Batwings rise from a rock above him, take aim with a Winchester, and blow the top of the Ranger's head off.

Cole jerked his own rifle, took steady aim, and killed Batwings. He watched him pitch from the rock and tumble to the cañon's floor. Bullets chewed up the ground around Cole, but he had gone into the cold-blooded state of mind of a killer—everything moved in slow motion. The remaining gunfighters were mere targets for him calmly and efficiently to knock down. Old instinct took over, his aim steady and true, he began to kill them in the rocks until the last one threw down his rifle and ran.

Cole dismounted and kneeled beside Teddy Green's body.

"Teddy," Cole said, "you damned fool."

Then he searched Green's pockets. He has lost most of his things in the storm, but his Ranger badge was pinned to his undershirt, and around his neck tied to a leather thon, Cole found a small waterproofed packet. He opened this and found a tintype of Ella when she was young, her hair done up in reddish curls, a slight smile on her lips. Pretty and innocent. Cole stared at the picture for a long time, remembering the woman he'd kissed in the summer kitchen in autumn with the sweet scent of apples in the air. He realized, too, how much Teddy Green had loved her, enough to give his life for her when he didn't have to. Also in the packet was a letter. He opened and read it.

Dear Teddy,

I still think of you and miss you. I wonder every day if the Comanches that you so dearly love to chase, or some outlaws, will bring you harm. I worry about you constantly. I was so in love with you when first we met, and you with me. I was just a girl but knew my own heart. How did such a heart become broken? How did our love become separated? Why wasn't I enough for you? Questions I still ask myself in my loneliest hours. But I know the answers. I know that you were born needing to do the right thing, that you were born with a sense of honor that few men have. That for you to see injustices done was simply intolerable. And your duty and your honor proved a greater power over you than did my love, though I've no doubt that you loved me. Denver is a city full of passion and life, though my own life has not been easy, my sins many—these, the price I've learned to pay for this freedom. Would that you leave your beloved Texas and join me, I would give up this life and become your wife again. But I know how utterly unhappy you would be here, just as unhappy as I'd become there on the frontier. These are matters of the heart and my heart wanted to tell your heart that I shall always love you, even though I could not love you enough, or you could not love me enough, for us to be together forever. Think of me, and never let me out of your heart for very long.

Your Ella

Cole placed the tintype back in the packet with the letter and slipped them into his pocket along with the badge. They didn't deserve to be lost and scattered in some lonely cañon, as lost as bones and dust.

"Dammit, Teddy Green, why didn't you love her enough?" were the only words to express Cole's grief at the loss of a good man, and maybe a good woman, too.

Harve saw Cole return without Teddy Green in tow.

"He still up the cañon?"

Cole nodded.

Harve shook his head. "Son-of-a-bitch. You get the others?"

"All but one."

He took a deep breath and let it out. "We lost a good one," he said.

"I know."

"What now?"

"Let's saddle a horse to that hack and take Teddy to Gonzales for a proper burial."

"What about Ella?"

"I think I know where she is," Cole said.

"Huh?"

"Call it a feeling."

Together the three righted the hack, cut loose the dead horse, and hitched the hack to Teddy Green's mount, then took it up the canon, and loaded his body into it.

The fat Mexican sheriff, Carlos Delgado, was just coming out of a café when he spotted the three of them.

"Hey, you went off to find *Señor* Feathers," he said, "and what you found was a Negro and a buggy. That's pretty good."

"Shut up," Cole said.

The sheriff blinked.

"Stay clear of me, you understand?"

The sheriff glanced at Teddy Green's corpse in the hack. "You kill heem?"

They continued down the street until they found a store front advertising an undertaker.

"We'll make the arrangements," Cole said, "then this is where we part company, Harve."

He looked stricken. "Why, John Henry? We ain't found Ella yet."

"Because that's the way I want it, partner."

Harve reached in his pocket and took out his wallet, removed several bills, and handed them to Cole.

"You'll need it ... traveling expenses."

"Thanks."

"I'll see to it that Teddy Green gets a proper and fine funeral. You go on and do what needs doing. Just one thing."

"What's that?"

"I'd appreciate a wire sent to me in Denver to let me know how it turned out."

They shook hands. Then Cole shook Isom Dart's hand. Dart thought he would go back and bury Tom Feathers. He felt he owed him that much.

Harve told Dart that either he would have to take him along or take a little money to help with the expenses. If it was no offense, Dart said, he'd prefer the money. Harve said he wasn't offended.

Cole turned his horse back toward San Antonio, prodded by nothing more than a feeling that was aching in his bones like a fever.

CHAPTER THIRTY-ONE

"Vaudeville Variety Theater and Gambling Saloon is where you'll usually find him, if he ain't here," the bartender at the Golden Spur said. "Doc ain't here, he's usually there … loves the comics."

Cole figured that if anybody knew the underside of San Antonio, it would be Doc Holliday and so Cole needed to search him out.

He crossed the street, cut across Market Square, and angled his way opposite the Alamo Plaza, where some sort of festival was taking place. Dancers wearing red-trimmed skirts and peasant blouses clicked their heels to a mariachi band; the men were dressed in black with silver conchos adorning the legs of their trousers, and big sombreros. The music was lively and quickened the blood and the evening sky was streaked with crimson clouds.

Cole found the Vaudeville and asked the man at the ticket window if Doc Holliday was in attendance. He was a short, balding man with heavy jowls shaved to a clean pink.

"Have not seen him yet," the man said. "However, I do expect him. The Rose of Cimarron is playing tonight … she's a wonderful singer, you know."

"What time do you expect him?"

The man pulled a watch from his pocket, snapped open the lid.

"He's usually here around eight ... unless, of course, him and Kate are getting into it."

Big Nose Kate was Doc's common-law wife. Cole asked the man where they resided and he said over a butcher shop on South San Saban Street.

"Which way is that?"

Cole followed the directions. The street was, like almost every street in San Antonio, cluttered with ox-drawn wagons. The buildings were mostly of stone or stucco, pockmarked by the weather. Cole found the address and climbed the outside stairs and knocked on the door.

He waited a few moments and knocked again, then the door opened and Kate stood there in a chintz robe clutched with one hand. Her hair was uncombed and it looked like she'd been crying.

"Oh," she said. "I was expecting someone else."

"Doc here?"

"He's not here," she said, her voice hoarse, the way a voice ravaged by liquor and cigars will get. "Fact is, I thought you were him."

"Doc usually knock on his own door?" Cole asked.

"Who are you?"

"Guess you don't remember me, Kate. I'm John Henry Cole. We met in Deadwood some time back."

She was a large woman, large and sad—her love for Doc having cost her a lot. "I think I do remember ... vaguely," she said. "Doc's got so many friends, so many acquaintances ... seems to me you were looking for him back in Deadwood, too."

"It's a different reason this time. Do you know where he is? It's important that I talk to him."

"Try the Golden Spur," she said.

"Already have."

She shrugged; her face was bloated. "Then he might be at the Vaudeville Theater."

"Tried there, too."

"Well god damn him," she said, and began to close the door but not before Cole could wedge his boot in.

"I'll call the police if you try and molest me," she warned.

"I'm not trying to molest you. I'm trying to find out where Doc is and I'm not leaving until you tell me."

"Well, he's not here."

Cole gave her a hard stare to let her know he wasn't budging.

A sob caught in her throat. "Try Fanny Porter's sporting house down the street. He has a particular little red-haired whore he enjoys there … apparently I'm not enough for him. Now leave me the hell alone!"

Cole removed his foot and she slammed the door hard. He heard the lock click from the inside. Then he heard sobs that quickly became wails.

The light of evening had gone from crimson to black silver. An almost golden dust seemed to have descended on the city, and lights in windows were winking on. Cole descended the steps and went up the street, looking for Fanny Porter's sporting house.

It might have been any one of a number of bagnios, for he came to a block where a red light glowed in almost every window. He picked one at random and knocked and a young Oriental woman with black hair nearly to her hips answered. She was pretty and small and wore a tight-fitting green dress.

"Yes, come in," she said.

"Is this Fanny Porter's?"

"Why you want to go there? You come in, we got everything you need right here. We got white girls and Negro girls and China girls. You don't need to go no place else. Come in, come in."

"I'm not looking for a girl," Cole said. "I'm looking for a man."

He realized what that sounded like the minute he'd said it. The Celestial clasped her hand to her mouth and giggled.

"Oh, we don't got no men for you. Why a nice handsome fellah like you want a man for when you can have cute girl like me?"

"No, you don't understand," Cole said. "Just tell me which way to Fanny Porter's."

"She got no men for you. No, no. She don't have no men like that. Come in, you see, girl be OK for you now."

Cole turned and left, her laughter still burning his ears. He knocked on the next door and this time a large black man who looked like he could bend a crowbar without breaking a sweat answered and stared at him. "You got forty dollars?" he said. "That's the price of admission you want to come inside, sample the ladies. You ain't got forty dollars, keep on moving … this ain't no crib joint like most the places up and down this here street."

"I'm looking for Fanny Porter's," Cole said.

"This is Fanny Porter's. You got forty dollars, or ain't you?"

"No, I don't."

He started to close the door.

"But I got this."

He stopped when he saw the Colt Peacemaker aimed at his nose.

"I'm looking for Doc Holliday. He around?"

He looked at the iron for another second and said: "Please, step in, suh. I'll go fetch Doc."

The scent of lilacs and cigar smoke is a smell that reeks of loneliness and desperation and the room was filled with it. So, too, does the clink of whiskey glasses and loud laughter, red drapes and wilted flowers dropping from cheap vases. Cole looked around, remembered a time when a place like this was exciting, remembered his first time in a whorehouse in Abilene not nearly this fancy. Barely seventeen he was and with some others just off their first cattle drive. They'd been thinking about it all the way from the Brazos and found it exciting. But what it turned out to be was just a spare room over a saloon—an iron bed and a hollow-eyed woman who wanted $3. Yet for a jug-eared, whiskey-soaked kid it was exciting. Now it simply seemed to Cole to be a sad place for a man to have to find refuge in, to have to find some sense of himself.

A woman with platinum hair and a mole on her left cheek descended the steps leading from the upper floor. She was barely dressed in a lavender kimono that parted at the top enough to show the mounds of her breasts. She looked to be all of maybe twenty years old unless you looked into her eyes—the eyes were a lot older.

"Howdy, slick," she said. "You come for any particular gal, or will I do?"

"I'm waiting on a friend," Cole said.

"Well, while you're waiting won't you buy a lady a drink, only cost you a dollar, honey."

"Dollar for cheap watered-down whiskey? I hope you got a lot of charm."

She smiled. "I got enough," she said. "But I can see I can't fool no hardcase such as yourself, sugar. Where you hail from, somewhere in the South? I'm from Alabama."

"This what you did in Alabama?"

She snorted, said: "Hell, no. I was a preacher's wife in Alabama."

"That must have been some church."

She laughed, then suddenly looked sad. "If I could go back with my head up, I would, but I'm afraid it's too late for salvation."

"Well, salvation comes in many forms, but I'm not one. Thanks for the offer, sis."

She snorted again. "How'll you know what you're missing, if you don't give it a try?"

"I got a feeling I know what I'm missing. Thanks, anyway."

"John Henry Cole."

Cole turned to the rasp of Doc Holliday's voice. He stood in a doorway in just a nightshirt and trousers, the galluses down, stocking feet, a glass of whiskey in his hand, his arm around an ample woman with hair as red as autumn leaves. Surprisingly, except for the hair, she looked very much like Big Nose Kate.

"I need to talk to you."

"I'm in the middle of something. Joseph says you pulled a pistol on him, threatened to blow out his brains, he didn't come retrieve me."

"Joseph exaggerated. I only meant to shoot him in the knees, if he didn't tell me where you were."

Doc smiled. "Can it wait ten minutes?"

"If it could, I wouldn't be standing here."

"OK, OK," he said with a wave of his glass. "At least let this poor pilgrim get dressed. I see you met Phoebe." He indicated the woman with the platinum hair.

"This poor sucker a friend of yours, Doc? Well, if I'd known, I'd have thrown him a free one."

Doc shook his head. "You'll have to excuse Phoebe," he said. "She's a mite loose-mouthed. She's lost all her gentility somewhere along the way."

"Hell, that and a whole lot more, Doc!" The woman's voice was full of regret.

"Be gone with you, sister, this man and I have personal business to discuss." Holliday's gaze had suddenly turned serious.

Cole waited until Doc went back inside the room with his lady, then emerged, fully dressed. He reeked of whiskey and cheap perfume.

"Let's go into the parlor, where we might have some privacy," he suggested. "And where I might have a drink to settle my hash. Young Jasmine in there is enough to make a man nervous with anticipation of her comely charms. *Coitus interruptus* will fray a man's nerves every time."

Cole waited while he poured himself a drink, declining an offer to join him.

"What is it you'd have of me, sir?" he said at last.

Cole took out the tintype and showed it to him. "You ever see this woman, Doc?"

He looked at it, brought it closer to the lamp, where the flame glowed white.

"Well ... she has a certain resemblance to someone I've seen about recently," he said.

"Tell me where."

"First let me ask you why you thought I'd know her?"

"Call it a hunch, Doc."

"Because you think I'm a man who knows everyone and everything that has to do with the dark side of humanity."

"I'm interested only in finding this woman."

He looked again. "She's a new girl ... just showed up here in the district a day or two ago, recent acquisition of Madame Lu over on Water Street, near the river. Lu's a high-class Chinawoman, sells everything but herself, charges high rates. She also runs a dope den."

Something hammered at Cole's heart. "Take a good look, Doc. Are you sure it's the same person?"

He looked again, nodded his head. "I'm fairly sure, but not a hundred percent. The lady in question was a bit more drawn, older, hair a bit lighter … but, she bears a strong resemblance."

"How do I find this place?"

Cole felt as if his blood was on fire as he walked from Fanny Porter's down toward the river. A heavy fog had begun to settle over the city and the only distinct sounds were the ringing of his spurs as the fog closed in the nearer he got to the river.

Somewhere in the shadowy mist a sudden burst of laughter shattered the stillness, then stopped as quickly as it had begun. He was remembering the answer Teddy Green had given him the time he had gone into the tenderloin of Ogallala looking for Ella: *I thought maybe, I might find her there.* Teddy Green knew something about Ella that Cole hadn't until he'd read the letter taken from Green's pocket—her reference to her life in Denver, the sins she'd alluded to, the loneliness. It was what gave Cole the hunch to come looking for her here now. That, and the feeling he'd gotten the last time he'd walked these streets. Sometimes all a man has to go on is the feeling in his gut. If Doc Holliday wasn't mistaken, then Cole's hunch had proved right. He hurried his step.

The lights on the bridge were shrouded in fog. A set of stone steps led from the bridge to the street below—which had to be Water Street, according to Doc Holliday's directions. Cole reached the bottom, heard the lap of water along the banks, the splash of a fish. To his right he could barely make out the shapes of buildings, most without light, others farther down too enshrouded to see. Holliday had said to look for a door that had Chinese lanterns and a red dragon painted on it. That's what Cole was looking for when suddenly several shapes emerged from the fog.

"Where you bound to, mister?" one of them asked.

Cole's warning instincts went up immediately. He was reaching for the Peacemaker when something struck him from behind, something hard that sent him reeling until a fist smashed into his ribs and another into his jaw almost simultaneously. He went down, spitting blood under a rain of blows and curses, hands grabbing at his pockets while others smashed into him. The Peacemaker, knocked from his hand, Cole reached for the Starr single-action—the one he'd taken off Batwings in the cañon fight—jerked it from where he'd positioned it at the base of his spine and shot one of the feet nearest his face. The owner screamed when he blew off his toe. He fired blindly and heard another yelp that he'd been shot, then the running of footsteps fading into the night. Cole thought at first it was the fog closing in on him, then, too late, realized it wasn't.

CHAPTER THIRTY-TWO

John Henry Cole awoke to a dull ache, his head buzzing. When he went to move, everything hurt. He rolled over and sat up, found himself sitting on a hard bunk in a jail cell, the smell of human waste nearby. In the cell next to him slept a man with a long, tangled beard, his mouth open in a steady snore. The smell was coming from a bucket under his cot.

Cole's left eye was nearly closed. He could feel the lump when he went to rub it with the heel of his hand. His ribs ached every time he took a breath. He couldn't tell if it was daylight or still dark—there were no windows, just a row of cells, lanterns hung on hooks from the stamped tin ceiling.

His weapons were gone and so were the contents of his pockets. He'd been robbed and his mood was black. He thought of the letter and the tintype and how he'd hoped to return them to Ella. Now they were gone.

An iron door leading back to the cells cranked open and a fellow with a black vest, white shirt with garters on his sleeves, and trousers tucked inside his mule-deer boots came strolling down the aisle. He looked in at the man in the cell next to Cole and said: "Jesus, Bart, you stink worse'n a cow's butt!"

Then the man stopped in front of Cole's cell, took a key, turned it in the lock, and jerked open the door. "Come'n out."

Cole followed him into an office where three others stood or sat around—all wearing badges, two drinking coffee, one cleaning his boots.

"Have a chair, *amigo*," the man with the gartered sleeves said as he sat down behind a desk across from Cole. Cole saw the contents of his pockets spread on the desk—saw Teddy Green's Ranger badge, the packet with the letter and tintype—and he was relieved they hadn't been stolen. "You're mighty careless for a Ranger," the man said. "Letting a bunch of trash jump you down on Water Street. Lucky them boys didn't cave in your skull and throw you in the Guadalupe. Pull two or three bodies a week out a that river."

"I shot one in the foot," Cole said. "Maybe shot another one, too. If you find a man with his toe shot off, you'll find one of them."

The lawman looked at the other deputies, then back at Cole.

"How come I don't know you?" he said. "I know practically every Ranger around these parts, but I ain't never seen you before."

"I'm out of Houston, looking for someone," Cole said. A lie was good only if it worked to your advantage.

"Houston, huh? I suppose you know Bob Sugar, captain with the Rangers over there."

Cole nodded. "Good man," he said.

"You've got that right," the man said, and extended his hand for Cole to shake.

"Cal Morris," he said, "chief of police. Some of my deputies were cruising the river area, heard the gunshots, and found you cold-cocked. Most get cold-cocked down on Water Street ain't so fortunate, are they R.J.?" He looked at the deputy cleaning his boots, who nodded.

"I've always been more lucky than smart," Cole said.

"You don't look so danged lucky. Who was it you say you were looking for?"

Cole nodded toward the tintype. "That woman."

"She commit a crime in Houston?"

"She's wanted for the investigation of a murder there."

He picked up the tintype, studied it for a moment, then laid it back down. "Jesus, pretty woman like that," he said.

"Yeah, I know."

"So you figure you'd find her down on Water Street?"

"I heard she might be in the area somewhere."

"You carrying a warrant for her arrest? 'Cause I didn't see no warrant papers among your personal effects."

"I'm not out to arrest her," Cole said. "I just want to ask her some questions. Not likely she did the killing, but she may have a handle on who was involved."

"See, the way it works, any arrests to be made in San Antone, me or one of my men make 'em. You Rangers want 'em, you come here first, ask for my assistance … sorta what I consider professional courtesy."

"You're right," Cole said. "Next time I will. But like I said, I'm not wanting to arrest her, just to ask her some questions. That OK with you, if I do that?"

He seemed to relax a little. "You want us to help you find her?"

"Not yet. Let me see if I can run her down. If not, I'd be grateful for the assistance. I'm sure you boys got lots better things to do than find a woman."

One of them snorted.

"I can't think of a thing better'n finding a woman, can you, Cal?" the one cleaning his boots said.

Morris grinned, took a cigar from his waistcoat pocket, one that had already been lit and snuffed out once, and screwed it into his mouth. "Maybe the first thing you ought to do is find yourself a sawbones, have him look at that face."

"That bad, huh?"

"You'd scare babies and old folks. Looks like maybe those thieves broke your nose, too."

"Thanks," Cole said. "You mind I gather up my things and get in the wind?"

"No, go right ahead."

"I had some weapons on me when I got jumped last night," Cole said. "A Colt, a Deane Adams, a Smith and Wesson, and a Winchester."

Morris opened a drawer, took out the Dean Adams, Smith & Wesson, and Winchester, and laid them on the desk next to the tintype, badge, and packet that held the letter.

"Didn't find a Colt. Those boys probably grabbed it up and run off with it. Probably will use it to kill or rob someone with."

"Loss of a pistol, a broken nose, cut eye … I'll settle for that," Cole said, and took up his belongings.

"Water Street's a bad place to go alone day or night," Morris said. "But I guess you already figured that out."

"Thanks, Chief, maybe sometime, you ever get to Houston, I'll be able to return the favor."

He sniffed, said: "Hell, don't hold your breath waiting for me to show my face in Houston again. Last time I was there, I caught the clap. If you ever caught the clap, you know what I'm talking about."

"*Adiós.*"

"Take care, pardner," he said.

It was good to breathe fresh air again, and in the light of day, even seeing it with only one eye, the world looked new and full of hope. Cole headed back to Water Street.

He was perhaps two blocks from the jail when he heard someone call his name. He looked around and there, standing across the street at the edge of the plaza, was Roy Bean, Cleopatra's former boss, pimp, and sweetheart. He'd asked Cole once whether or not he thought there was opportunity in Texas. Cole had told him he thought there was for an enterprising man.

"John Henry Cole," he said. "I'd recognize that lanky frame of yours anywhere." He was a short, pudgy man with dark eyes and just recently it looked as if he had begun growing a beard. He dodged two or three mule trains crossing the street. "Holy mother of pearl! What happened to you?" he asked.

"Fell off my horse."

"Ought to learn to ride better."

"You look like you've fared well for yourself, Roy. Fancy coat and pants like that have to cost a man fifteen, twenty dollars."

Bean flushed with pride. "You were right about Texas. More opportunity here than lice on a dog." He was carrying a book, a big book. "Taken up study of the law," he said, shifting the book from under his arm to his hands. "Figured I've been on one side of the law long enough, I ought to try the other … more money in it than running whores and selling liquor to jaspers. Bought me a patch of land down along the Pecos … lawless country, the kind that needs a man of my adjudication, a word I learned in this here book."

"Glad to hear things are working out for you, Roy, but I've no time to talk about it right now."

"You living in San Antone?"

"No, just here to find someone."

"What about Cleo?" he said. "She still with that gamy-legged fellow she run off with?"

"He's dead. She's fixing to go East."

He shook his head, spat the chaw he'd been grinding in his cheek, and said: "Fuss. I wisht she could see me now. She might not want to run off to the East, if she knew I was a prosperous and righteous man."

"I'm sure. See you around, Roy."

"You need anything, I'm staying at the Alamo Hotel until tomorrow, then down to the Pecos!" he shouted as Cole headed toward the river.

When Cole reached the spot where he'd been waylaid, he glanced at the ground, saw some dried blood on the rocks near the walking path and knew it was his. He felt like he'd been leaving pieces of himself all along the trail since leaving Cheyenne, but he was close to Ella now—he could feel it—and that was all that mattered.

Eventually he found the place Doc Holliday had described the night before—Madame Lu's. He saw a door with a red dragon painted on it. He knocked, waited, knocked again. A small Oriental woman who looked as ancient as time itself opened the door and looked up at him.

"We close, you come back tonight, OK?"

"I'm looking for this woman," Cole said, showing her the tintype.

She barely glanced at it and said: "She no here."

"Look again," Cole insisted. She started to close the door, but he held it open.

She looked at him with alarm. "You go now, I find the policeman you don't go."

"I'm looking for this woman, her name is Ella, and I know she's here. I'm not leaving until I see her."

She weighed all of seventy pounds. "Lu, Lu!" Her voice was more like the screech of a barn owl than human.

Another Oriental woman appeared, younger, good-looking. "What is it, Nana?"

"Him," the old woman said. "He cause trouble."

"What do you want?"

Cole showed her the tintype. "Her," he said.

She looked at Cole, this beautiful Asian woman whose skin was as smooth as ivory and eyes like black silk. She said first to the old woman: "It's OK, Nana. You go drink your tea. I take care of the gentleman."

Then, when the old woman left, the younger one invited Cole in and led him to a front parlor. "Please, you no cause trouble."

"You go bring Ella to me and there will be no trouble."

"This is very difficult, what you ask me to do."

"Tell me where she is then, and I'll go get her."

"You no understand."

"I've come a long way to find her. You can go get her or I will."

"She not well."

"More reason I should find her."

"Please," she said, touching Cole's wrist as he began to move past her to go and search the house. "Let me explain something, OK?"

"You've got one minute."

"This lady, she not free to go."

"Time's up. I'll find her myself."

Cole started to move past her again.

"You try and take her, he will kill you," she said.

"You mean Gypsy Davy?"

"Yes."

"He might not care for the results if he tries. Where is she?"

The woman wore a dress of green silk that whispered with her every movement. "He will kill me, if you take her."

"Not my problem, lady. You should have thought of that before you got involved."

"He gave me no choice. He said he would kill me and kill my nana if I didn't take her in. He said he would cut our throats."

"What do you expect, you associate with cut-throats to begin with? Maybe you should find a new line of work."

"I can't …."

"I'll find her myself. Tell me this. Is he with her now?"

She shook her head. "No, he hasn't been here for two days."

"Where is she?"

"You take her and go!" she said abruptly. "I show you her, you take her and get her out of here, as far away as you can."

Cole followed her to the back of the house, past several doorways, some partly open. Inside one of the rooms Cole saw a woman lying on her side on a pallet on the floor, her eyes half open, her lips wordlessly moving. The pungent odor of opium was thick in the air. When they reached the back of the house, they went out a rear door to a small building where the woman took a key from her pocket and turned it in the lock.

"You kept her locked up?"

"He tell me to. He say … 'You make sure she don't run away. You make sure nobody get to her.'"

Cole pushed the woman aside and stepped into the dim interior. He could again smell the pungent stench of opium. Several thin blades of light pierced the cracks between the wallboards. In a matter of seconds his eyesight adjusted enough that he could see the figure huddled in the corner of the room. His heart hammered hard.

"Ella." He whispered her name as he crossed the room and kneeled before her. In the stripes of light, he could see glimpses of her eyes. She had the frightened look of a startled animal, one that had been trapped.

"Ella, it's me, John Henry."

A sob broke from her throat, an utterance of fear as he reached out and touched her arm. She shivered from the touch.

"She sick," the Oriental woman in the doorway said. "I told you ... very, very sick."

Cole started to come closer, to draw her into him, but she recoiled, murmuring words that were unintelligible, small sounds like those of a child that had been whipped. Cole's hand struck something on the mattress beside her—a glass pipe that shattered—spilling its contents of water.

"You've got her doped," Cole said over his shoulder to the woman. "No wonder she's sick. How long has she been like this?"

"Three days, maybe. Not me, him. He tell me do it, so I do. He tell me make her smoke opium, so I do. He tell me I no do what he want, he kill us all."

"Jesus," Cole muttered, not believing what he was hearing or seeing. "Go get me a blanket," he said to the woman. When she didn't move for a moment, he got angry. "Go get me a blanket or what he threatened to do to you will be nothing compared to what I'll do!"

She hurried away.

"Ella, it's John Henry Cole. You remember me. I know you do." He touched her hands, took them in his as gently as he knew how, and held them. She tried to resist, but then let herself go limp almost as quickly. She had no real resistance left in her. Cole continued to say her name, telling her his, hoping that somehow it would break through her fear and confusion. She sobbed and shook and his heart ached at the sight.

The woman returned with the blanket, tossed it to Cole, and said: "Here, you hurry, take her, and get out! He come, I tell him you here, tell him you come trying to steal her, I try and stop you. I don't care he kill you!"

Cole took the blanket and wrapped it around Ella and picked her up. She was frail, a quaking of bones, and he carried her out of the building and into the light. The anger in him welled up at the full sight of her. She was pale, nearly bloodless except for the darkness around her eyes. Her hair was tangled and dirty; the cotton shift she wore was stained. She was unwashed, and she covered her eyes quickly against the light, crying softly.

"You better hurry!" the Oriental woman chirped. "He come back soon, find you with her, he kill you, kill all of us!"

Cole walked the six or so blocks from Water Street to the Alamo Hotel with Ella in his arms, ignoring the looks of passers-by, ignoring everything but his own anger and need to protect Ella from any further depredations.

The man behind the desk of the Alamo came around and said: "Hey, you can't bring her in here! Why, looks like she's in need of a doctor, and this ain't no hospital!"

"Which room is Roy Bean's?"

"Pardon me, sir, but you'll have to leave."

"Mister, I set this woman down, I'm drawing my pistol and killing whatever son-of-a-bitch happens to be in my sights. Now you tell me where Roy Bean's room is! Better still, you take me to him."

Roy Bean answered the desk clerk's first knock, saw Cole holding Ella, and stepped aside.

"Sorry for the intrusion, Mister Bean," the desk clerk said. "But this feller insisted. Should I call the police?"

Roy Bean handed the man a pair of silver dollars and said: "No, these are friends of mine. Why don't you go down to the bar and bring us a nice bottle of whiskey. Charge it to my account. Bring up some hot water and some clean towels while you're at it."

The clerk took his leave as Cole was laying Ella on the bed.

"Friend of yours?" Bean asked. "She looks in bad shape."

"She's in trouble. She'll need a doctor."

"I'll go tell the boy to get one of those, too."

Roy Bean left the room and Cole was alone with Ella at last, no one and nothing standing between them any longer.

She lay curled up in a ball under the blanket, still shaking, still whimpering. Cole stroked her hair and spoke to her, told her how sorry he was that this had happened. He wasn't sure if the words meant anything to her or not. It didn't matter—they were words he needed to say to her, words he'd been needing to say for a long time. "Ella, I never should have left you when I did. I was a fool."

Maybe it was the words, or maybe the simple fact he'd not abused her but sat there and stroked her hair, for she calmed and lay silently beneath his hand. Cole had to fight back tears, seeing her like that. In that moment of peace, of her stillness, he couldn't even vow vengeance on the man who'd done this to her. All he could do was avow: "Ella, I love you. Don't leave me."

She opened her eyes once, looked at him, then closed them again.

CHAPTER THIRTY-THREE

"How long you figure she'll be like that?" Roy Bean asked.

They were sitting on the gallery of his place—a wooden courthouse, store front, and whiskey den he'd paid Mexicans to build. It was in an empty, aimless land, except for the nearby Pecos River. A land of mesquite and Gila monsters and enough bad *hombres* to keep Roy Bean in business as a self-appointed judge with a handful of hired Mexican *vaqueros* to act as officers of his court. There were a few other buildings nearby that comprised a village of sorts. Upon his arrival Bean had pronounced the place Langtry after the well-known actress, Lily Langtry—a woman he adored but one he'd never met. He kept a photograph of her above his bed and another above the bar.

Ella preferred to keep to herself in a spare room the judge had fixed up for her. Cole had accepted Bean's invitation to bring her to this place of refuge. Cole was torn between wanting to protect and care for Ella, and wanting to go find Gypsy Davy and kill him. But Roy Bean had exercised his judgment by stating that if Cole went after Gypsy Davy, he'd be leaving Ella alone with no one to protect her. "That *hombre* has outfoxed you before, John Henry," Bean had observed back in San Antone. "There's nothing to say he couldn't do it again. It's best you and Ella come with me down to the Pecos country. Let the hand of fate take care of Gypsy Davy … sooner or later he'll come to a bad end." It had been a solid enough argument.

Now here they were, nearly a month later. Roy Bean had paid a Mexican woman to feed and care for Ella's every need, and in that respect Ella was thriving. But she continued to remain silent, refusing to talk about what had happened to her and Cole hadn't pushed it.

"I wish I knew," Cole said, in answer to the judge's question about Ella's mental condition.

Bean was ciphering figures in a ledger book held on his lap. "Fines," he said, wetting the stub of his pencil before each entry. "Figure three dollars if convicted of petty theft. Five for wrongful shooting or stabbing. Ten for illegal whiskey peddling … anything that don't come through me … twenty for stealing a horse, and twenty-five for contempt of court. That should do her to begin with. I can change it around later if I need to. Now all I need is for some *hombres* to break the law."

Maybe it was the sameness of the day-in, day-out existence they'd come to live, but Cole was feeling restless, worried that Ella might not ever be the same woman she had been, worried that he might not ever find out the truth of what happened to her. He needed to understand. "I think I'll go in and check on her, Roy."

Bean scratched around in his beard, which by now was flourishing into a nest of gray wires. The big straw sombrero pulled down low over his eyes and the silver pistol in his belt made him look like a real hardcase. "Image is everything," he'd said the first time Cole had seen him in his frontier clothes.

Ella was sitting by the window, her face to the light, when Cole entered the room. She didn't turn to look at him—she never did.

Cole took a chair and pulled it close. "How're you feeling?"

"I'm OK."

"Would you like to go for a walk? We could walk down by the river."

She sat silently, her hands folded in her lap, as though she were posing for a portrait. Perhaps it was the way the light caught in her hair or the way it touched her cheek or the soft curve of her neck, but Cole had never seen her look more beautiful.

"We could just walk," he said. "You wouldn't have to talk. Neither of us would. It might be good to get out of the room for a bit."

Still she didn't move or say anything. Cole stood to leave, his hand reaching for the doorknob when she said: "OK."

Roy Bean was telling his Mexican deputies how it was important that they not hang a suspect until *after* he'd tried them. His Spanish was poor and their English non-existent and he was gesturing a lot with his hands. He stopped when he saw Cole and Ella emerge. Cole thought Bean was nearly as happy as Cole was to see her finally leave the building.

"We're just going to take a little walk down by the river," Cole said. Later he said: "Do you want to take my hand, Ella?"

She didn't reach out, so he took hers, and she didn't resist.

They walked in silence. When a jack rabbit hopped from one mesquite bush to another, she stopped and stared at it for the longest time. Then she allowed Cole to guide her the rest of the way to the river.

They found a stand of cottonwoods where leaves fluttered in the warm wind, and sat on a flat rock at the river's edge. A yellow bird trilled from a perch among the reeds.

"I like it here," Cole said. "Quiet and peaceful. I come here when you're sleeping and think to myself this would be a good place to build a little house, raise a few kids maybe. Roy Bean may have discovered something here."

Her gaze followed the water's current. On the far bank, a large branch lay half submerged, tickling ripples, while the dry end made a resting spot for a dozen small turtles. Cole saw plenty mule deer tracks near the water's edge and the sun dazzled off the river's surface like diamonds. A fish flopped downstream, and Ella started and said: "Oh."

"It's OK," Cole said, touching the back of her hand.

She looked at him and said: "John Henry."

"Yes."

Her eyes searched Cole's. "I ... I ...."

"No need to talk just now, Ella. Just enjoy the peace. Listen to the river, hear how sweet."

Her fingers closed around his.

"It will be OK, Ella. Everything will be OK. There's nothing to worry about."

As the shadows were growing long, they returned to Roy Bean's. It never ceased to amaze Cole, the number of signs the judge had painted and nailed up, advertising his business, one declaring him Law West of the Pecos—a man whose courtroom was an upturned whiskey barrel and a folding table, and if it rained hard, he held court inside instead of out. Bean sat there, peacefully snoozing, dreaming, no doubt, about Lily Langtry, a man content in the world he'd created for himself. Cole realized then that Bean was a lot smarter than most.

"Would you care to take supper with me outside this evening?" he asked Ella. "The judge would be most appreciative of the company, and it looks like it's going to be a beautiful sunset." She seemed uncertain for a moment, then nodded, and Cole felt that possibly, at last, she was starting to come back from whatever dark world she'd plunged into.

They sat around the long table the judge had his deputies station in the yard while Mexican women served them tortillas, *frijoles*, pan-fried *nopales*, steaks from a young steer the judge had ordered butchered just for the occasion, and champagne from his personal stock.

Bean ate with his hat on but with his cuffs rolled up and a napkin tucked in the throat of his shirt. He ate with relish and drank the same way and toasted God and Texas several times over.

"Why Texas is better'n ten Wyomings thrown together," Roy Bean said. "I don't know why I didn't leave that country long before now. This is what I call fat living."

Ella ate in small bites, her mood silent, as Roy Bean regaled the table guests with tales of Lily Langtry and how he planned on meeting the actress someday to express personally his affections for her beauty and talent.

"Most beautiful woman ... present company excluded, Miss Ella ... in the whole of the universe."

Ella smiled at this and the judge clapped his hands.

"Well, you look lovely tonight, Miss Ella. As lovely as the moon and stars all rolled into one. Let's have us some music! Hector, grab up your fiddle and you and Rodrigo get to playing some."

The one took up his fiddle and the other a guitar and began to play a Mexican ballad. Ella seemed taken with the music and inclined her head on Cole's shoulder while Cole held her hand. The judge lit a cigar and smoked it as nightfall descended. In the distance, the song of the river joined the music and for the first time in a long while he felt happy and had a sense of peace.

Eventually Cole walked Ella to her room and kissed her forehead and started to leave, but this time she clung to him and said: "Not yet."

He held her close to the strains of the music, coming from the yard. Several of the deputies had begun to sing in Spanish. They stood like that, holding each other in the darkness. Cole could feel the ticking of her heart through his shirt as the warmth of her body pressed against him.

"Don't leave me tonight," she whispered.

"Are you sure?"

She drew him to the bed, and he lay down with her. She folded herself into his arms and it was enough.

* * * * *

Another week passed. Ella and Cole took daily walks down to the river. Roy Bean always made sure that at least two or three of the Mexican deputies kept them within sight, for he was uncommonly sure that sooner or later Gypsy Davy would make an attempt to get Ella back. Cole was of the same mind but had asked the judge to order his men to maintain a discreet distance.

"We give her the impression we're worried about Gypsy Davy coming for her," Cole had said, "it's likely to push her over the edge."

"Be my pleasure to try him, find him guilty, and hang him for you, John Henry. First I'd fine him twenty dollars, then hang him." Cole had asked the judge to be cautious in his comments concerning the madman while in the presence of Ella.

Then one afternoon, as they sat on the rock at the river's edge, she said: "I want to talk about it … about him."

It was a moment that Cole had anticipated, but now that it had arrived, he wasn't certain he wanted to hear about it. "Sure?" he asked.

She nodded, stared for a time at the water, then said: "David is my half-brother and he thinks that he is in love with me."

Cole understood now about the same last name.

"Before I came to Cheyenne," she said, "where I met you, I'd lived in Denver. I was still married to a man but had been separated from him for some time." Images of Teddy Green floated into Cole's mind. He wondered if he should tell her now or wait.

"I thought I could find a sense of myself," she continued. "I was foolish, of course. What I was looking for didn't exist, something I've since come to realize. My troubles have been long-standing, David and his unnatural desire for me being the source of many of my troubles. I suppose that when it didn't work out between my husband and me, it only confirmed my suspicions that I was unworthy of a decent man. Then in Denver, I fell to a new low."

She took a deep breath. This confession was difficult for her.

"I became a prostitute," she said. "I had beauty and charm but little else to sustain me. I met a rich man who introduced me to other rich men ..."

"You don't have to tell me this, Ella. I don't care what has happened in the past."

"Yes," she said, "I do need to talk about it."

He took her hand.

"It wasn't as bad as you might think. I lived well, was never abused, and was highly thought of by many of these men. My secret was well kept and I got invited to many parties. This life also did something else for me ... it helped me forget what had happened, to forget my half-brother. The last I knew he was in the East, attending medical school, and I figured that whatever his childhood fantasies had been about me, he'd probably outgrown them. Anyway, it was a safe world for me, in a sense, and I wasn't terribly unhappy with it except for one thing ... having left my husband."

"I know."

She looked searchingly at Cole.

"He came to Cheyenne, looking for you regarding some murder in

Denver, your involvement in it. He asked me to help him find you. If it wasn't for Teddy Green, Ella, I wouldn't be here. I wouldn't have known." Before she could say anything further, Cole took the packet with the letter and the tintype he was still carrying and handed it to her. "I took this from him the day he was killed."

She gasped at the touch of them, held them in her hands as gently as fragile birds. "He's dead?"

"I'm sorry I have to be the one to tell you."

Moments passed with only the sounds of the river and the occasional splash of a turtle sliding off a limb into the water.

"Should we talk about this another time?"

She shook her head. "I won't grieve for him just yet," she said. "I'll grieve in private, not in front of you, John Henry. I loved him, and I love you. It wouldn't be fair to you or respectful of Teddy to grieve openly."

"I understand."

"The man I first met in Denver who introduced me around to the others was the son of a federal judge. He also introduced me to the opium dens. In a way, it was an escape from what I'd become … a high-priced whore, but a whore nonetheless."

"What happened?"

"Life soon turned into a haze for me. And then, Davy showed up in Denver, insisting that he wanted to marry me, insisting that I go away with him. I refused, of course. He wormed his way into the circle I'd been involved with, his charm and wit and cleverness too much for them to resist, just as I had been too much for them to resist. He threatened to expose me, our past, if I made an effort to openly spurn him. But Tyron became jealous of Davy's attentions toward me and, of course, I couldn't tell him the truth, nor could I convince my half-brother to leave me alone. It came to a terrible tragic end one night outside an opium den. Davy killed Tyron in a fit of rage, mutilated him."

The words broke from her as she began to weep. Cole held her in his arms.

"He threatened to expose me, if I didn't run away with him, and say that the killing was a result of an illicit love triangle, that I'd killed Tyron when he caught me with my lover … my half-brother. He fled then, telling me to meet him in San Francisco. That's when I went to Cheyenne, hoping that he would not find me again. Then, after the fire, I went to Nebraska."

"I can figure the rest. He came looking for you in Nebraska, you got word, and asked Tom Feathers to help you escape again."

"Yes, a wire had arrived at my aunt's house from Davy, telling me that he was coming for me, that it was useless to try and hide from him. So I went to poor Tom. He was the only one I could turn to."

"Davy would have you no matter what?"

She nodded, wiped the tears from her eyes.

"No matter what. Even if he had to keep me drugged, even if he had to break my spirit by having other men violate me."

"It's over," Cole assured her. "He won't touch you again."

She looked up at him with her pale green eyes, eyes that no longer trusted. "No, he'll find me again. Nothing can stop him."

"You're wrong, Ella."

"Promise me something," she said.

"What?"

"That if he comes, you will kill me, that you won't let him take me."

"I won't let him take you. I promise."

That night, as Cole lay beside her in the bed, he wondered if he had made a promise he wouldn't be able to keep.

CHAPTER THIRTY-FOUR

Two more weeks and nothing out of the ordinary occurred, except that some of Roy Bean's Mexican deputies caught a wanted felon, a man by the name of Charlie Dick, on whom the judge had a Wanted poster for a Union Pacific train robbery.

Roy Bean was so pleased to have his first real criminal case to preside over that he put on a fresh shirt and combed his hair. The deputies had hog-tied Charlie Dick and had to crow-hop him up the steps to the gallery of the Jersey Lilly, as it was called.

One of the deputies who could speak the best English told the judge they'd caught the man trying to steal a horse, but once Roy Bean took a good look at him, he remembered the Wanted flyer and charged the man with his rightful crime of train robbery.

Charlie Dick was a large, dark-eyed man with black brushy eyebrows and he stared defiantly at the judge. "You ain't got no legal right to try me," he said. "That train I was supposed to have robbed was in Kansas. This here's Texas."

"I reckon a tally whacker like you would know the law," Roy Bean said. "I reckon you studied *Blackstone*, read his book and all, and know all there is to know about the legal system, jurisprudence and all that."

"Huh?" Charlie Dick said.

"I reckon 'cause you're so gol-dang' smart, you got caught trying to steal Hector's horse whilst he was inside a whorehouse, not knowing of course that Hector's horse is stone-blind and that he'd walk you around in circles."

"He was a gol-danged hammerhead, or I'd've got clean away."

"Well, I want to abide by the law," Roy Bean said, "and see you get a fair trial, so I'm appointing you a defense counsel before we get started."

"Defense counsel?"

"Hector," the judge said to his Mexican deputy, the one who could speak English the best, "since it was your horse this man tried to steal and you're the only one speaks a lick of *Americano* around here besides myself, I appoint you to defend this crook in my court. You got the floor first."

Hector Gutierrez was a slender man of some fifty or sixty years of age who had met enough *gringos* in his time to have picked up a working language.

"*Sí, Juez* Bean." Then Hector looked at Charlie Dick as if to say: "I'm sorry, *señor*, but I don't understand too much about the law."

"This is a joke!" Charlie Dick cried. "Might just as well take me out and hang me as to have this damned greaser sum-bitch be my lawyer."

"I fine you five dollars for use of abusive language in my courtroom," Roy Bean said, and hammered the folding table with the butt of his pistol. "Any more outbursts in my court by the defendant will result in …" He paused and thumbed through his law book, then said: "Contempt of this court, which will cost you another five dollars."

"Well, you just as well might fine me a thousand dollars," Charlie Dick said disgustedly, "'cause I ain't got a red cent."

"A thousand it is," Roy Bean said, rapping his table twice more with his pistol. "And in lieu of cash payment, the court shall confiscate those fancy spurs you're wearing. Where'd you get 'em … off the heels of a dead man's boots?"

It went like that for as long as Roy Bean could stretch it out. He didn't want his first court case to end too soon, not knowing when his deputies might catch another lawbreaker. Finally, however, the judge pronounced the man guilty of robbing the Union Pacific and trying to steal Hector's blind horse. He ordered his deputies to deliver the man to the jail in Del Río along with a request for the reward money.

"I think the judge's bark is worse than his bite," Ella said, having witnessed the trial.

Roy Bean's spirits were high, having presided over his first real case, and he announced at the supper table that evening that he had decided to go to Chicago to see Lily Langtry perform on stage.

"It's a dream come true," he announced, his eyes misting over at the very mention of her name. "Miss Ella, you and John Henry are invited to join me."

Ella looked at Cole.

"Would you like to go?" he said.

"No." Then turning her attention to Roy Bean, who was seated at his customary position at the head of the table, she said: "I think that you should go alone and see her." And he knew exactly what she meant and was grateful for the encouragement.

Later, when Ella was inside, Roy Bean and Cole sat on the gallery and smoked.

"I'll make sure there's enough deputies to keep an eye on your back," Bean said. "I sent half with Charlie Dick, and Ramon has to go down across the border because his mother is dying, but that still leaves Juan, Rodrigo, Hector, and Xavier. All good men who can shoot."

"Thanks," Cole said. "But if Gypsy Davy hasn't shown himself by now, I doubt that he will. I expected him last week, the week before that, but who knows? Maybe he's dead, maybe in jail somewhere."

"My thinking, too," Roy Bean said. "I expected to see him long before now. You say the son-of-a-bitch has long dark hair?"

"That's the description I have of him. I've never met him."

"Well, I told my boys they see any *hombre* with long dark hair to shoot first and take depositions later."

"You looking forward to Chicago, seeing Lily Langtry?"

He sat there, his legs crossed at the ankles, holding the stub of a cigar between his teeth. "In a way I am, and in another way I ain't. You know how it is. You had this dream all your life, then you get a chance for it to come true. Part of you wants it, but part of you don't, because once it comes true, it ain't a dream any more."

"I understand that."

"Just thinking about it makes me breathe hard."

* * * * *

Roy Bean left early the next morning for San Antonio, where he would catch a train to Chicago. Once he'd gone, the whole place seemed quiet as a stone. He'd ordered the bar closed because none of the remaining deputies knew how to make change in case anyone stopped by for an iced beer or cigars. The four deputies drew straws to see which went fishing and which stayed behind to keep an eye on things, meaning—according to the judge's orders—Ella and Cole.

Ella said: "Let's pack a picnic lunch and go down to the river and watch the men fish."

Cole figured she knew the reason all of the deputies hadn't gone fishing and wanted to give them an opportunity to enjoy themselves while the judge was away. They made sandwiches and took some iced beer, enough for everyone, and walked to the river, the deputies trailing behind, with their rifles and fishing poles.

The sky was as blue as Cole had ever seen it, and Ella seemed happy and held his hand. It was as though none of the past had ever happened, as though they were just a couple who were beginning to fall in love.

They spread a blanket beneath the cottonwood trees and had their picnic while the deputies fished.

"Look," she said, "Hector has caught a catfish."

It seemed to delight her as much as it did Hector. Then Hector's head exploded in a bloody spray and he pitched into the river, the catfish still flopping from the end of his line.

"Run!" Cole commanded, but Ella seemed paralyzed.

The other three deputies dropped their fishing poles and scrambled for their rifles but Rodrigo was cut down by a bullet to his spine. Cole pulled

Ella to cover behind one of the cottonwoods as he watched Xavier and Juan snatch up their Winchesters and take a kneeling position of defense.

Across the river from a crop of rocks, Cole saw the glint of a rifle barrel, then it was gone. He called to the deputies in Spanish to lay down a line of fire toward the rocks while he took Ella out of harm's way and back to the house. They took aim and began firing.

"We have to make the house," Cole said. She just looked at him. "Ella, he won't get to you, I promise."

She nodded, and he took her wrist and told her to move ahead of him and run as fast as she could. He shouted for the deputies to do a slow retreat but to keep up enough firepower to protect themselves. Part of Cole felt like he was running out on a fight, but Ella's safety was more important to him than any sense of pride and duty. He had only one duty and that was to her.

They reached the house, and he gave her one of his pistols and told her to go inside to her room, lock the door, and stay there.

"John Henry ..."

"He won't get to you."

She looked at the pistol he'd placed in her hand. "If he does, I know what to do."

He kissed her and went back outside, running toward the river. Halfway there he met Juan and Xavier who were doing a quick retreat.

"He quit shooting," Juan said in Spanish.

"I think maybe we killed him or something," Xavier said.

"What you want us to do, *jefe?*" Juan asked.

"Get to the house, one in front, one in back, and keep an eye out," Cole said in Spanish, the only language they knew.

"What about you, *jefe?*" Juan wanted to know.

Cole looked at them and saw the earnest, loyal eyes of men who Roy Bean was probably paying too little to risk their lives. "The woman," he said. "If he gets past me, don't let him get to her. If you can't kill him, you kill her."

They exchanged looks, then nodded.

"We won't let him get her, *jefe,*" Xavier promised.

"Good, get going."

Cole made his way to the river and took up a position behind one of the thick cottonwoods where he could take clear aim at the rock outcropping. Hector's body had already floated downstream and Rodrigo lay face down as though he were taking a *siesta* there on the warm bank.

Cole waited for any sign of movement from the rocks and asked himself after an hour what the hell was going on until he realized that Gypsy Davy wouldn't still be there. He was too crafty for that. He'd eliminated two of them, then in the confusion had made his escape. Cole cursed himself for not having figured Gypsy Davy's next move and retreated back to the house.

That's where he found them, Juan and Xavier, their throats slit, and his heart sank.

The door of the courthouse flew open and Gypsy Davy stepped out onto the gallery, one arm around Ella's waist, a small but deadly blade pressed to the side of her neck.

"Don't be foolish," he said. "Throw down that rifle and rid yourself of those pistols."

Ella looked at Cole, her eyes reflecting utter despair. Cole had failed her again.

"Seems we all want her," Gypsy Davy said. "Enough that we're willing to die for her. Are you willing to die for her, sir? Better yet, is she willing to die for you?"

"What sort of man would kill the woman he supposedly loves?" Cole asked.

Gypsy Davy's face flashed anger, then amusement. "Love? What would you know about it? Love is not wanting to live without the object of your affection. If I cannot have Ella, then nobody will."

"You're a coward," Cole said. His anger boiling as much at himself as it was at Gypsy Davy.

He laughed. "Do you think by calling me names that will somehow save your life or hers? Honestly, Ella, what sort of rustic have you taken up with? A man who can't even protect you, just as the last one and the one before that weren't able to protect you. Only I can do that, my darling. You should know …"

It was as though his knife-hand simply exploded, followed by the sound of rolling thunder. The blood splatter covered Ella and instinctively she screamed as Gypsy Davy was knocked backward, releasing his grip on her. Cole was on him in an instant, hammering his face, the bloody stump of his hand flailing wildly, trying to hold Cole off.

Whether from pain or fear or both, Gypsy Davy drove his full weight against Cole in one mad charge, and they went over the railing and landed on the ground, hard, with him atop Cole. The force knocked the wind from Cole's lungs and in that instant Gypsy Davy grabbed a Derringer from his pocket and stuck it in Cole's face. Cole slapped the hand away just as he pulled one of the triggers, the shot grazing Cole's cheek. Gypsy Davy's strength, however badly wounded he was, was unbelievable.

Cole struck him twice in the jaw, knocking him off, and scrambled to his feet. Gypsy Davy was coming up with the Derringer when Cole slammed a forearm to the side of his head at the same time as he drove a knee into his face. Gypsy Davy flopped on his back and lay still.

Cole staggered to Ella's side. "Are you all right?"

She was desperately wiping the blood from the side of her face. "Yes, yes!" Her voice was filled with terror. "What happened …?"

Cole didn't know. Then he heard the sound of a rider, the soft clop of hoofs on the hardpan, and looked around. It was Harve Ledbettor! He dismounted, carrying a Winchester. "Hell of a shot for a one-armed man," Cole said.

"Not such a good shot, considering I was aiming to blow off his pumpkin," Harve said. He looked at Cole, then at Ella. They both knew the risk he'd taken. An inch or two off the mark, she would have been dead. Cole tried not to think about it, because he knew that sooner or later Gypsy Davy would have killed Ella—if not with a knife, then some other way not as kind. As though he had read Cole's mind, Harve said to Ella: "I didn't have a choice. I hope you know that." She gave him a knowing look, and he said: "Well, I guess we're done here. I guess we can all go home now …"

A bang like the slap of a screen door sounded, and Harve spun sideways, sinking to the ground. Cole came around instinctively, drawing the Deane Adams, and shot Gypsy Davy, the little pearl-handled Derringer clutched in his fist. His body jerked once, then lay still.

Harve sat there in the dust, clutching his hip, blood trickling through his fingers.

"Damn it to hell and gone," he moaned. "He's as bad a shot as me."

"Why'd you come back?" Cole asked, kneeling beside him, stuffing his fancy red kerchief in the wound in his hip.

"Aw, hell, John Henry. When'd I ever listen to anybody?"

"Maybe you will now."

Harve looked at the patch job, grinned weakly, and said: "You think Cleo would cotton to a one-armed man who's got himself a limp?"

"It's what's in here, partner," Cole said, tapping his shirt pocket. "I think she'll like you clear down to her shoes."

"Well, maybe I'll stop in Cheyenne on my way back to Denver and see does she like soirées."

CHAPTER THIRTY-FIVE

Roy Bean asked: "Where's all my deputies?" John Henry Cole told him what had happened. He sat down on the top step of the gallery and said: "Holy Jesus ... they're all dead?"

"They didn't have to die," Cole said. "They stayed because they were loyal and good men."

Bean removed his top hat, the one he'd worn to Chicago with the fancy suit, and fanned air on himself. "Hector was the only one could speak any English," he said. "I'll miss him something terrible. The others, too. They might not have spoke English, but they played dominoes good and knew how to catch fat catfish."

"I hope you'll see if they got families, that they're taken care of, Roy."

"Not to worry, we're all like family here. Got to be, we're all we got ... just each other."

"I didn't mean to visit harm on you or your men," Cole confessed.

Bean shook his head. "I invited you, remember?" They sat there for a few moments, then he said: "Ella, she OK?"

"She'll make it, Judge."

"She inside?"

"No. She went back to Nebraska. She had an aunt who lived there.

There's a home waiting for her. Some place peaceful. The only one here besides me is Harve Ledbettor, still healing up."

"What about you?" Bean asked. "You going to join Ella?"

"Maybe someday, Judge. She needs time to bury the dead."

He took a deep breath, let it out. "Damn if I couldn't stand a drink. You?"

They drank liquor on the gallery and watched the first rain in weeks drip off the eaves.

"I never got to see Lily," Bean admitted. His cravat was twisted, his fancy shirt dusty. "She'd gotten ill and the performance got canceled. I paid a stagehand to let me sit in the theater even though I knew she wasn't coming. In my mind I could see her up on the stage, singing a song just for me. Later I'd take her flowers and ask her to escort me to dinner where we'd eat oysters and drink fine champagne and laugh and talk the night away."

"I'm sorry you didn't get to see Lily."

"I am, too, in a way. Thing is, I still got her here," he said, tapping a stubby finger to his heart. "She'll always be there. I don't suppose you can probably understand that ... a man foolish as me?"

"I understand what you mean, Judge."

"What're your immediate plans?"

"Hadn't thought about it, Roy. Why do you ask?"

"Well," he said, "it'd be nice to have a deputy that spoke some *Americano*, somebody I could play dominoes with whilst waiting for lawbreakers."

"You offering me a job?"

"You needing one?"

the end

About the Author

Bill Brooks is the author of twenty-five novels of historical and frontier fiction. After a lifetime of working a variety of jobs, from shoe salesman to shipyard worker, Brooks entered the health care profession where he was in management for sixteen years before turning to his first love—writing. Once he decided to turn his attention to becoming a published writer, Brooks worked several more odd jobs to sustain himself, including wildlife tour guide in Sedona, Arizona, where he lived and became even more enamored with the West of his childhood heroes, Roy Rogers and Gene Autry. Brooks wrote a string of frontier fiction novels, beginning with *The Badmen* (1992) and *Buscadero* (1993), before he attempted something more lyrical and literary in the critically acclaimed: *The Stone Garden: The Epic Life of Billy the Kid* (2002). This was followed in succession by *Pretty Boy: The Epic Life of Pretty Boy Floyd* (2003) and *Bonnie & Clyde: A Love Story* (2005). *The Stone Garden* was named by *Booklist* as one of the top ten Westerns of the decade. After that trio of novels, Brooks was asked to return to frontier fiction by an editor who had moved to a new publisher and he wrote in succession three series for them, beginning with *Law For Hire* (2003), then *Dakota Lawman* (2005), and finishing up with *The Journey of Jim Glass* (2007). *The Messenger* (Five Star, 2009) was Brooks's twenty-second novel. *Blood Storm* (Five Star, 2011) was the first novel in a series of John Henry Cole adventures. It was praised by *Publishers Weekly* as a well-crafted story with an added depth due to its characters. Brooks now lives in northeast Indiana.